DATE DUE

FE 23 '05	FEB 6 - 2018	
MR 23 '05		
AP 21 '05		
JE 7 '05		
AG 3 '05		
JE 1 '06		
JY 8 6 06		
JE 1 6 '10		
NY 0 1 1		
NOV 0 2 2010		
2 MAR 8 - 2017		

Wisconsin

Book One

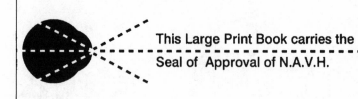

This Large Print Book carries the
Seal of Approval of N.A.V.H.

<u>Wisconsin</u>

Book One

Second Chances Abound in Two Romantic Stories

Andrea Boeshaar

Thorndike Press • Waterville, Maine

Published in 2004 by arrangement with Barbour Publishing, Inc.

Thorndike Press® Large Print Christian Romance.

The tree indicium is a trademark of Thorndike Press.

The text of this Large Print edition is unabridged.
Other aspects of the book may vary from the original edition.

Set in 16 pt. Plantin by Al Chase.

Printed in the United States on permanent paper.

Library of Congress Cataloging-in-Publication Data
Boeshaar, Andrea.
    [Haven of rest]
    Wisconsin : second chances in two romantic stories
/ Andrea Boeshaar.
      p. cm.
    "Book one."
    Contents: The haven of rest — September sonata.
    ISBN 0-7862-7073-X (lg. print : hc : alk. paper)
    1. Wisconsin — Fiction. 2. Large type books.
 I. Boeshaar, Andrea. September sonata. II. Title:
September sonata. III. Title. 05-28
PS3552.O4257H38 2004   THORNCHR Ron
813'.54—dc22   (THONGAIE)   2004059414

1|05
$27-95

<u>Wisconsin</u>

Book One

As the Founder/CEO of NAVH, the only national health agency solely devoted to those who, although not totally blind, have an eye disease which could lead to serious visual impairment, I am pleased to recognize Thorndike Press* as one of the leading publishers in the large print field.

Founded in 1954 in San Francisco to prepare large print textbooks for partially seeing children, NAVH became the pioneer and standard setting agency in the preparation of large type.

Today, those publishers who meet our standards carry the prestigious "Seal of Approval" indicating high quality large print. We are delighted that Thorndike Press is one of the publishers whose titles meet these standards. We are also pleased to recognize the significant contribution Thorndike Press is making in this important and growing field.

Lorraine H. Marchi, L.H.D.
Founder/CEO
NAVH

* Thorndike Press encompasses the following imprints: Thorndike, Wheeler, Walker and Large Print Press.

The Haven of Rest

Chapter 1

Uncle Hal's lawyer, Jim Henderson, had been a family friend for as long as Amie could remember. She'd been in his Wausau, Wisconsin, office only once and she recalled being impressed by its neat and stately appearance. Jim himself was a noble sight, with his bushy, white hair and hawk-like features. He'd always reminded Amie of the second President of the United States, John Adams, with a bit of Albert Einstein mixed in. As a little girl, she had felt thoroughly intimidated around him, assuming he was a stern and intolerant man. But in all of her twenty-six years, she'd come to learn that Jim and his wife, Helen, were kind people and good friends. Even now, as they both sat in her parents' modest but tastefully decorated living room in Chicago's Lincoln Park area, she sensed Jim's concern and compassion as he began reading her uncle's will.

Jim had to have known that traveling to Chicago on a Sunday afternoon was the only way he'd get the busy Potter family together for this somber event. Not all of them had schedules permitting the six-hour drive north to Wausau during the week — and Amie had the tightest timetable of everyone. Her position as a creative consultant for the Chicago firm of Maxwell Brothers' Marketing and Development Company gave her little or no flexibility. And for some reason, Jim stressed the importance of her attendance at the disclosing of Uncle Hal's last will and testament.

"To my sister, Lillian," he read from the document in his hands, "and to her husband, John, I leave ten thousand dollars."

Amie raised her brows in surprise at the generous amount. Her mother, too, looked quite taken aback.

"Mercy!" she exclaimed, shaking her head disbelievingly. "Wherever did Hal get that kind of money?"

Jim smiled patiently. "Investments. He liked to dabble in the stock market and it proved quite profitable for him."

"Well, knock me over with a feather!" Lillian Potter exclaimed, combing back her silver, chin-length hair with well-manicured fingers. "And to think he's lived like a pauper all these years."

"Don't feel sorry for Hal. He was very

10

happy," Jim stated, wearing a hint of a smile just before his gaze fell back to the will. "And to Dottie I leave my mother's jewelry."

Amie smiled, hearing her twenty-three-year-old sister gasp with pleasure. As girls, Lillian had told them that she and Hal had split their mother's jewels after her death. Grandma Holm had wanted to be fair to both her children, even though she knew Hal hadn't much use for women's jewelry.

"To Stephen, my favorite nephew —" Jim paused to chuckle since everyone knew the youngest Potter was Hal's only nephew. "— I leave my Chevy Caprice."

"Awesome!" eighteen-year-old Stephen declared. His golden-blond hair, the same color as Amie's, shone brightly, and the smile on his face reflected the happiness he obviously felt at receiving such a gift. Stephen had been pleading with their father for "wheels" that he could take to Northwestern University next month when the fall semester started and he'd begin his freshman year. Now he had them.

"And to Amie," Jim stated, causing her stomach to flip in a peculiar way, "I leave my gas station and entire property in Tigerton, Wisconsin."

The room fell silent and all eyes turned on her. Dottie wore an expression of pity, Stephen, a look of confusion, and her parents' countenances scarcely masked their horror. As for Amie, she felt terribly disappointed. Why would he leave her a gas station? Maybe Uncle Hal hadn't liked her after all. . . .

Over the years, Amie had been sure her uncle favored her above her brother and sister. He remembered her birthdays, whereas he tended to forget Dottie's and Stephen's. At Christmastime, all three received gifts from Uncle Hal, but Amie's were always the biggest and the best. It used to be a point of contention among the two other Potter children. And every year around Easter, she would get a card from Hal wishing her a happy "spiritual birthday" because it was her uncle who'd led her to a saving knowledge of Christ when she was twelve years old.

But she must have done something to displease him before his death to warrant such a bequest. Although try as she might, Amie couldn't think of what!

"Oh, I'm sure there's got to be some mistake," Lillian said, turning to Jim with a frown of confusion creasing her silvery brows. "That run-down gas station? He left it to Amie? Why, I don't think it's even in working order."

"Yes, it is . . . for the most part. And there's no mistake," Jim countered emphatically. "Hal told me, himself, even before we'd put anything in writing, that he wanted Amie to have the service station."

"What in the world is she supposed to do with it?" John Potter asked incredulously, sitting and resting his forearms on his knees. As always, he was smartly dressed, wearing a red polo shirt and khaki pants. He shook his white head that, in his younger days, had been as blond as Amie's and Stephen's. "My daughter doesn't know the first thing about running a gas station — not that she'd want to. Look at her. There she sits, sugar and spice and everything nice. Can you see her running a filling station? I don't even think she's put gas in a car in her life. She usually gets Stephen to do it . . . or Dottie . . . or me!"

"Oh, Dad, I've filled my car's gas tank plenty of times," Amie replied, disliking the way her father had just made her sound so inept.

He shot her a teasing grin while Dottie and Stephen burst into hysterical laughter. Meanwhile, she sat by bristling. So she wasn't aggressively competitive like her younger sister, who wore her dark hair short and was majoring in sports medicine. So

Amie liked her hair long and softly curled. So she liked feminine-looking clothing, lace and frills; she used make-up, bubble bath, and fingernail polish. So what?

"Princess," her father cajoled, "you've got to admit, it's awfully amusing. You and a . . . a gas station."

Her family laughed again and even Amie had to smile this time.

"Jim, are you certain there's been no mistake?" Lillian asked, doing her best to swallow her merriment.

"I'm positive," the attorney replied. "Hal specifically stated that he wanted Amie to have his gas station and its surrounding acres." Jim shifted his weight in the powder blue wingback chair. "Now, Amie," he said, looking over at her and wearing an understanding expression, "you can sell the place or keep it and hire someone to manage it. There's a fine man who's worked with Hal for the past thirteen years — ever since he was sixteen. Tom Anderson is his name. He roomed with Hal in the two-bedroom apartment above what used to be a Laundromat years and years ago. Now it's just filled with junk." Jim grinned. "That was Hal's other hobby — collecting junk. You name it; it's probably stuffed into some part of those two buildings."

He paused, obviously seeing the confusion on Amie's face. "Let me explain. There are two buildings on Hal's property, the service station with an attached garage and a two-story building that houses the Laundromat area, along with Tom's and Hal's apartment . . . well, now it's just Tom's place."

A sheepish look crossed Stephen's face. "Was there, um, a particular reason why my uncle and this guy shared an apartment?"

Jim chuckled good naturedly at the implication. "No. They were just good friends. Hal was like a father to Tom ever since he was a teenager." He paused and cleared his throat. "In a way, Amie, you've inherited Tom, too."

"Great," she replied, unable to keep the discouragement out of her voice.

"There, there, take heart, my dear," Jim told her. "Tom is a nice fellow. Honest. Hard working. With his help, you might be able to figure out how to actually make Hal's place into a profitable business." He paused, looking around the room at all the Potters. "I believe you folks met Tom at the funeral a few weeks ago."

"Oh, I know who you're talking about," Dottie said, giving Amie a rap on her shoulder. Leaning toward her, she added,

"He was that geek with the dark brown wavy hair and mismatched suit who looked like he'd just stepped out of a rerun of 'The Partridge Family.' "

Stephen hooted. Amie couldn't recall meeting anyone of *that* description.

Jim cleared his throat, appearing slightly agitated. "Look, Tom's a good man. He's intelligent, even though he's only got a high school education. But I know lots of folks with college degrees who don't have a lick of common sense."

"True enough," Helen Henderson agreed, speaking up for the first time in a long while. Round and jolly looking, she possessed a wide, double-chinned face and short auburn hair that was teased back off her forehead. "Tom's a smart fellow. Why, I remember Hal saying he would have been valedictorian of his senior class if it hadn't been for —" She stopped short after receiving a look of warning from her husband. "Oh, never mind," she added, in an obvious attempt to cover her blunder. "It's a long story anyway."

"Tom didn't move into the apartment with Hal until about two years ago," Jim offered, apparently feeling the need to explain the situation. "It was right after his youngest brother turned eighteen and went off to college and Tom sold the family property. Being the eldest in his family and with his mother dead and his father being a . . . well . . . he liked to tip the bottle, to put it politely. Tom kind of raised his siblings, and Hal kind of raised Tom." Jim smiled broadly and glanced at Amie. "Tom will be glad to help you out, whether you decide to sell Hal's station or let him manage it."

Amie sighed glumly.

"I imagine you'll want to at least inspect the place before you make a decision." Slipping his hand into the pocket of his dress pants, Jim pulled out a key, dangling from a chain sporting a plastic rainbow trout the size of a large paperclip. "This is for the safe deposit box at the Tigerton bank. In it you'll find the deed to the property and such."

He handed it to Amie, who turned the key in her palm, still marveling at her inheritance — or curse — whichever the case may be. What was she ever going to do with an old service station filled with junk and an "outdated" attendant?

"Amie?"

She looked up, meeting Jim's serious regard.

"I sincerely hope you'll come to appreciate what Hal left to you. He loved you very much and spoke fondly of you."

"Thank you," she replied halfheartedly. "I hope I'll come to appreciate it too."

The scorching July sunshine beat down on Tom Anderson as he watched the 1980 Caprice drive away, heading south on Highway 45 with Hal's nephew at the wheel. The sun reflected off the red taillights, and as he saw them disappear into the distance, Tom hoped the guy would take care of the vehicle. Hal had babied his eighteen-year-old automobile with frequent oil changes and tune-ups. Tom wasn't so sure Stephen Potter would be as responsible. He'd seen the expression on the kid's face when he first viewed the Caprice — Tom could only describe it as utter disappointment.

Must've been expecting a newer model, he thought dryly.

Turning and heading for his apartment, Tom thought about Stephen's sister Dottie. She'd driven them up from Chicago to get the Chevy. They'd both come to claim their inheritances, and while Stephen seemed dissatisfied with the car, Dottie had appeared wide-eyed and calculating after tucking Hal's jewelry box under one arm. She surveyed Tom's apartment with interested chocolate brown eyes, inquiring over several pieces of wooden furniture, the tea cart, cane-backed chair, coffee table, and matching end tables. Then she asked about their ownership. Hal had purchased them at various rummage sales or found them sitting on the side of the highway with the trash. But Tom had repaired, sanded, stained, and varnished them. They'd both enjoyed them, so he honestly didn't know who possessed legal rights to the items.

"Well, no matter," Dottie had said, lifting her chin haughtily. "Amie owns the place. I'll just ask her if I can have them."

Tom climbed the steep, narrow steps to the apartment he used to share with a man who was more of a father to him than his biological dad. He walked through the kitchen where the red-and-white rubber-tiled floor had obviously seen better days. In the dining room, an aging air-conditioning unit rattled noisily in the window, surrounded by cracked plastered walls. The worn, pea green carpet covering the dining and living room floors needed replacement badly. That was the next thing Hal had wanted to do — rip up the carpeting. But that was before his heart attack last month, and now Tom never felt more depressed in his whole life.

The only consolation he found was thinking about Hal in heaven, walking the streets of gold with the Savior, Jesus Christ. His friend was in a much better place than here in this dumpy apartment, in this nothing little town.

Collapsing onto the green, floral sofa and ignoring the ancient springs' groans of protest, Tom thought about the stocks and bonds Hal had left to him. He supposed he could cash them in, take the money, and run for his life. Leave Tigerton behind along with the nightmarish memories of his life here. But where would he go? What would he do?

In his hopeless state of mind, Tom couldn't fathom that answers to those questions even existed. Picking up his Bible from the coffee table, he opened it and flipped through the Psalms. Finally, he began to read: "The Lord is my shepherd; I shall not want. He maketh me to lie down in green pastures: He leadeth me beside the still waters. He restoreth my soul. . . ."

Chapter 2

Amie had postponed this trip for as long as possible. She'd been dreading this day ever since she'd found out about her inheritance. Dottie said she was "in denial," and perhaps that wasn't too far from the truth. But she had tried to argue the point anyway.

"I'm a creative consultant," she'd retorted. "I am not a financial wizard, nor am I well informed about gas stations!"

"Then just sell it, Amie. What's the big deal?"

What's the big deal? Amie repeated the question to herself now as she drove her red BMW up US-41. She passed farms, wheat fields, cornfields, and Holstein cows, and she marveled at the tranquility that filled her being when she left the bustling city of Chicago behind. Entering the state of Wisconsin, she drove on the outskirts of Kenosha, Racine, and Milwaukee Counties. An hour later, she was just north of Oshkosh when she crossed a long bridge spanning Lake Butte des Morts. Amie smiled at how the sunshine sparkled off the clear blue water as it cavorted around motorboats and fishermen. About fifteen miles later, she exited the interstate in the town of Appleton and found her way to Highway 45.

What's the big deal? Amie sighed, running those words through her head once more. How could she possibly explain to Dottie and the rest of her family that after spending time in prayer and consulting with her pastor, she didn't have peace about selling her uncle's gas station? Her family members were not believers, and Amie had tried discussing other important matters with them in the past, such as her college education. They'd never understood why she'd chosen a Bible college over a state university. And, while her parents thought it was "nice" that she had her "religion," her siblings made it clear that they didn't want any part of Christianity.

Driving on, Amie passed more farms, more cornfields, and then drove through a host of small towns. Finally, she traveled the last stretch of Highway 45 into Tigerton, crossing the Embarrass River on a tiny suspension bridge. To her right, Amie noticed the brand new Amoco gas station and sandwich shop being built on the edge of town. She wondered how her uncle's rundown place would ever compete with such a modern establishment.

Just one more thing to consider, she mused, reaching her destination at long last.

Hot August sunshine bounced off the concrete garage of Uncle Hal's filling station. At one time, the building had been whitewashed, but it now stood in drab gray, chipping and peeling. Amie climbed out of her car and stretched the muscles in her legs while scrutinizing the exterior of the other building. It had always reminded her of something out of an old western movie, with its false, squared-off front that loomed higher than the roof of the second story.

"Can I help you?"

Amie startled at the sound of the male voice coming from behind her car. She pivoted and found herself looking into a pair of the most mournful hazel eyes she'd ever seen.

"Yes, I, um, I'm Hal's niece," she stammered. "Amie Potter." She smiled politely before adding, "That's *Am*ie . . . as in *Am*ish. My mother grew up in Marion . . . you know, the neighboring town? And I was named after her favorite art teacher."

"Yeah, I know who you are."

Surprised at his remark, Amie brought her chin back, considering the man standing before her. Parted down the side, his dark brown hair hung in waves past his ears and had obviously outgrown any particular style long ago. His chin was stubbled, but his arms were smooth and suntanned, their color accentuated by the white tank top undershirt he wore tucked into badly oil-stained blue jeans, and on his feet were soiled work boots. Gazing down at her own sandals, Amie wondered if the guy's toes were frying in his shoes on this ninety-degree day.

She looked back up into his face, unkempt, but not at all unbecoming, and forced a polite grin. "You must be Tom."

"Uh-huh."

She nodded, and then several uncomfortable moments passed.

Amie cleared her throat nervously. "Any chance there's a restroom nearby? I just finished a four-hour drive up from Chicago. . . ."

Tom looked over at the decaying garage. "There's one in there, but the plumbing doesn't work anymore." He shifted his sad, green eyes back to Amie. "You're welcome to use the one upstairs in my apartment, though."

"Oh, well, that's awfully kind of you, but, um . . ." The thought of going into a strange man's apartment — especially if he intended to show her the way — sent a shiver of panic slicing through her.

As if sensing her discomfort, Tom added, "I'm refinishing a piece of furniture around back, but the door to my place isn't locked. Go on up and help yourself. Bathroom's right off of the kitchen."

Amie smiled gratefully, relaxing somewhat. "Thanks."

Walking briskly toward the western-styled building with its green-speckled asbestos-tiled siding, Amie entered the tiny, dank hallway and made her way up the narrow staircase. She found the lavatory easily and marveled at its interior. She assumed the place would be dumpy and dirty — like it was outside. But it was remarkably clean.

Minutes later, she washed up, left the bathroom, and then curiously inspected the apartment her uncle had shared with Tom. Again, she was impressed by its tidiness. There wasn't anything in sight that seemed in need of dusting, and the potted plants in the living room looked adequately watered and healthy. Amie groaned inwardly, thinking of her messy condo in Chicago.

She'd left dirty dishes in the sink; the place hadn't been vacuumed in at least two weeks, and any plants she'd ever owned died within a month of her care — or lack thereof. If anyone dropped in on her unannounced, the way she'd done to Tom today, Amie thought she'd die of embarrassment.

Suddenly Amie recalled her sister's pleading for the refinished antiques that added charm to this dilapidated dwelling. Little wonder Dottie wanted them. They were objects of beauty. Carefully, almost reverently, Amie ran her hand across the smooth top of a chest — a hope chest — that sat beneath the dining room windows.

"Did you get lost?"

For the second time in fifteen minutes, Amie jumped. This guy seemed to have a knack for sneaking up on people!

"Sorry," she said, chagrined that she'd been caught snooping through his apartment. "I should have asked for a look around, although you did tell me to 'help myself' if I recall." She gave him a friendly smile, hoping to dispel any irritation he might have with her.

Tom just eyed her speculatively. "I told your sister that I wasn't sure who owned the furniture. Hal bought a lot of it and found the rest, but I fixed it up." His gaze moved past her, to the living room, and he expelled a weary-sounding breath. "But I've decided that I don't care what you take. Take it all, for that matter." He looked back at her and, despite the discouragement in his voice, a slight smile curved his thin but nicely shaped lips. "Except I don't think you're going to get much of anything packed into that little hot rod of yours."

Amie grinned. "Well, I've got a news flash for you, Tom. I wasn't planning on packing anything into my . . . *hot rod.*"

He shrugged and Amie all but forgot her earlier concerns about being alone with Tom in his apartment. There was something very disarming about him. Perhaps it was his sorrowful eyes. They were shaped like teardrops that had fallen sideways, and gazing into their aqueous green depths caused Amie to feel a great measure of pity for the man. He had the perpetual expression of one on the brink of a good cry.

"You miss my uncle a lot, don't you?" she asked softly.

Tom's nod was so subtle that Amie barely saw it, and for an immeasurable second, they both stood there staring dumbly at each other.

Finally, Amie's nerves got the best of her,

and she gave in to her lifelong habit of babbling incessantly.

"I never really knew my uncle. Not really. I mean, he came to visit during the holidays, and I remember sitting on his knee as a little girl. Once every summer, my family and I made a brief stop here in Tigerton to see Uncle Hal on the way to our lakeside cabin in Minoqua, but that's about as much as I saw of him. And then, after I became a teenager and had my driver's license, I was usually more interested in hanging around with my friends than visiting with an older relative. I don't mean that in any form of disrespect; it's just one of those senseless teenager things." She paused for a breath. "And now I sort of wish I had known Uncle Hal better. Maybe I'd know *why* he left me his property and *what* he intended for me to do with it!"

A slow grin spread across Tom's face. Then, much to Amie's surprise, he actually chuckled. She couldn't help noticing that his teardrop eyes were transformed into little smiles as he squinted when he laughed. A little thrill passed through Amie to think that she'd had something to do with the metamorphosis.

"Hal said you could talk circles around most women."

Amie's surge of joy turned into a huff.

"Oh, he did, did he? Well, it's too bad my uncle isn't here so I could properly thank him for the compliment."

"He didn't mean it as an insult," Tom assured her. "Hal thought it was funny."

"I think it's horrible! Not that Uncle Hal thought my chattering was funny, but that I have to chatter at all!" With hands on her hips, she shrugged. "It's a nervous thing with me — especially if I'm around people who don't do much talking. I guess I kind of make up for it, you know? I talk for the both of us. Although, I've got to admit, my rambling does come in handy when I give presentations. Once I had to impress the president of an oatmeal manufacturer with my ideas on building oatmeal's popularity with the general public — kids especially. That was really tough! I mean, what kid do you know who likes oatmeal? I hated it when I was a child. Still do —"

Amie paused midsentence. "See, I'm doing it again."

Pursing his lips thoughtfully, Tom nodded. "Yep, you sure are."

"You could shut me up, you know, by participating in the conversation."

"Participate?" Tom raised dark brown eyebrows. "I haven't been able to get a word in edgewise!"

29

Amie sucked in her lower lip, wishing she hadn't made such a fool of herself. She sent up an arrow of a prayer: *Lord, help me have a quiet spirit.*

Tom's expression was somber once more. "You want to see Hal's room?"

"Bedroom?" Amie swallowed down a second wave of panic — her other "bad habit." Ever since that night three years ago, she was afraid of being alone with a man, save for family members, of course. Never again, she'd vowed, would she allow herself to get into a vulnerable position. The last one cost Amie her virtue! Yet, it seemed she'd done exactly that today; she'd let down her guard and here she was — alone with Tom, a guy her sister called a "geek," and a man her brother dubbed a "grease-monkey." Worse yet, she knew practically nothing about him or his character.

"No, thanks, Tom. I don't need to see any more of the apartment," she hastily replied. "I really need to get going." She marched toward the kitchen, heading for the door. "I have to go to the bank, check out some things. I'm sure you understand."

Amie heard him silently trailing her, which only increased the alarm pumping through her veins. She practically ran down the precarious stairwell and out to her car.

But as she reached the BMW, Tom caught her elbow.

"Hey, are you okay?"

By now, Amie was shaking badly and had worked herself into tears, but she nodded anyway.

"I wasn't making fun of you upstairs or anything." Tom smiled, albeit slightly. "I thought all your talking was rather . . . refreshing." His words faltered as Amie swatted the errant tears, hoping he wouldn't see them. But by the stupefied expression on his face, she knew he had.

"Are you okay?" he asked once more, looking considerably more concerned this time.

"Oh, I'm fine," Amie fibbed. "I get this way sometimes. Must be stress or something." After fumbling with her car keys, Amie managed to unlock the door. "I'd better get to the bank before it closes."

"It's only three o'clock; you've got plenty of time. On Friday nights, the Tigerton Bank doesn't close till seven."

"Good." Amie climbed into the driver's seat.

"Need directions?"

She grimaced. "Oh, yeah, that might help."

Tom explained how to get into town and

described the location of the bank. "It's across the street from the pharmacy."

"Thanks."

"When you come back, I imagine that you'll want to see the books."

Amie tipped her head questioningly. "Books?"

Tom nodded. "The financial records on this place."

"Right."

He stepped back and Amie shut her car door. As she pulled out of the ramshackled gas station, she caught Tom's worried frown in the rearview mirror. *He must think I'm totally nuts,* she thought, following his directions to the bank, which wasn't far. *I have to be more careful,* she decided, as she parked and turned off the engine. *I have to quit babbling and stop panicking!* She hesitated before leaving her car, knowing she couldn't do either without God.

"Claim a Bible verse," Pastor Bryant had said when counseling her about the anxiety attacks — even though she couldn't get herself to tell him *why* she'd been having them. "Claim God's promises," he'd advised.

Amie looked at her dash where this week's verse was taped. She'd been trying to memorize Scripture, writing verses on index cards, and keeping them in her car. Currently, she was working on Philippians 4:6–7: "Be careful for nothing; but in every thing by prayer and supplication with thanksgiving let your requests be made known unto God. And the peace of God, which passeth all understanding, shall keep your hearts and minds through Christ Jesus."

"All right, Lord, I'm declaring this passage as Your promise to me."

After several minutes in prayer, Amie sighed, concluding that she felt calmer already. She squared her shoulders. *Now, about Uncle Hal's safe deposit box . . .*

Tom eased himself down onto the shaded concrete stoop outside the station and popped the top off a cold soda. Taking a long drink, he stared beyond the old gas pumps and thought about Amie Potter. She was as pretty as her college graduation picture, the one that sat on Hal's dresser — maybe prettier. He took another swig. Definitely prettier! Her hair was the color of a golden wheat field, and her brows were like two upward flaxen slashes above her cornflower blue eyes. And her figure — couldn't say she was fat. And she wasn't too slim. Just somewhere in between. In Tom's estimation, Amie Potter looked like a woman a man could hold onto without breaking in two. He liked that idea, although he sure wasn't any kind of expert on women. With the exception of two younger sisters — who didn't count in the matter of romantic relationships — women were foreign territory to him, especially Amie.

And what in the world happened to cause such a reaction in her? What had she said? Stress? Could be. Or maybe it was one of those female things. His sisters, Lois and Jeanne, used to become veritable barracudas at certain times of the month, and Tom had personally witnessed their transformation. He'd almost been glad when they had run off, one right after the other. However, such glee didn't last long before reality set in: Lois and Jeanne had left him with an alcoholic father and two younger brothers to look after.

Taking another swallow of his cola, Tom wondered where his sisters were. He hadn't heard from them since they left home some ten years ago. He hoped they were happily married and raising packs of kids. He hoped they'd escaped from their childhoods, their pasts.

He wiped the sweat off his brow. At least Matt had a good chance at life. His youngest brother was the first of the Andersons to attend college. He'd gotten a grant and a scholarship — he'd be fine. He'd succeed. On the other hand, his other brother, Phillip, had followed in their old man's footsteps — his drinking and carousing had landed him in jail. Tom went to visit him every couple of weeks, and praise God, Phil had come to a saving knowledge of Christ not long ago. Hal once said that sometimes God had to throw a man into prison in order to save his soul. Perhaps he'd been right.

Tom rose from the cement stoop, drank the last of his cola, and pitched the can into the plastic recycling bin. He decided he'd best pull out the financial stuff so it would be ready for Amie when she returned from the bank. A good portion of the records was on his computer, but he could readily print off anything she asked to see. Turning toward his apartment door, located right next to the closed-down Laundromat, Tom entered and started up the steep steps, suddenly wishing he'd been the one to run off at sixteen years old, instead of his two sisters. Sometimes bearing the weight of responsibility was more than he bargained for, especially in a tiny town like Tigerton.

Chapter 3

In the solitude of one of the bank's offices, Amie read and reread her uncle's letter, marveling at its contents. *He remembered,* she thought with tear-filled eyes. *I had long forgotten, but Uncle Hal remembered. My hotel.*

She swallowed her sadness, smiling now as the memories came rushing back. Amie had always wanted to build and operate her own hotel. As a little girl, she had fantasized about holding tea parties in the beautifully decorated lobby — just as she and her mother had done one year for Amie's birthday at the Palmer House in Chicago. Amie couldn't have been more than five years old at the time, but the grand hotel with its quaint charm had greatly impressed her. Queen of the Hotel, that was the title Amie had always coveted, until she was in her teens and realized the ridiculousness of it all. She had to go to college and learn to do something practical with her life. Hadn't her father drummed that into her brain enough times? And, of course, he was right. She had a marvelous career. Dreams of tea parties and hotels had long ago been stacked away with childhood storybooks and baby dolls.

She glanced at her uncle's letter, still resting on her fingertips. *Use my land, Amie,* he'd written. *Raze the old gas station, Laundromat, and my apartment, and build yourself one dilly of a hotel!*

"Oh, right, Uncle Hal," she murmured inwardly, as if somehow he could hear her. "Like this town is ready for a Palmer House." Amie rolled her eyes heavenward. "A truck-stop, maybe. But a hotel? I don't think so. And surely there's a Holiday Inn or something around here."

She studied the letter once more, focusing on the paragraph about Tom Anderson. Her uncle had written: *Tom is my son in the faith. I had the pleasure of leading him to Christ when he was a teenager. He is a good Christian man, and that is why I left him over half of my investments.*

"A good Christian man," Amie murmured aloud, lifting her gaze, contemplating the information. While she hadn't known her uncle well firsthand, she'd known a great deal *about* him. Her mother often spoke of how "religious" her brother was, always adding that she'd never heard a bad word out of his mouth. Amie recalled the numerous times her mother phoned Uncle Hal when she needed encouragement. And her father frequently said his brother-in-law was a good judge of character. If Hal Holm stated that Tom Anderson "is a good Christian man," then Amie felt certain it was true. In the next moment, she realized her earlier fear of the man was unwarranted. A sense of relief swept over her.

She looked back at the letter. *And Tom Anderson inherited over half of Uncle Hal's investments?* she mused incredulously as she simultaneously wondered at the dollar amount.

Suddenly a knock sounded at the office door. "Miss Potter?" It opened to reveal the kindly lady who'd helped her obtain Hal's safe deposit box. "Is everything all right?"

"Just fine, thanks." Amie smiled politely. "I'll be finished up here shortly."

"Very well." The portly woman with curls in her light-brown hair turned to leave. "If there's anything else you need, just give me a holler."

"Thank you."

The door closed and Amie folded the letter. Gathering the contents of the safe deposit box, she realized she possessed the other portion of her uncle's investments — whatever they were worth.

She stuffed the papers and Hal's letter into her shoulder bag, sticking her tiny purse in there too. However, leaving the bank, she didn't feel any closer to knowing what to do with her inheritance than when she first entered nearly forty-five minutes ago.

Amie threw a quick glance up the street. It was obviously the main drag and traffic was picking up. To her left there was a clinic up on the hill, next to the river. The pharmacy was across the street. The next block boasted a sign that read, MARKET SQUARE MINI-MALL. If *that* was a mall, Amie was the queen of England! It hardly compared to anything she was used to shopping at in Chicago. Except she couldn't help noticing the mouth-watering smell of fried chicken emanating from the place or the delicious-looking ice cream cones that four kids were holding as they fairly tumbled out the main entrance.

Gazing farther up Cedar Street, Amie spied an outdated telephone booth on the corner, the likes of which she hadn't seen in at least ten years. Farther yet was RON'S FOODLAND. But what Amie didn't see anywhere was a hotel.

Get it out of your mind, Amie Potter! she berated herself, marching to her car. *This town wouldn't know what to do with a hotel. This town looks poverty-stricken and it's . . . dying!*

An elderly man passed her on the sidewalk and stared openly. "Say," he called after she'd passed him. "Aren't you Hal Holm's niece?"

She stopped, turning slowly. The man had a stocky build and wore a snug-fitting light blue polo shirt. "Yes, sir. I'm Amie Potter."

He grinned broadly and etchings the years had made in his tanned face seemed to deepen. "Well, sure, I recognize you. I remember when you were this high!" he said, holding his hand level with his right hip.

Amie forced a polite smile. "I'm sorry, but I don't remember you."

"Ernie Huffman."

"Pleased to meet you, Mr. Huffman."

He kept grinning. "You visiting?"

"Sort of. My uncle left me his filling station, and I'm trying to get that part of his estate settled."

"I see. Well, I'll leave you to your business, then."

With a polite nod, she continued her short jaunt to the car. Disengaging the alarm system, she opened the door and was met by a blast of suffocating heat. She instantly regretted not opening a window, even slightly. By the time the air-conditioning completely cooled the car, she'd be back at Hal's station. A lot of good it was going to do her then!

Amie drove through town, halting at the junction of Highway 45. The sun bore down on the BMW as she waited for a break in the late Friday afternoon traffic. The road was filled with travelers. Watching them, Amie noticed at least four campers heading north, most likely for the weekend. A couple of cars pulling boats whizzed past, followed by an automobile towing jet skis.

Tourists.

Lots of them.

"I'm not building a hotel in this town!" she said out loud as if debating with someone sitting in the passenger seat next to her. "If I were smart, I'd sell Uncle Hal's property, cash in on those investments, and take a cruise this winter. Chicago winters are pathetic."

A car's horn honked from behind her, and Amie realized the traffic rendered her access onto the highway. She waved in apology and stepped on the accelerator. She had to cross the little suspension bridge again before arriving back at the gas station.

Pulling into the lot, she immediately noticed a car parked at the pumps. Its hood was up and Tom stood beside a gray-haired man, both of them staring at the auto's motor with grave expressions.

"So you can't fix it?" she heard the stranger ask as she walked up to where he and Tom stood.

"Sorry, Russ," Tom replied evenly. "Cars these days have computers, and I don't have the equipment to work on them. Gotta take it back to the dealer in Wittenberg."

"But they'll charge me a fortune!"

He shrugged. "Sorry."

The older man muttered while Tom dropped the hood.

"Why don't you get yourself some of today's modern tools, Tom, so you can fix my car?"

"Guess I'm not interested in fixing cars anymore."

Russ sputtered off a lengthy complaint. It was then he spotted Amie, and the sudden expression on his face seemed to border on shock and curiosity.

Tom inclined his dark brown head in her direction. "This is Hal's niece, Amie Potter."

Russ was immediately all smiles. "Well,

how-de-do! Wel-come to Tigerton."

"Thanks," she said, unable to keep from smiling herself.

"You know, Tom," he said conspiratorially, yet loud enough so Amie heard, "it's Cash Night in town. If you're inside a local business when your name is drawn, you can win money."

"Yeah, I know, Russ," Tom replied, sounding disinterested.

"Well, I was thinking — the bowling alley's got great burgers. You ought to take her out to eat there tonight. Maybe knock over a few pins while you're at it." He elbowed Tom and winked pointedly. "Match made in heaven, eh?"

Amie puzzled over the remark, then decided to just laugh at the old man's antics. However, one look at Tom's face said he wasn't amused — although he didn't look particularly annoyed either.

Her uncle's words came back to her. *Tom is my son in the faith . . . a good Christian man . . . I left him over half of my investments.*

Amie wondered if he'd like to invest in a hotel.

Except she wasn't building one.

No! She would not build a hotel! The very idea was absurd!

"I think you insulted her, Russ," Tom

said, drawing Amie out of the inner battle that was pulling her apart. "She's from Chicago. She doesn't want to eat at some two-bit bowling alley, especially with a guy like me."

He looked over at her, and those sad, green eyes melted Amie's heart.

"I'm not insulted," she quickly replied. "On the contrary. I'm starved. I'd love a hamburger from the bowling alley. No, make that a cheeseburger." She frowned questioningly. "Do they have double cheeseburgers there? And chocolate shakes?"

Half a grin curved his mouth, challenging her. Now she'd have to see him smile — or, better yet, laugh!

Amie put her hands on her hips and lifted a brow in feigned insolence. "And my next question is: Are *you* buying?"

That did it. Tom chuckled, his gaze falling to the cracked pavement beneath his dirty work boots. Then, looking at Russ, he waved an abrupt good-bye. "See you later."

"Oh, yeah, sure." Russ wore that previous look of surprise on his face. "See you later, Tom." He nodded at Amie. "Nice meeting you."

"Same here," she called, watching as he climbed slowly into his car.

When he drove away, Amie turned to Tom. "Did I embarrass you? Sorry if I did."

"No, you didn't embarrass me." His expression had returned to dismal, his hazel eyes so sorrowful. "But I think you'd best be aware of the way talk spreads around a small town like this one. I mean, I wouldn't put it past Russ to spread the word that you and I are . . . dating or something after what just happened."

"Oh, who cares what people say," Amie said with a flippant shrug of her shoulders.

"Well, unfortunately, what people say about you in this town is who you are." With that, Tom turned and walked into the tiny office attached to the garage.

Amie followed. "So, does that mean I have to go find a hamburger by myself?"

Tom didn't reply to her tart remark but found his way to the other side of the counter on which a myriad of papers were stacked, along with a grimy adding machine and telephone. Finally he looked at her with such a probing gaze that Amie was tempted to turn away. But she didn't. She met his stare undaunted.

"Look, Amie," Tom said at last, "I don't think it's a good idea if you go anywhere with me, okay?"

"Why?" she couldn't help asking. And

then it hit her. "Oh, I get it. You've got a girlfriend . . . or a fiancée, huh? I understand. I wouldn't come between a couple for a million bucks, even if we are just two friends eating a hamburger at the same table."

"But that's my point. In this town two people can't eat at the same table without folks speculating about something more going on between them."

"Oh . . ."

She glanced out the smeared plate-glass window as unexpected disappointment pricked her heart. She was so tired of eating by herself, save for the "power" lunches she had with clients. It seemed to Amie that everyone had someone special with whom they shared their lives, except for her. All her friends from college were married and raising children. Dottie was engaged. Stephen had a steady girlfriend who was going with him to Northwestern University.

Guess it's dinner for one again, she conceded inwardly. After all, there was no point in agonizing over things beyond her control. She'd just learn to be content as a single woman.

"By the way, I'm not dating . . . or anything."

She pivoted, looking back at Tom. He

was pulling out hard-bound ledgers from underneath the counter. "Well," she hedged, "in that case, would it be all right if you and I ordered a pizza and ate it around back where no one could see?"

That slow, half grin reappeared, brightening Tom's countenance ever so slightly. "Amie, I don't care if people see me taking you out to eat. I don't even care if they think we're on a date. I'm just trying to protect your reputation in this town. I owe Hal that much." He shrugged. "But I suppose since you are his niece . . . and everyone knows he and I were friends . . ."

"What do you mean, 'protect my reputation'? Are you implying that being seen with you will ruin it? My uncle told me that you're a fine Christian man."

Tom's face fell, his gaze included. "Yeah, well, he was one of a kind. This town'll tell you that I'm the guy least likely to succeed. Always was. Always will be. You don't need to get pegged with the likes of me."

Amie opened her mouth, fully intending to scold the guy for having his own pity party, but then she remembered what Jim Henderson said the day he read Hal's will. Something about Tom's father being an alcoholic and Tom having to drop out of high school to raise his siblings. No doubt he'd lived a hard life. Then he lost his best friend.

Reaching out, she touched his tanned arm. "Tom, if my uncle said you're a fine Christian man, then I'd believe him over anything other people might say."

He looked up from the ledgers he'd been staring at forlornly.

Amie smiled sweetly. "Will you go get cleaned up and take me somewhere for a double cheeseburger and chocolate shake before I faint from hunger?"

Tom pulled his arm away and nervously scratched the back of his head. "I certainly hope you know what you're doing."

"Does that mean yes?"

"Yeah, sure," he replied, although it lacked enthusiasm. He walked around the counter in acquiescence and headed for the door.

"I haven't had a date in three years," Amie blurted. "And I can tell you right now, Tom Anderson, that you are two hundred times better than the last guy who took me out!"

"You can tell that already, huh?" he asked with a hint of sarcasm.

"There's not a doubt in my mind," Amie stated tenaciously.

He smiled from the doorway. "In that case, I'll even *pay* for your double cheeseburger and chocolate shake."

She laughed, watching as Tom strode purposely for his apartment. Maybe, if she was lucky, he'd even take a shower!

Chapter 4

While Tom cleaned up for dinner, Amie paged through her uncle's ledgers. As far as she could see, everything was in order. She noticed there wasn't much in the way of profits to report, but according to last year's accounting, the filling station didn't appear to be losing money.

Amie closed the hardbound book and began to investigate her newly acquired property. The office and attached garage weren't nearly as well maintained as Tom's apartment. Empty oil cans and various auto parts were strewn about the concrete floor of the garage, while clusters of paper and unopened mail occupied every available flat surface in the office. Amie wondered how a man could work in such a mess.

Stepping outside into the late afternoon sun, she walked next door and attempted a look into the old Laundromat. Through a dusty window, she saw that junk and more junk had been piled floor-to-ceiling, from one end to the other.

"Uncle Hal," she muttered inwardly, "what in the world were you thinking when you stored all this stuff in here?"

"He was thinking that it'd be worth something one day."

Startled, Amie turned and found Tom standing several feet away. She narrowed her gaze in annoyance. "Didn't anyone ever tell you that it's not nice to sneak up on a person?"

He shook his head, still damp from its obvious washing, although he hadn't shaved his stubbled chin. Then, putting a hand into the pocket of his clean blue jeans, he withdrew a set of keys. "Would you like to go inside for a better view?"

"No," she replied tersely to cover her embarrassment. "That's not necessary. Besides, I don't think there's room for a human being in there."

"Good point." Tom stuck the keys back into his pocket. "But a lot of decent furniture's in there that could be fixed up, if somebody had the time to do it."

Curious now, Amie peered back into the window. "What kind of furniture?"

"A couple of dressers, a bookshelf, a baby's crib, kitchen table, and matching chairs — some of them have broken legs, though, and I don't know if they're worth salvaging. There's a roll-top desk in there somewhere too."

"Wood furniture?"

"Uh-huh."

"Hmm . . . and here I had thought it was all junk." She turned to face him once more. "Why don't you fix those pieces up, Tom? You've obviously got the capability, from what I've seen of the antiques upstairs that you refinished."

"I've been working at it here and there."

An idea suddenly began to take form. *An antique shop . . . in the hotel.*

"Are you, um, still hungry?"

Amie gave herself a mental shake. "Hungry?" she answered. "I'm starving!"

"Well, let's go, then." Again he pulled out his keys. "I'll take my truck, and you can follow me in your car. We'll eat in Shawano, and then get a motel room."

"Excuse me?"

Tom stopped in his tracks, his face reddening with embarrassment. "For you," he quickly replied. "We'll get a motel room for you. See, there's no motel in Tigerton. Closest one's in Shawano." He cleared his throat uncomfortably. "I didn't think you'd want to drive back to Chicago tonight."

Amie nibbled on her bottom lip to keep

from laughing aloud. If she still had doubts about Tom's integrity, they were all gone now. The poor guy was blushing! When was the last time she'd seen a man actually *blush?*

She smiled, swallowing the last of her mirth. "Well, thanks. That's really considerate."

He nodded. "Thought we'd go over the books tomorrow," he added, still looking chagrined. "I've got this year's figures on my computer. I started printing them out, but didn't get finished."

"Sure. Tomorrow's fine."

Tom began walking around the side of the building. "I'll get my truck."

Watching him go, Amie was reminded of a country singer her sister had been madly in love with some ten years ago. Maybe it was Tom's outfit — the navy plaid, light cotton, collared shirt he wore with its long sleeves rolled to the elbow, the faded blue jeans and black cowboy boots completing the ensemble. Coupled with whiskered face and hair wet from shampooing, he looked somewhat cavalier. There was an uncanny resemblance between Tom and that country-boy singer whose picture Dottie had plastered all over her bedroom.

Well, why am I surprised? This town is about

as country as it gets, she thought wryly, strolling toward her car. As if on cue, she heard a cow lowing in the distance. *Right. I'm in the land of cows and country boys. Got it.*

Disengaging her car alarm, she climbed into the BMW, and within minutes, Tom pulled up in his red and black Ford Ranger. Amie was amazed yet again, having guessed he'd drive some sort of old rust-bucket.

"Ready?" he called out the window.

"Ready."

The trip didn't take more than twenty minutes, and upon her arrival, Amie noticed Shawano was larger than Tigerton and sported a wide variety of shops, restaurants — and motels. But she couldn't help wondering, as they both parked their vehicles, if Tom's ulterior motive for bringing her here — and taking two cars — was to escape unwanted gossip in his hometown.

"I like this place," he told her when they met on the sidewalk in front of a small, locally owned eatery whose sign read: ALLEN & ROSIE'S KITCHEN, PARKING IN REAR. He grinned slightly. "Hal and I used to come here a lot. Their cheeseburgers are made with real beef, and they make a mean chocolate shake — probably use real milk too."

Amie chuckled at his dry sense of humor

before returning a bit of it. "Are you saying you don't care for soybean and artificial dairy products? What kind of an American are you?"

"A healthy one," Tom replied evenly, holding the door open for Amie.

Entering the establishment, she appraised her surroundings. Red-checkered clothed tables lined the small but heavily populated dining room. On the other side of a spindled partition, stood an L-shaped counter, flanked by red and chrome swivel stools.

They waited by the door for a few minutes while a table was cleared, then sat down near the café-curtained plate window.

"This place is so quaint," she remarked. "I get tired of the large chain restaurants. They're all the same in every big city, and the food tastes alike."

Tom shrugged. "Well, as I said before, the food here's real good. They close at eight every night and don't serve liquor. Guess that's what I like best about this place. No liquor."

"Oh . . . ?" Amie glanced around and didn't see a bar, confirming Tom's comment.

"Disappointed?"

She brought her attention back to him as he opened his menu and began studying it.

"Not at all," she replied. "I don't drink — anymore. I used to. That is, I'd occasionally indulge in a small glass of . . . something. But then . . . well, it was about three years ago when I gave it up completely. My decision wasn't a result of a religious conviction, although God certainly showed me that bad things can happen when a person drinks and —" Amie paused, expelling a flustered sigh. "And I'm babbling again. Sorry."

Tom lifted his gaze, meeting hers, and she thought she saw a glimmer of understanding in those hazel depths.

Finally, he glanced back at his menu and closed it. "I think I'll have the same thing you're having. Double cheeseburger and a chocolate shake."

"Smart choice," she said, wondering if she'd ever get her irksome habit of babbling under control.

By the time they left the restaurant, it was just past six o'clock. A younger crowd seemed to dominate the streets now and music blared from passing autos. The weekend had arrived in this northern Wisconsin town.

"You want to find a place to stay now?" Tom asked. "There's a motel near the fairgrounds. I can drive you over."

"Can we walk? I feel the need for a bit of

exercise after all the food I just consumed."

He nodded. "It'll be a bit of a hike, but sure."

As they turned to go, a burly man approached them. "Well, well, if it isn't Tomboy," he said with a facetious ring in his deep voice. His hair was shiny black, but his craggy beard was the color of charcoal. As Amie stared at the large man before her, she was reminded of Popeye's foe, Brutus. "And who might this be?"

The man shifted his dark-eyed gaze to her, and Amie took a step closer to Tom. She fought down a wave of anxiety and forced herself to smile politely.

"I'm Amie Potter," she replied.

He grinned interestedly. "My pleasure. I'm Al Simonson." The man threw Tom a curious look and smirked. "You two long-lost cousins or something? No girl in her right mind would go out with this guy otherwise. Isn't that so, Tomboy?"

Turning to him, Amie noticed Tom's flushed face, and instantly the desire to thwart *Mr. Bigshot* was too overwhelming to resist. How dare this man belittle one of her uncle's best friends!

She took another step toward Tom. "We're not related at all. Actually, I'm in town for the weekend on business, and Tom

57

was nice enough to take me to dinner to-night." She looked up at him, wearing a sweet smile, and looped her arm around his elbow. "We met over at the gas station in Tigerton."

"You don't say . . . ?" He stood there non-plused.

Tom's smile reflected his embarrassment. "Al, she's really —"

"Dying to go for a walk," Amie put in hastily. "Come on, Tom. You promised me a stroll around town." She looked back at the gaping Al Simonson. "Nice to meet you."

She half pulled Tom down to the street corner where she burst out laughing while waiting for the WALK sign. He stared at her, a look of horror on his face.

"Are you out of your mind?"

"Probably . . . oh, now, don't get mad, Tom. That guy deserved it. Didn't you hear how he insulted you? What a jerk!"

Amie released his arm as they crossed the street.

"I've practically grown up with Big Al Simonson," Tom muttered, "and I can't believe what you just did." He glanced over at her. "You don't have a clue, do you? This isn't Chicago, Amie. People talk. Al is from Tigerton, and not only is he a large man, he's got a large mouth. By noon tomorrow, what just happened will be all over town."

"Relax, Tom. He'll find out who I am soon enough and figure everything out. It's not like I lied."

"Purposely deceiving someone is the same as lying, Amie."

She huffed at the rebuttal. "All right. Fine."

Tom stopped in midstride. Amie paused as well. And as she looked up at him, she saw the most miserable expression she'd ever seen on a human being. His gaze was out somewhere over her head, giving her a chance to scrutinize his features without him noticing.

He wasn't at all an unattractive man, she decided as questions piqued her curiosity. Why wasn't he dating? He seemed like a fine catch — for the right woman, of course.

"Why did that guy say those things, Tom?" she asked softly, so passers-by wouldn't overhear. "Why did he say that no girl in her right mind would go out with you?"

"I thought I explained all this earlier."

"You're the guy least likely to succeed? Bah!" She rolled her eyes. "And now I suppose you're upset because a rude man from Tigerton saw us together and he'll peg me as the woman least likely to succeed. Is that it?" With hands on hips, she lifted a defiant chin. "Well, I know differently, and I don't care what anybody says. I'm successful and you can be too. If God is for us, who can be against us?"

Tom stared back at her in reply, his expression unreadable.

Amie continued her discourse, "I haven't known you for more than a few hours, Tom Anderson, but even if this town thinks you're least likely to succeed, I don't believe it for a minute. You could be anything you wanted to be." She glanced up the street where they'd run into Tom's beefy pal. "But if it will make you feel better, I'll go try to find Al . . . I'll explain everything." She looked back at him. "Will that fix things?"

"Maybe." He narrowed his gaze. "You know, I can't figure you out. You go from feisty to fearful in a single bound. A few minutes ago, I could've sworn you were afraid of Big Al and now you're offering to go find him." He chuckled, looking thoroughly amused. "I suppose you'd take him on single-handedly, huh?"

"I'm a very outgoing, congenial person," she stated, sounding defensive to her own ears. "But every so often I have these moments of . . . of *trepidation*." She turned to walk away, slinging her purse over her shoulder. "In any case, I'm more than able to take care of myself in any given situation. So thanks for dinner and I'll see you tomorrow. And I'll find *Brutus*," she added sassily over her shoulder, "after I check into the motel."

Man, that guy has got to lighten up, she thought in exasperation. However, it only took her a few moments to realize that she had no idea where she was going. She stopped short and turned around, slamming into Tom.

"Oh, sorry."

He lifted his brows expectantly.

She swallowed hard, utterly embarrassed. "Guess I need you to show me where the motel is."

He smirked. "Right this way."

They walked the remaining blocks in awkward silence. Then, upon reaching the Best Rest Motel, she checked in, signed the necessary forms, secured the room with her credit card, and dropped the key to her room into her purse.

"All set," she announced to Tom who'd waited for her outside in the cooling evening breeze.

They hiked back amid the same uncomfortable mood. When they finally reached their vehicles, Amie turned off her car alarm using the mechanism built into her key chain and released the locks in the same fashion.

"Thanks again for dinner," she muttered, opening the door and climbing in. But when she tried to close it, Tom stood in the way.

She looked up at him with uncertainty.

"Do you think we could talk for a little while? I mean, I wouldn't want the sun to go down on our anger."

"I'm not angry."

"Neither am I," he said earnestly. "But, I think it'd be good if we settled a few things anyway."

"What sort of *things?*"

In reply, he reached for her hand, helping her from the car and impressing Amie with his manners once more. She immediately decided that touch of savoir faire made Tom Anderson seem more the gallant gentleman than the backwards country boy she had assessed him as before.

Now, if only he wasn't so melancholy . . .

"Should we go back into Allen and Rosie's for a soda or something?" he suggested. "At least in there we could hold a conversation without being in the public spotlight, and they're open for another half hour."

"Sure."

They entered the restaurant for the second time, and after they were seated, Amie and Tom ordered colas.

"About what happened . . . I'm sorry," she told him. "I should have kept my mouth shut. It's just that Al's insults upset me."

"Why? He wasn't insulting you. Besides, it's no big deal. I'm used to it."

Amie contemplated his answer as she sipped her soda. "That's terrible. You shouldn't have to put up with derogatory remarks from that . . . bully!"

Tom grinned wanly. "Whatever. Can we forget all that? I've decided you're right — Big Al'll find out who you are soon enough, and he'll know we weren't on a date. I actually wanted to talk about the gas station. I meant to bring up the subject at dinner but didn't know how to approach it."

She frowned, puzzled. "What about the gas station?"

"Well," he hedged, "I wondered if you knew what you wanted to do with it."

"No, not yet."

"I suppose you'll need to charge me rent."

"I . . . I don't know. I didn't think about that." She lifted a hopeful brow. "Wanna buy the place from me? I know Uncle Hal left you some money."

"Are you nuts?"

Frowning, she quipped, "I think you just hurt my feelings!"

He smiled, though it didn't quite reach his eyes. "I didn't mean to. It's just that if I buy that gas station . . . well, I'll be trapped. Stuck in a dead end."

"A dead end in a dying town?"

"Something like that."

"I see . . ." Amie thought about telling Tom her hotel idea. Except she really didn't want to be "trapped" either. But even if that wasn't the case and even if she could come up with the funds, which she couldn't, she'd never have the time to oversee such an undertaking.

"There's a lot of traffic on Highway 45," she ventured. Perhaps Tom would want to build a hotel. "I saw plenty of tourists heading north for the weekend."

"I don't want to buy the gas station, Amie, so get that notion out of your head."

"Okay." She sighed. "The truth is, I really never had peace about selling it anyway." She looked down at the ice cubes, swirling around in her glass. "In his last letter to me — the one I found in his safe deposit box today — Uncle Hal told me to raze the buildings on the property and put up a hotel." She lifted her eyes to gauge Tom's reaction. "It was always my dream as a little girl . . . to build a hotel."

"A hotel?"

"Yes. But what's incredible is I've really been thinking about it!"

"Building a hotel . . . in Tigerton?"

"Yep." Amie laughed at his astonished expression, which faded fast. Moments later, Tom seemed pensive.

"Think it would be a profitable business?" she asked.

"Might be."

A spark of aspiration rose up in Amie but dwindled just as fast as it had been ignited. "I don't have the time or money to build a hotel," she confessed, wishing she didn't feel so disappointed.

"Yeah, me neither."

Tom pushed his chair back and stood. Taking it as a hint that their meeting had come to an end, Amie did the same.

"Well, um, I hope you have a good night's sleep," he said, looking suddenly ill at ease. He threw a few dollars onto the table. "I guess I'll see you tomorrow."

"Yes, see you tomorrow."

In silence, they exited the quaint restaurant and without a word they parted, giving Amie the distinct impression that she'd said something terribly wrong.

Chapter 5

"What a dumb idea. I've never heard anything more harebrained in my entire life!" Tom ranted to himself as he paced the apartment. "What makes you think you can have a hand in running a hotel? You don't know the first thing about it! What are you thinking? As if a woman like Amie Potter would even consider *you* for a business partner." He collapsed into a faded, overstuffed armchair in the living room. "You, a loser. Son of the town drunk. Part of a dysfunctional family unit if there ever was one!"

He sighed, his feelings of depression escalating. He couldn't help thinking that his self-deprecation sounded a whole lot like Big Al's taunts. He'd heard them since junior high, and he was used to it, either way. Combined with the memory of his father's beatings, he didn't have much faith in himself.

"But I've got faith in God," he affirmed out loud, clinging to that delicate thread of hope that kept his head together when circumstances threatened to blow his very mind. Hal, friend that he was, had always told him faith in Christ was the key to everything in life. And he'd been right.

But now he's gone, Tom conceded glumly. He squeezed his eyes closed, shutting them against the onslaught of grief. *Oh, God! Why couldn't You have taken me instead? I'm the one who's so tired of living.*

Suddenly Amie's words from earlier that evening floated back to him. "If God is for us, who can be against us? You could be anything you wanted to be."

Opening his eyes, Tom gazed around his dingy living quarters and smiled sadly. She was so much like her uncle. Always thinking positive. He laughed. Why, she'd even stuck up for him in front of Big Al Simonson, just like Hal used to do. But she'd been scared of him too. Tom hadn't missed that. And he had to wonder — was the incident this afternoon, the one which sent her flying out of this apartment, a result of fear as well?

Naw, he decided. *Why would she be afraid of me?*

With his emotions in turmoil, Tom reached for his Bible. He opened to the Book of Genesis and took up reading where he'd left off yesterday. He didn't have to go far before God spoke to his heart from chapter 39, verse 2: "And the Lord was with Joseph, and he was a prosperous man."

Tom paused reflectively. The Lord prospered Joseph — a man who didn't have the greatest background either. Hadn't Jacob, Joseph's father, deceived Esau into selling his birthright for a cup of soup? Hadn't Jacob displayed favoritism toward his wife Rebecca over Leah, causing great strife between the sisters? Hadn't he done the same with his sons, favoring Joseph over all the rest and generating bitterness and hatred among his family? Yet, God loved Jacob *and* Joseph.

"If God is for us . . ." Tom murmured thoughtfully. Searching the concordance in the back of his Bible, he found the verse Amie had quoted. Romans 8:31: "What shall we then say to these things? If God be for us, who can be against us?"

"Okay, maybe this is a chance at a new beginning." His thoughts returned to the hotel idea, and a yearning such as he'd never experienced began spreading through him, like wildfire through dried brush. God was with him. The Lord would prosper him. And wouldn't it be something if he could show this town that Tom Anderson could be a successful businessman? What a testimony of Christ's saving power!

All right, Lord, I'll do it, but You're going to have to work out all the details — like convincing Amie to build the place and persuading her to let me be her partner.

Amie toyed with the earring she'd looped around her middle finger while she spoke with her father on the telephone. "I know it sounds crazy, Dad. But after I read Uncle Hal's letter, I just couldn't get the idea out of my mind. I want to build a hotel up here."

"Well, honey, you know I'm all for adventure, particularly if it pertains to business." He chuckled. "I don't call these things 'business ventures,' I call them 'business *ad*ventures.' "

She laughed softly.

"But your mother may not be as supportive as I am, you understand. She hated country living. When we met in college, all she talked about was moving to a big city and staying there so her children would have the opportunities she didn't."

Amie rolled her eyes. She'd heard the story a thousand times if she'd heard it once. "Dad, I'm not talking about *living* here, although there are days when my life is so hectic that I've thought about moving somewhere quiet, slow paced."

"In that case, try North Carolina," he quipped. "I was there on business last week and even the fast food is slow."

"Oh, Dad," Amie chided him, smiling. "Be serious now."

He chuckled. "All right. Well, let's see . . . money? That's your first concern."

"I might have an investor. But I emphasize the word 'might.' " She paused. "His name is Tom Anderson. He's a nice guy. Very helpful, and I think he'd be the perfect person to run the hotel." *I just have to convince him of it,* she added silently.

"Okay, Princess, I trust your judgment."

"And Uncle Hal left me some of his investments. I don't know what they're worth, though."

"Stocks? Mutual funds?"

"I don't know. Let me get them."

Amie fished through all the papers she'd acquired since opening her uncle's safe deposit box yesterday. One by one, she read them to her father who promised to do some research for her.

"I'll also talk to my friend, Bill Reeser, the architect. I'll see if he can come up with a few designs for us to look at."

"Thanks, Dad. Let him know that I want my hotel to include an antique shop, banquet hall, café, and indoor swimming pool."

"Anything else?" he asked on a facetious note.

"Well, rooms, of course."

"Very funny, young lady."

"A veritable chip off the old block, huh, Dad?" she teased.

He chuckled. Then, after a moment's pause, he asked, "Why an antique shop . . . and all the rest? Perhaps those could be added later."

"Oh no, Dad. We'll need those things to draw tourists. Antique shops are big up here, and Tom is fabulous at refinishing furniture. It'll be a great attraction for the hotel. After the tourists stop, we'll have to feed them, so we'll need the café — and, of course we'll have to offer a continental breakfast to our guests. I thought the indoor swimming pool could be a community attraction. We can rent it out for special occasions like kids' birthday parties. The same with the banquet hall."

"Take a breath, Amie," her father joked. "You're going to hyperventilate."

She pursed her lips, realizing she'd been babbling like a silly little brook. "Sorry about that. I guess I'm just excited."

"I guess. But it's not the worst thing in the world to be enthusiastic about a new business adventure, you know."

She smiled. "Thanks for understanding."

"You bet."

"Will you talk to Mom for me?"

"Soften the blow, you mean?"

"Something like that." Amie wondered if her mother would be the next to hyperventilate.

"Yes, I'll speak with her. Don't worry."

"Thanks, Dad."

Amie hung up the telephone and took a deep breath, experiencing God's peace that passed all understanding. This was God's will. She was certain of it.

Ever since last night, after meeting with Tom over colas, she hadn't been able to sleep or even concentrate. It was as if there were a disturbing, nagging swell in her chest that wouldn't go away.

Until she made her decision.

She would build a hotel.

Smiling, she grabbed her purse and left the motel room for her uncle's gas station and yet another meeting with the reclusive Tom Anderson.

"I have to talk to you."

The words were spoken in unison.

Amie giggled. "You first."

"No, no, ladies first," Tom insisted.

"Well, okay."

She climbed out of her car and stood beside Tom, who had immediately met her as she drove into the station. He looked rested and his eyes seemed to have lost some of their sadness. He was dressed better than yesterday when she'd first seen him, and he appeared showered and shaved.

She tipped her head. "Could we talk over coffee . . . and maybe a sweet roll?"

Tom grinned. "You eat a lot for a woman, know that?"

"Excuse me! I haven't had breakfast yet!"

He laughed in a way Amie had never heard. She narrowed her gaze. "Why are you so happy today?"

"I'm not so happy," he replied, a hint of a smile still on his face. "You're just awfully fun to tease."

"Yeah? Well, remind me never to let you and my father in the same room together. He loves to tease me too."

Tom appeared a bit chagrined, glancing at the pavement before looking back at her. "I've got a pot of coffee upstairs and some doughnuts." He assessed her thoughtfully, then added, "If that's okay with you."

She hesitated, but just for a moment. "That'll be fine. Thanks."

As she followed Tom to the front door, a nightmarish recollection flashed through

73

her mind. *Stop it,* she warned herself. But in the next moment, her step faltered as she remembered something more — it was a statement made by one of the women leading a Bible study at church. "Good girls don't get raped," she'd declared adamantly. "It's the girls who put themselves in compromising situations who end up getting hurt."

The woman might have been more sensitive, had she been aware of Amie's past. Nevertheless, those words haunted her. Had she put herself in a "compromising situation" three years ago? Yes. Obviously. And it was all her fault.

Don't think about that now, she chided herself again. But it was no use; she couldn't seem to shake the horrible memory of that night.

"Tom?" Amie reached for his arm, fighting down the sudden panic.

He stopped and turned expectantly.

"Do you think we could . . ." She scanned the property. "I mean, it's a nice day, and . . ."

"Want to have coffee at the picnic table around back?" he asked as if divining her thoughts.

She nearly fainted with relief. "That'd be great."

He nodded. "Be right back."

The shaking began as it always did; however, by the time Tom returned carrying a mug of coffee in each hand and a box of chocolate doughnuts under one arm, it had dissipated. Her composure was back. Amie watched as he pulled out packets of powered cream and sugar before sitting down at the picnic table.

"Wasn't sure how you like your coffee," he explained, taking a seat at last.

"Cream and sugar — both." She managed a smile, grateful that Tom didn't treat her like some lunatic. But perhaps he hadn't noticed.

"Okay, you start."

She ripped open a creamer and cleared her throat. "I've decided to build a hotel," she blurted. "And I've decided that you're going to help me. Now, don't argue, Tom. Hear me out, first. I don't mean to be presumptuous; it's just that I *need* you . . . to run the antique shop in my hotel — *our* hotel." She gave him a shy smile. "See, I, um, need your money too."

Tom gawked at her in obvious disbelief.

"I know I'm dumping all this on you, but I really think it'll be a great investment for the both of us." She looked at him askance. "What do you think?"

"I think . . ." He shook his head. "I can't believe what I'm hearing. That's what I think."

Amie winced. "You don't like my idea?"

"No! I mean, yes. Yes, I like your idea." Tom seemed temporarily abashed. But then he grinned. "That's exactly what I wanted to talk to you about. Building your hotel."

"*Our* hotel," she corrected him.

"Our hotel." He scratched his head. "That sounds weird." His hazel eyes suddenly searched her face for several long moments. "I'd like a chance at this," he said earnestly. "I'd like a partnership. I don't know anything about running a hotel and . . . and an antique shop . . ." He paused. "An antique shop." He spoke the words reverently, and an almost dreamy expression appeared on his face.

"I take it you approve of that notion."

"Sure!"

Amie chuckled and sipped her coffee. This was the most reaction she'd ever seen from him.

"I'm a fast learner," Tom continued. "Maybe I could take some management courses to get my feet wet, so to speak. I won't let you down."

"I see," she stated lightly. "You're not a bad salesman, either." Lifting a doughnut from the box, she added, "You're hired."

"So are you," he retorted, extending his right hand. "Partners?"

Amie smiled broadly. "Partners."

Chapter 6

Amie and Tom spent the remainder of Saturday going through the Laundromat, sifting through everything Hal had collected over the years. They quickly agreed they were off to a good start in gathering merchandise for their antique shop.

"I know a farmer who'll let me rent part of his shed for storage," Tom said, looking around at all the pieces of furniture. "He won't charge much. I'll start hauling stuff over next week. Obviously, I'm going to have to empty the buildings before we can get a demolition crew out here."

Amie nodded, wondering what she'd ever do without Tom helping her out and offering to be a partner. Besides the financial aspect, her career wouldn't afford her the time to haul and sort. She was glad Tom would be here to do it.

Later, after a picnic supper of microwaved hot dogs — Tom playing the gourmet cook — he allowed her to go up to the apartment alone and box up her uncle's personal belongings.

Entering the bedroom, Amie's gaze immediately fell to the framed photographs on the dresser. One was her own college graduation picture and, next to it, was a photo of Tom, his hair much shorter. He wore a suit that looked as if it had seen better days and, standing beside him, was a younger-looking man in a graduation robe. Both men sported broad smiles.

Setting down the frame, she considered the other snapshots. A woman's black-and-white portrait — probably Hal's wife. Amie recalled hearing the tragic story of the young woman's drowning while on their honeymoon, but it wasn't something her uncle candidly discussed, and as a little girl, she'd often wondered about the incident.

Opening the dresser drawers, Amie emptied them. Then she removed all the clothing from Hal's wardrobe, deciding his garments could go to charity. Glancing around the room, she determined the oak bedroom set that Tom had sanded and varnished could go to Dottie since she'd been coveting some of the furniture. Tom already said he didn't care. Anything in this room was hers to do with as she pleased.

The packing of books on the wooden shelf

became her next task. Boxing them up, Amie noticed the three hard-bound journals. *Uncle Hal kept diaries,* she mused, feeling somewhat surprised. He'd never seemed like the kind of man who'd record his thoughts. Marveling at her find, she ran a hand across one volume's smooth red surface. She leafed through it briefly, and then purposed to read all three of the memoirs when she had a free evening or weekend — whenever that might be.

Placing the books into the box, she finished loading the others before gently laying the photographs on top.

Wiping her dusty hands on her colorful broomstick skirt, Amie surveyed the room one last time with a pang of sadness. Much of her uncle's life had just been packed into three large boxes.

Sunday dawned another glorious summer day. Tom invited Amie to attend worship service in a tiny country church in Morris, an outlying, rural community. Amie remembered it well. It was the church in which her uncle's funeral had been held.

Sitting in the hard, wooden pew, she was once again captivated by the charm of the sanctuary, from its polished planked floors to the antiquated pipe organ in the far right corner. Amie found it amazing that the simplicity of her surroundings roused in her an inexplicable sense of inner peace.

Moments later, the youthful-looking pastor began the service with prayer, after which the congregation stood, opened their hymnals to page 270, and sang:

> *My soul in sad exile was out on life's sea,*
> *So burdened with sin and distrest,*
> *Till I heard a sweet voice saying, "Make me your choice!"*
> *And I entered the Haven of Rest.*

Although she'd sung this song dozens of times, today the words touched a tender chord in Amie's heart.

> *I've anchored my soul in the Haven of Rest,*
> *I'll sail the wide seas no more;*
> *The tempest may sweep o'er the wild, stormy deep —*
> *In Jesus I'm safe ever more.*

The pastor returned to the pulpit and delivered an enlightening message, but all the while the hymn's lyrics swirled around in Amie's head.

The Haven of Rest.

Suddenly she knew what to name the hotel — that was, if her partner agreed.

After the service ended, Tom introduced Amie to the minister, his wife, and their four darling little girls, Emma, Carol, Ellen, and Lucy.

"I'm sorry you have to go back to Chicago so soon," Katie Warren, the pastor's wife, said. "I hope you'll visit us again sometime." Her voice sounded as soft as the light brown curls looked in her hair.

Amie smiled. "I'll probably be back in a couple of weeks."

"Oh? Is there more to do in settling your uncle's affairs?"

"Yes, quite a lot more, actually," she replied. "Tom and I . . . well . . ." Amie didn't want to say too much about their hotel endeavor at this point. There were still the legalities to straighten out. "I guess I'm not exactly sure where to start." She turned to Tom. "Probably the Village Hall, don't you think? We're going to need some kind of permit."

"I'll find out," Tom answered. He moistened his lips and looked at the pastor. "There's, um, something I'd like to talk to you about."

Jake Warren's auburn brows shot up in surprise. "Why, Tom, you little sneak!" He chuckled jovially, his gaze moving between the two of them. "Hal's niece, huh?" He whacked Tom on the back affectionately. "I sure was fond of your uncle," he said to Amie. "He spoke of you often. And now you're going to marry our Tom — Hal would have been pleased as punch!"

"I beg your pardon?" Amie gasped.

Tom's hazel eyes were as wide as saucers as he grasped the pastor's meaning. "No, no, Pastor," he quickly tried to explain. "You've got it all wrong. We're not getting married. Not yet. I mean, to each other . . . we're not." He swallowed hard and Amie fought the urge to giggle. "We're building a hotel. Amie and me . . . partners. Business partners. That's what I wanted to speak to you about. You know . . . to get godly counsel."

"Oh, I see." The disappointment on his freckled face was clear, and Amie felt her face flush in embarrassment.

"Oh, I'm sure you two'll end up getting married someday," Katie stated sweetly. Then she frowned. "Oh. I didn't mean it that way. To each other. Necessarily." She cleared her throat uncomfortably. "I meant, I'm sure that someday you'll get married to whomever God has chosen for you."

Amie nodded for the sake of propriety.

But, after her past, she'd begun to wonder if there was a decent Christian man alive who'd want to marry her.

Folding her arms tightly, she let her gaze wander around the chapel. "This is such a pretty little church," she murmured, desperate for a change of subject.

"We love it here," Katie told her, her own relief apparent.

"Well, Tom," Pastor Warren began, "drop by anytime and we'll discuss whatever is on your heart."

"Thanks," he said with a slight grin.

They both turned to leave when a plump, elderly lady with tightly coiled gray hair approached them. "Did you say you're getting married, Tom?" she asked. "How wonderful!" Turning to Amie, she added, "Tom is such a nice young man. It's a pity he's had such a hard life. I'm so glad he's finally found a pretty girl to settle down with."

"Thank you, but, um —"

"We are not getting married, Mrs. Jensen," Tom fairly hollered into the poor woman's left ear. "She's hard of hearing," he explained with a quick glance at Amie.

"Oh."

"This is Hal's niece, Amie Potter," he continued loudly. "She's here for the weekend . . . on business."

The elderly woman frowned. "You're not getting married? Bette Jo Christensen said she heard you were. She heard Pastor Warren say that, just now."

"Good grief," Tom mumbled irritably.

Amie couldn't conceal her mirth a moment longer and burst into a fit of laughter.

Tom shook his head and then hugged the old lady around the shoulders. "A misunderstanding, Mrs. Jensen. Have a good day."

"Thank you, Tom." She pouted slightly. "I just wish you were getting married." With one final glance at Amie, she added, "He really is a nice young fellow."

"Yes, I know he is," she replied, following Tom to the door. When the old woman became preoccupied with talking to another parishioner, Amie turned to Tom. "I noticed *she* doesn't have a low opinion of you."

"Mrs. Jensen was my kindergarten teacher. She still thinks I'm the best finger painter in all of northern Wisconsin."

Amie chuckled softly as they descended the many steps leading to the gravel lot.

"This isn't funny," he told her on a note of exasperation. "Do you understand now what I mean about gossip starting and spreading around here like the Bubonic Plague?"

"Don't fret, Tom," she countered sassily. "Perhaps Pastor Warren will make an announcement from the pulpit next Sunday and dispel the rumors. Or maybe he can take out an ad in the local newspaper."

He shook his index finger at her. "You're gonna be sorry you laughed about this, Amie. Mark my words."

She rolled her eyes. "Lighten up, Tom. It's a hoot." His expression remained grim, so she continued, "You and I haven't done anything to bring gossip down upon our heads. This is harmless — a comedy of errors — and it'll get straightened out soon enough."

"Yeah, sure," he replied, looking none too convinced.

"By the way, I thought of a name for our hotel."

He lifted his brows expectantly. "Oh? And what's that?"

"The Haven of Rest." She smiled proudly.

He repeated it a couple of times. "I like it. The Haven of Rest."

"Great." They stood behind Amie's red BMW. "Well, I guess I'll see you in a couple weeks," she said, opening her purse and pulling out her keys. "I'm sorry I can't get up here sooner. I'm so busy at work."

"That's okay. I've got your e-mail address and phone number, and you've got mine."

A couple of boys, obviously junior-high age, suddenly peeked around the van parked next to Amie's car and began to make smooching noises. Tom took a deep breath, his face reddening with indignation.

Amie didn't even attempt to hide her laughter as she disengaged the alarm system. "Just remember," she said, climbing into her uncomfortably hot car, "self-control! Fruit of the Spirit and all that."

"Easy for you to say, *Miss Chicago*. I'm the one left here to deal with this mess."

She gave him a careless shrug, just to tease him all the more.

But then, as she made her way down the little dirt road, heading out to the highway, it occurred to her that not even Tom Anderson, a man who thought of himself as a loser, would want a woman like her for a wife. Chaste and virtuous, that's what single Christian men were looking for in a woman.

Amie thought about the singles group she belonged to at church. They were forever pledging their purity until marriage when the pastor spoke on the topic. But each time the altar call signaled such a response from her, she felt like a hypocrite.

She stepped on the accelerator. Tom was right. This situation was not funny. Not funny at all!

The next week passed quickly for Amie. She barely had time to think, let alone make decisions about the impending hotel project. Her boss, Tim Daley, dumped two new accounts on her, forcing her to put in twelve-hour days at the office and take work home at night. Finally, on Sunday afternoon, otherwise known as "family time," she was able to get her mind off Maxwell Brothers' Marketing and Developing Company for at least a few hours.

"You look a bit peaked, dear," her mother said, furrowing her silver brows in concern. "Are you eating enough?"

"Mom, I could live off my fat for months," Amie teased.

"Nonsense."

"She'll eat tonight," John Potter told his wife. "I'm throwing steaks on the grill."

"Oh, yum!"

Her father winked. "Just for you, Princess. And after dinner, I'll show you the sketches Bill Reeser drew up for your hotel."

"Great." She took a seat in her parents' newly remodeled kitchen. The brightly papered walls added splashes of color to the otherwise stark-white room. Seeing her mother's immaculate countertops made Amie feel like a terrible housekeeper. She'd been too busy and, as a result, her condo was a complete disaster.

"Sweetheart, your father told me all about your plans — and you know how he loves a challenge, but I wish you'd reconsider," Lillian said, pulling a pitcher of lemonade out of the refrigerator. "Property values are rapidly depreciating up there. The community is largely impoverished."

"Then perhaps my hotel will help the local economy."

"Perhaps," Lillian stated carefully as she poured the chilled drink into two frosted crystal glasses. "Or you could lose everything, Amie. You're taking quite a risk."

She shrugged. "Nothing ventured, nothing gained."

Her mother lifted a well-shaped brow. "Nothing ventured, nothing lost."

Amie chose not to reply as she accepted the offered glass of lemonade. She'd known her mother wouldn't be much of a cheerleader. She'd even surmised that Lillian Potter would try to talk her out of building the hotel. However, her mind was made up.

"Mom, look, it isn't like I'm making some

rash decision. I've thought about this . . . prayed about this."

"All right, dear," Lillian remarked, looking skeptical.

"Hey, how's Stephen doing?" she asked, attempting to distract her mother from the subject of the hotel. "Does he still like college?"

"Loves it. Got an A on his first biology quiz."

"Good for him."

"He's always done well in school. In fact, when Stephen was in first grade —"

Dottie suddenly burst through the back door, capturing their attention.

"Amie, you've got to be nuts!" she declared loudly. "Dad just told me you're building a hotel in Tigerton. Of all the places in the world, why you'd choose that town is beyond me!"

"Lemonade, dear?" Lillian asked her younger daughter, who nodded as she marched over and stood beside Amie.

"You ought to have your head examined," she rambled on. "And when can I pick up my furniture?"

Amie sighed. So much for a peaceful evening with the folks at home.

Chapter 7

When Amie got back to her condo, she felt somewhat discouraged. She wondered if she had, indeed, made a mistake in deciding to build a hotel. Only her father seemed enthusiastic, but she quickly reminded herself that was the way it usually was with her family. Seldom did her mother and Dottie agree with Amie's decisions, and for some odd reason, their lack of support overshadowed her father's exuberance.

Setting her purse on the kitchen table, Amie walked into the spare bedroom that served as her home office. She flipped on the computer and began to check her E-mail messages, feeling pleasantly surprised to see one from Tom.

Hi, Amie,
  Hope you had a nice weekend. Here's the update so far. I got most of Hal's junk cleared out of the two buildings. A lot of it was trash, but

the majority of it can be salvaged. I had to rent a storage unit in Shawano. Herb Mahlberg's shed was too small. (By the way, I set aside more furniture for your sister.)

I should be moved out by the end of August. Pastor Jake said I could move into the church basement temporarily. The Tigerton town council meets once a month. If the vote goes through, the property should be ready for demolition some time in October. I talked to a couple of construction companies, and both said they could start building in the spring, provided the plans have been approved by the state. Guess we'd better get the plans together.

Smiling, Amie immediately typed a reply, informing Tom of the structural designs her father's friend had drawn up. She promised to mail him copies and described the layout she liked best. *Nice work, Tom,* she wrote. *You're a fast mover! What would I do without you?*

She clicked on SEND and sat back in her chair, suddenly feeling excited about this endeavor again.

Tom stood across the highway as the last

of the golden leaves on the elm trees rustled overhead. The temperature was in the mid-fifties and the gusty wind had a nip to it. He glanced at his booted feet and the surrounding dried vegetation. Fall had arrived, and everything was dying off. Even the October sunshine had grown distant.

At the sound of roaring machinery, he turned his gaze back to the gas station and garage where he'd worked for the past thirteen years of his life. The huge gasoline tanks had been dug out last week and now the final razing of the buildings would occur.

Shaking his head in wonder, Tom forced himself to remember. That's why he'd come here today — to watch and reminisce. One last time, then never again. He caught his breath as the bulldozer slammed into one of the walls. It seemed like a million years ago since he'd walked into Hal's office and asked for employment.

"So you want a job, huh?"

"Yes, sir," Tom had replied, feeling more than a little intimidated. Everywhere he'd applied, he'd been turned down. This was his last chance, and it had taken him over an hour to get his courage up enough to walk in. Halvor Holm, known around town as "Hal," had a reputation for being a harsh, no-nonsense guy. Tom had never known anyone who'd asked him for a job. No one had the audacity! However, Tom felt desperate. He'd been rudely awakened to the fact that if he didn't support his family, nobody else would. It was up to him. His youngest siblings were counting on him — particularly six-year-old Matthew.

"Know anything about cars?"

"Just that you gotta put gas in 'em."

Hal pursed his lips in thought. "Gotta put oil in 'em too. And a few other things."

"Yes, sir." He looked up into Hal's grizzled face, thinking his Norwegian blue eyes were almost startling in contrast. Then they scrutinized him so hard that Tom squirmed.

"Aren't you one of those Anderson kids?"

Reluctantly, he nodded. Once more, his reputation had preceded him. It looked like this job was shot too.

"Your younger brother busted my window the other day. Pitched a rock clean through it."

Tom shifted uncomfortably. "I, uh, didn't know that. Must have been Phillip. I . . . I'll see that he comes back and fixes it."

"Hmm . . . you do that. And I suppose you're not aware that your dad stole fifty dollars from me either. He took it right out of the till while I was fixing the pop machine out front. That guy's got a lot of nerve, I'll say!"

"He stole your money?" Tom's stomach flipped. He'd wondered where the groceries came from. And the bottle of whiskey.

"What's that bruise under your eye? Were you in a fight? Are you one of those kids who uses his fists instead of his brains?"

Any further hopes for a job flew straight out the broken window. "I'd better get going. Thanks anyway."

"Now, hold on a second."

He paused.

"I asked you a question," Hal said sternly, "and I expect an honest answer. Whether you knew about the broken window and the money doesn't matter to me as long as you tell me the truth."

"I didn't pick a fight. My pa hit me," Tom blurted, staring Hal straight in the eye. "But he didn't mean it. He was drunk. He's not a bad man, he's just . . . just not been right since Mom died." He swallowed his shame over what his family had become. "As for the window and the money, I didn't know about either one, till now."

After a moment's deliberation, Hal nodded. "Okay. I believe you." He rubbed his whiskered chin. "You still in school?"

"Uh-huh."

"Can you drive?"

"Legally?"

Hal grinned wryly. "Yeah, legally."

"I don't have my license, but I can drive. Real good too."

"Well, we're going to have to get you your license, son."

Tom's brows shot up. "We are?"

"Yep. I'll need you to fetch parts once in awhile."

"You will?"

Hal extended his wide, oil-stained hand. "You got a job if you want one."

The bulldozer made another hard hit against the side of the apartment building and Laundromat, pulling Tom's thoughts to the present. The splintering of wood and the spray of shattered glass echoed in the chill of the autumn afternoon. They weren't unfamiliar sounds, and suddenly he recalled a time when his father hurled a kitchen chair across the room, destroying one of the few framed photographs that hung on the wall, but not before it struck Tom in the shoulder. Hal's place had been a safe haven for him back then — a place where he went to lick his wounds. It was also where he'd come to a saving knowledge of Christ.

Under Hal's fatherly and biblical counsel, Tom had learned to forgive. He'd also re-learned how to laugh.

So many memories were made and stored up there, Tom reflected, as a good portion of the old apartment building crumbled. *Nearly as many memories as there was junk!*

Even so, he couldn't say he was completely grieved to see the decrepit structures knocked to the ground because with them went his past. There was only one thing left to do now: Rebuild.

Amie climbed out of her car and inhaled sharply when she saw the flattened land that had once accommodated her uncle's filling station. The frosty November wind blew her hair into her face. She pushed it back in vain. She couldn't imagine why she was so surprised to see the buildings gone. Tom, her faithful partner, had phoned her on the day of the demolition. Since then, he'd kept her up to date on everything from finances and town hall meetings to calls inquiring about the state's approval of their hotel plans. Still a little part of her was sad to see her uncle's place actually . . . gone. Only a thin white layer of snow covering two mounds of brown dirt hinted at where buildings once stood on Uncle Hal's property.

"But it's my property now," she reminded herself. "Mine and Tom's."

Glancing at her watch, she gasped. If she didn't hurry, she'd be late for the Thanksgiving dinner at the Warrens'!

Jumping back into her car, she sped down County Highway J and on into the rural town of Morris. Farms, fields, and gently rolling hills stretched out before her. She made a turn and then another, passing the little white country church. Finally, she reached the Warrens' driveway.

Accelerating up the hill, she spotted Tom's truck and cringed inwardly. On several occasions, he'd accused her of living life in the "fast lane," and Amie couldn't deny it. She seemed to rush everywhere she went, and more often than not, she was late in getting there. Recently, however, she'd come to hate her hectic schedule and frequently felt like a caged gerbil, spinning its wheels.

Last night, she'd promised Tom she wouldn't be late today — but she was.

Throwing the car into park, Amie grabbed her purse and coat, then practically fell out of the BMW in her haste. As she reached the front porch of the single-story ranch home, the door opened and Katie Warren smiled kindly.

"Welcome, Amie."

"Thanks," she replied, breathlessly. "Sorry I'm late."

"Oh, you're not late. I just took the turkey out of the oven."

Amie smiled gratefully as the slim brunette hung up her wool, full-length coat. She turned and smiled. "Come with me. I want to introduce you to all our guests."

Following her hostess into the parsonage's modestly decorated living room, she noticed two elderly, white-headed ladies sitting on the couch along with a bald, wrinkled man who was propped at the other end. To her right, an attractive, young, and very pregnant woman with shoulder-length, frosted hair looked as though she'd sunk into the armchair, and Tom was perched on the piano bench across the room.

Amie sent him a subtle wave, immediately aware of his haircut and clean-shaven face. In reply, he mouthed, "You're late."

She grimaced.

"This is Mrs. Helen Baumgarten," Katie began, "and Mrs. Louise Gunderson and her husband, Harold. And over here," she added, indicating the expectant mother, "is Mrs. Nancy Simonson whose husband, Al, is deer hunting. Now, I'll leave you all to get acquainted while I finish preparing dinner. Everything's just about ready."

After Katie left the room, Amie acknowledged everyone with a polite nod and a smile. She strolled over to the piano bench, taking a seat next to Tom who, unlike herself, hadn't overdressed for the occasion. Amie figured they made quite a contrast with him wearing a pair of faded jeans and a navy, long-sleeved shirt and her in a black-and-white checked Christian Dior dress with matching jacket.

She shifted her weight on the hard bench and gave Tom a tiny smile. For some odd reason, she felt suddenly awkward around him, even though they'd been corresponding for months. She chanced another peek in his direction, deciding his facial features seemed much different than she remembered. He looked well-groomed, his handsome features quite apparent now that they weren't hidden behind whiskers and long hair. His hazel eyes didn't seem so sad — so haunted. But curiously, Tom's improved image only boosted her perplexing emotions. Why did she feel shy and self-conscious around him when, by phone or E-mail, she'd been very comfortable? It was as though they'd gotten to know each other a little better on the inside, but they were still strangers on the outside.

"Lots of traffic on the road today?" Tom

asked, his arm inadvertently brushing against her shoulder.

Amie gave him a guilty look. "No, I just slept through my alarm."

"I told you . . . ," he stated softly, a teasing light in his eyes.

"I know. I know . . ." She immediately recalled how last night, when she'd telephoned to ask directions to the Warrens' house, he'd warned her not to stay up late, working on her newest account. He predicted she'd oversleep — and she did. "I guess I should have listened to you."

She suddenly caught a whiff of his pleasant-smelling cologne and remembered what he'd said in one of his previous e-mail messages. *It feels strange not to reek of gasoline anymore.*

"So, you guys are getting married, huh?" Nancy Simonson half asked, half stated, her light-brown gaze alternating between the two of them.

"Married?" Amie brought her chin back in surprise. "Is that silly rumor still floating around?"

Tom threw her a dubious glance as his entire countenance reddened.

"I take it that's a 'yes.' "

He grinned wryly. "Yes."

"Yes, you guys are getting married?"

Tom groaned. "No, we're not getting married. Yes, the rumor is still floating around."

Nancy furrowed her brows, looking confused.

"We're just business partners," Amie expounded further, quickly sucking her bottom lip between her teeth so she wouldn't start chattering incessantly.

"Oh," Nancy replied. "Yeah, I guess I'd heard that too."

"If you aren't getting married, are you *engaged* to be married?" Mrs. Baumgarten, the sturdier of the two aging women, asked. "Couples these days seem to have to think about it for a long time." She nudged the frail woman beside her. "Don't they, Louise?"

"Mercy, yes!" she exclaimed shakily. "Why, I just read an article in 'Reader's Digest' on that very subject."

"Well, don't think about it too long, sonny," old Mr. Gunderson at the end of the couch piped in. "You might lose your sweetheart to another fella. Women don't like to wait, you know. They want a commitment."

"Yes, sir, I'll remember that," Tom replied, giving Amie a helpless shrug. It seemed he'd given up trying to explain the circumstances surrounding their relationship.

But the gleam in Nancy's eyes seemed to express her understanding of the situation.

And then Amie began to wonder . . . Simonson. Al Simonson. Where had she heard that name before?

"Have we met?" she asked the young mother.

"You met Al in Shawano," Tom cut in. "Remember? Big Al?"

She thought it over and suddenly the image of Popeye's friend, Brutus, came to mind. "Oh, yes."

"How did you meet Al?" Nancy wanted to know.

"It was last summer. Tom and I were in Shawano . . . on business," Amie stated carefully so no more misunderstandings could erupt. She felt like her nerves were getting the best of her and she decided not to say another word, lest she babble on for hours.

"Al was there for a baseball tournament," Tom explained. "He'd told me about it a couple of days before we saw him. Guess his team ended up winning too."

"Right," Nancy said with a roll of her eyes. "The baseball tournament."

"So you're from Chicago . . . Amie, is it?" Mrs. Gunderson asked.

She nodded.

"Is your family there too?"

Again, she merely gave a nod, not trusting herself to reply in words.

"Amie's folks went to Hawaii for Thanksgiving," Tom informed them, much to Amie's relief. "Her sister is celebrating Thanksgiving with her fiancé, and her brother is away at college." He glanced over at her. "Did I get that right?"

Another nod.

"Oh, my! Well, I'm glad you came up here for the holiday," said Mrs. Baumgarten. "Now you don't have to be alone."

The word "alone" reverberated in Amie's heart. Even as she reminded herself that Jesus always stood beside her in spirit, she couldn't deny the fact that she felt lonely. Sighing inwardly, she came back around to the same conclusion: Singleness was her God-given lot in life. Her cross to bear. But, oh! How she'd love to be married and expecting a baby like Nancy.

Suddenly seven little girls ran into the room, laughing, jumping, and squealing. Four of the children Amie recognized as the Warrens' girls, and the rest, she assumed, belonged to the Simonsons.

"Mama says dinner's ready," Emma announced. She was obviously the oldest of the group, therefore, the spokesperson.

Everyone rose from their places, and Amie watched as Tom politely extended a hand to help Nancy up from the deep-seated armchair.

"Why, thanks." She turned to Amie. "I guess chivalry isn't dead after all." She paused before conspiratorially adding, "You'd never know that by the way my husband acts. When Betsy, our youngest, was born, Al said he hated girls. Can you believe that? He *hates* them!"

With a shake of her head in reply, Amie looked at Tom who was currently helping the senior citizens to the dining room.

Nancy followed her gaze and continued, "Back in high school, Tom had a crush on me. But I didn't know it until a few years ago. He never even asked me out! What was I supposed to do, read his mind?" She paused, gazing at him thoughtfully. "I wished you would have asked me on a date, Tom. I should have married you."

Something tugged at Amie's heartstrings as she wondered whether Tom ever got over his crush. Then she berated herself for even pondering such things! Tom Anderson's personal life was none of her concern. They were partners — professional business partners!

She glanced over at him while he seated Mr. Gunderson. The discomfort Tom obviously felt about this topic was clearly etched on his features.

"Don't even go there, Nancy," he told her. "We're all praying for Al. Once God saves his soul, he'll do right by you and the kids."

"Yeah, sure," she replied doubtfully.

"Now, Nancy," Mrs. Baumgarten said with admonition in her voice, "we're to pray *believing* that God will do all we ask. Why, my great niece had a spouse who was an awful carouser, but once he became a Christian, he turned into a wonderful family man. The same can happen for you."

At that moment, Pastor Jake Warren entered the dining room carrying the turkey, already sliced and on a porcelain platter. Setting it down on the table, he looked over at Amie. "Well, hello! I'm sorry I haven't been much of a host. Katie's kept me busy in the kitchen."

"No need to apologize," she stated, forcing herself not to say any more.

"Now *there's* a family man for ya!" Mr. Gunderson declared. "It's only out of love and sacrifice that the good pastor helps in the kitchen." He laughed, producing a hoarse, wheezing sound.

"Thanks, Harold," Jake replied jovially. Then he clasped his hands together. "Okay, the girls prayed over their food and are eating in the kitchen, so let's thank the Lord and dig in!"

"Amen!" the old man exclaimed.

Everyone chuckled and Katie entered the room. They took hands, Tom holding Amie's left and Nancy, her right. Then the pastor began to pray. But all the while, Amie couldn't stop thinking of how warm Tom's fingers felt as they enveloped her own.

Lord, I'm behaving so foolishly. Help me to control my emotions — and my tongue. Give me laryngitis if You have to, Father God. Do anything to keep me from babbling like an idiot because I'm . . . I'm . . . oh! I don't know what's the matter with me!

When Tom gave her hand a gentle squeeze, Amie knew the dinner prayer had ended. Lifting her head, she opened her eyes and found him gazing at her curiously.

Finally, he indicated the chair he held out for her and grinned sheepishly. "Are you going to sit down or eat standing up?"

She quickly took the seat, her heart pounding in embarrassment, and immediately concluded that this afternoon would be a long one!

Chapter 8

Amie walked out to her BMW in the frozen night air with Tom at her side. A full moon guided their way. "You really didn't have to see me to my car, but thanks."

"Sure."

She looked up, amazed at how sharp and clear the stars appeared without Chicago's city lights and pollution hindering their brilliance. "Wow," she breathed, "get a load of God's creation."

Tom briefly gazed at the twinkling sky. "It's something, all right."

Reaching her vehicle, Amie attempted to disengage her alarm, only to realize she'd never set it. "I was in such a hurry . . ."

"What?"

"I didn't activate my car alarm."

"Nobody would steal your . . . *hot rod* around here," he teased, the moonlight illuminating his features. "In fact, Pastor Jake has a habit of leaving his keys in the ignition when he parks his minivan."

Amie blinked in wonder. "I couldn't do that in Chicago."

"No doubt."

Opening the door, she threw her purse onto the passenger seat.

"Okay, one more time," Tom said earnestly. "How 'bout staying overnight with the Warrens like you planned? It took you a good four hours to get up here, and it's another four to get home . . . that's a long drive for a turkey dinner. Why don't you get some sleep and leave tomorrow morning?"

Amie sighed. "I can't."

"You can't? Or you don't want to?"

"I *can't*. I've got so much work at the office."

"Amie, you've got to slow down. You look . . . worn out."

She rolled her eyes. "And *you* sound like my mother."

He stuck his hands into his heavy jacket. "Well, see, that just proves I'm right."

With a derisive little snort, she climbed into her car and started the engine.

"Hey, let me ask you something before you go."

"Sure." She got back out and closed the door. "I should let my car warm up anyway."

He nodded and seemed to carefully weigh

his next words. "Is everything okay, Amie? I mean, you haven't changed your mind about the hotel, have you?"

"No!" She smiled. "I mean, yes, everything's fine and, no, I haven't changed my mind."

"The rumor about us . . . you, know, about us getting married," he stammered, "is it bothering you? I've done my best to set things straight, but folks keep asking me the same questions!" He groaned dramatically. "I just can't believe it!"

"That piece of gossip doesn't upset me, Tom," she stated contritely. "But I do feel badly for you, having to deal with it."

He waved away her comment. "Aw, I don't care anymore either."

"You might if you knew about . . ." Then her words faltered. How could she tell him about what had happened? Shame flooded her and her face grew red. "Oh, never mind."

Amie hadn't ever talked to anybody about what had happened to her three years ago, and the desire to share her past with a friend who'd understand was getting more and more difficult to suppress. After all of their phone calls and E-mails, she was beginning to wonder if maybe *Tom* would understand.

Knock it off, Amie, she inwardly berated herself.

"If I knew about . . . what?" Tom persisted.

"Just forget it."

He narrowed his gaze. "Did Nancy's talk about her marital problems bug you?"

"Not at all." Amie shook her head. "Everything's fine!"

"Well, *something's* wrong!" Tom countered, sounding close to exasperation. "You haven't said more than a dozen words today. That's not like you!"

"I was trying not to babble," she confessed. "You know how I get when I'm nervous. I can't seem to shut up! I didn't want to do that today. I always feel so stupid afterwards. . . ."

She clamped her lips together while Tom chuckled softly.

"Amie, nobody would have cared if you 'babbled,' " he said at last. "Least of all me."

"Thanks."

Tom shifted his weight and the snow crunched beneath his boots. "Well, all right, then . . . um . . . call me when you get home so I don't worry."

"Yes, *Mother,*" she replied facetiously, feeling more like her old self for the first time all day. "Oh, and by the way, I don't think the people of Tigerton look down their noses at you, Tom. Everything I heard about you this afternoon pertained to your good attributes and nothing less." She paused, collecting her wits. "It only affirmed what I already knew."

He glanced at the cold, hard ground, before meeting her gaze again. "Thanks. And maybe you're right — I mean, about the folks around here." He paused momentarily as if collecting his thoughts. "My father was an alcoholic — the town drunk, to be blunt. I always felt like people held me responsible for the bad things he did when he was drinking because I was the oldest. The kids at school never let me forget that the Andersons were 'trash' and somewhere along the line I believed them."

"Oh, Tom." Amie's heart ached for him.

"But I've been counseling with the pastor about it. Got a lot of things settled." He chuckled lightly. "Now that I'm living in the church basement until our hotel gets built, I've had plenty of opportunities to talk with Pastor Jake — while we paint the sanctuary and repair the pews, among other things."

"I'm glad for you . . . that you have someone like the pastor to confide in."

"Yeah."

She smiled, a little envious. "Well, I'd better get going . . . besides, it's freezing out here!"

"Didn't mean to talk your ear off."

"You didn't," Amie assured him. "In fact, I'm glad you told me more about yourself. It helps me get to know you better. After all, we are business partners and business partners should know each other, right?"

"Right."

"And I'm babbling again."

Tom laughed. "I think your habit is rubbing off on me!"

Giving him a hooded glance, Amie climbed into her car again and he politely closed the door after her. Backing out of the driveway, she tooted the horn twice before speeding toward the highway. But for many miles, she speculated whether the day would really come when she could finally tell somebody about that horrible night.

The snow fell heavily and Amie watched it from the third floor window of her downtown Chicago office. Common sense told her to leave work and park her car safely in the underground garage attached to her condominium lest it be buried by a plow. But she didn't dare leave early. Not today. Something was up. Amie sensed it.

All day she'd had a feeling of impending doom, and she knew the reason why. She'd blown an account last week, and although it hadn't been entirely her fault, upper management wasn't pleased. Worse, her ears still burned from her boss's severe reprimand a few days ago. She couldn't blame him for being angry with her. In spite of putting in nearly sixty-five hours a week for two months straight, she hadn't been able to produce an acceptable marketing strategy for Wagg's Dog Food. Every slogan she dreamed up sounded too cliché for her clients' liking. *Your pooch's tail will wag when you serve him Wagg's Dog Food.* She sighed inwardly. It had been the best she could do, but it was far below her usual standard. Even Amie knew that.

Just then Tim Daley, director of the marketing department, entered her office, and she solemnly turned from the window.

"It's a winter wonderland out there," he stated, wearing a plastic smile. It was a sure sign that unpleasant business followed.

"What's up?" she asked, her heart hammering anxiously.

"We–ell," he closed the door and sat down in the adjacent chair, "I had a long talk with Kirk Maxwell, and we've decided that in the best interest of the company we

. . . we have to let you go. I'm so sorry. And here it's right before Christmas too."

"Let me go?" Amie suddenly felt as if her whole world was crashing down around her.

"I tried to go to bat for you," Tim insisted, "but Kirk was adamant . . . and you know Kirk."

"Okay, I know I blew a big account," she said desperately, "but it won't happen again. Give me another chance. I'm a hard worker. Haven't I proved that to this company?"

"You *were* a hard worker. You were one of our best creative consultants." He shook his golden head sadly. "But I've been watching you lately. You're here, but you're not. Your mind is elsewhere. Personally, I think you're distracted by that hotel nonsense. It's all you talk about."

"My hotel has nothing to do with my position here," Amie stated vehemently, wondering why she felt the need to defend that part of her life. Except she wanted to save her job with Maxwell Brothers' Marketing and Development Company.

"I disagree."

She closed her eyes, seething inside.

"Look, I'm sorry," Tim said. "I wish things were different. But there is good news: Kirk prepared a severance package

116

that'll get you through the holidays."

"Great," she replied evenly. Rising from her desk chair, she scanned the small office through tear-filled eyes. "I guess I'll need some boxes so I can pack my things."

"Sure. I'll go see what I can find." He stood and walked out of the office, leaving Amie with a bitter taste in her mouth and a sinking feeling in her heart.

Tom glanced at his watch and realized Amie had been talking for a half hour straight! He shifted the telephone receiver to the other ear. Shortly after Jake summoned him to the phone and Amie told him about losing her job, a complete and utter helplessness engulfed him. What could he say to console her? *Help me, Lord,* he prayed silently.

"Can you even believe such a thing? Those jerks!"

"Listen, you've got to calm down. You're only going to make yourself sick by rehashing everything that happened this afternoon."

"I can't help it. I just had to talk to somebody. That's why I called you. Oh, maybe I shouldn't have bothered you with this."

"No, Amie, I told you before; it's okay."

"What am I going to do?" she lamented.

"I'm ashamed to tell my family that I got . . . *fired*. How humiliating!"

He heard her begin to weep softly and his heart broke. "Aw, Amie, don't cry. Everything'll be all right. Things might look bad, but God's still in control."

Tom knew the words were trite and over-used, yet they were the only ones he could think of.

"How will I pay my mortgage? How will I live?"

"Sell that condo and move up here!" he blurted. An instant later, he wanted to bite off his tongue for saying such a foolish thing.

"Sell my condo?" Amie sniffed. "Yeah, I guess I could do that."

"Well, think about it," he said lamely. "Pray about it."

She paused momentarily. "You know it might work, Tom. I could sell this place and live with my parents until the hotel is built. Maybe God wants me to put all my energy into our venture, instead of killing myself for those ungrateful scoundrels at MBMD."

"Yeah, maybe. I'll admit, I've been worried about you, burning the midnight oil and all."

"Yeah, and a lot of good it did me!" She paused. "Do you think we could work together, Tom?" she asked in a broken little voice that tugged on his sensibilities in the most peculiar way.

"Of course," he replied adamantly. "We're already working together."

"But I mean . . . if I moved up there?"

"Sure." *Except the architectural plans include just one apartment,* Tom wanted to remind her, since he had no intention of living in the church basement forever. On the other hand, he didn't want to make her feel any worse.

"I always thought of myself as the proverbial 'silent partner,' " she admitted. "I figured I would continue with my career in Chicago and just check on my investment from time to time while you'd run the hotel."

Tom didn't know how to reply. He'd assumed much the same; however, the thought of having Amie around wasn't an unpleasant one, other than they'd have to decide which of them got the apartment. "Everything will work out."

"Promise?"

"Promise." He detected in her voice that she needed to hear something that she could hang onto, and suddenly a Bible verse came to mind. " 'All things work together for good —' "

" 'To them that love God,' " she finished for him, " 'to them who are called according to His purpose.' Romans 8:28."

Amie breathed a sigh, sounding much more relieved. "Oh, Tom, I knew you'd make me feel better. You're becoming such a good friend! Thanks."

"You're welcome," he said, his confidence on the rise. "Anytime."

Chapter 9

The hurt won't go away. I can't sleep at night because every time I close my eyes I see my beloved Rachel bobbing in the ocean, gasping for breath. Why couldn't I have reached her in time? Why did she have to die? She was a good swimmer . . . how could she have drowned? We'd only been married nine days . . .

Amie reached for a tissue and dabbed her eyes. Reading the first volume of her uncle's journals was not the light entertainment she'd needed. Although, from his writings, she was able to learn much about him. It seemed he was a very sensitive man, one with big ideas, but at the same time straight-forward, even blunt, when it came to voicing his opinions. Amie felt proud of him when she read how he'd rallied against a wealthy citizen of Tigerton who wanted to build a shameful dance hall at the end of town — and Uncle Hal won!

But that was before World War II. He'd been twenty-six years old when he enlisted in the Air Force. He got shot down and spent several months in a military hospital in London. There he'd met Rachel.

I never had much use for religion, Hal had written, *and now I wonder if there even is a God, because if He really existed, He wouldn't have taken away the one person who meant everything to me.*

Mulling over what she'd just read, Amie realized her uncle must have become a believer later in life. No doubt the Lord used that tragedy to bring Uncle Hal closer to Himself.

The telephone rang, startling her from the colorful floral-printed sofa. She rose from her comfy position, berating herself for not having her portable phone within an arm's distance, and walked to where it lay on the dining room table.

She pressed the TALK button. "Hello?"

"What are you doing, you bum? Lying around, eating bonbons, and watching soap operas?"

Amie rolled her eyes. "Hi, Dad."

He laughed. "Say, Princess, one of the guys at work here had a secretary quit. Want a job?"

"Secretary?" She wrinkled her nose distastefully. "No way."

"But why?"

"B.O.R.I.N.G."

"Now, Amie, I'd like you to at least consider this tremendous employment opportunity. Buzz is a great guy to work for."

"Oh, yeah," she replied smartly, walking over the lush, off-white carpeting and making her way back to the couch, "then why'd his secretary quit?"

"She didn't get enough roses on Secretary's Day; I don't know why she quit! But, just between you and me, she was something of a ding-dong."

"I don't know, Dad." Amie collapsed into a pool of multicolored throw pillows. "I really just want to concentrate on building the hotel, and then I'll work there. Tom suggested that I run the café while he manages the antique shop, and we'll both check in guests. Of course, we'll need to hire other personnel too."

"Well, that's just peachy, but you can't even *start* building until at least . . . what, June? And then it will take months to actually construct the place." Her father paused. "Amie, you'll be lucky if you're able to hold a grand opening next Christmas Eve. That's a year from tomorrow. What are you going to do with yourself till then?"

She smirked. "Lie around, eat bonbons, and watch soap operas."

"Very funny, young lady!"

This time *she* laughed.

"Now, look, I'm serious —"

"Thanks, but no thanks."

"Paid benefits and eight dollars and fifty cents an hour."

"What? I can't live on that!" She shook her head, marveling at her father's ludicrous proposition. "That's a mere third of my salary at MBMD."

"Honey, let me remind you that you're selling your condo and moving in with Mom and me."

She relented somewhat. "Yeah, I suppose I won't have too many expenses —"

"Any money you make you can put toward your hotel adventure. Buzz is aware that you wouldn't be around forever."

"Hmm . . ." Amie paused and began to consider the offer. "Can I pray about it?"

"Of course. I'll give you till five o'clock." With that her father hung up.

Amie glanced at the mahogany grandfather clock in the corner of her posh living room. *Thanks, Dad,* she thought sarcastically.

It was four-thirty.

★ ★ ★

Tom sat at the dining room table of the Warrens' home and sipped his coffee.

"Dessert?" Katie asked.

"No, I'm stuffed after that meatloaf dinner." He smiled graciously. "You're a great cook."

She blushed, looking pleased. "Why, thank you."

"Yeah, sure beats frozen entrees, hon," Jake teased his wife.

"Oh, you!" she replied with a tiny laugh before walking into the kitchen.

The girls had finished eating long ago and were now playing in their bedrooms. Periodically a high-pitched giggle floated down the hallway, and as much as Tom dined with the Warrens lately, he was used to hearing it. He was also getting a taste of how a healthy family behaved, although up until the age of twelve, his home life wasn't the dysfunctional mess it had become after his mother died.

"All set for the holidays, Tom?"

He lifted his gaze to the pastor. "I think so."

"Did Amie decide whether she's going to drive up for Christmas?"

"Yep. She said she'd come." He sipped his coffee. "Her family doesn't know the

Lord, and they celebrate by going to Florida for a couple of weeks."

Jake furrowed his auburn brows. "Weren't her parents recently on vacation in Hawaii?"

"Yeah, but I guess that was more business than pleasure. Amie's dad had to work, so her mom just went along."

"I see." He sat forward, his forearms on the table, as a lock of his reddish-brown hair flopped onto his high forehead. "And Amie doesn't want to go to Florida with her family?"

"Nope. Guess she never does. She told me she usually finds someone from her church family to spend Christmas with, but this year she didn't have the time to ask around. So it all worked out that she'll come up here."

A surge of anticipation coursed through Tom's veins — as it did whenever she phoned or e-mailed lately. He wasn't quite sure what to make of these tumultuous feelings he'd developed for Hal's niece. He hadn't experienced anything like them since high school. Surely he was too old to have a crush on Amie like he'd had on Nancy. Regardless, he didn't think any more than a professional friendship was warranted, under the present circumstances. Besides,

Amie Potter was a woman way out of his league.

"So," Jake said, his cobalt eyes gleaming with mischief, "are you planning to take Amie . . . out . . . somewhere?"

He smirked. *Suddenly half the town is playing matchmaker*, he thought cynically. Glancing at the pastor, he answered, "I'm not planning any candlelight dinners, but Amie and I have an appointment on Saturday to see an attorney and legalize our partnership. That's about as 'out' as I'm taking her."

"Tom, you old romantic, you!" Jake razzed, getting up from his chair. "An attorney open on Saturday, huh?"

"It's Jim Henderson, Hal's lawyer, and I guess he's doing us a special favor since Amie will be in town and because he'll be on vacation for the next two weeks."

"I see; well, it's good to hear that Amie can spend Christmas with us, anyway," Jake stated more soberly now. "I know Katie will look forward to having her around for a few days. It's nice that she doesn't have to rush right back to Chicago."

"Uh-huh." Tom stood, following the pastor's lead; however, a host of clamorous emotions still wreaked havoc in his heart. He went from infatuation with Amie to

127

grieving Hal's death — and seemed to stop at everything in between!

"You ready to take a look at my van?"

Tom gave himself a mental shake. "Ready when you are."

"Great. I can't get the thing started. Don't know what it could be . . ." Jake paused, giving him a friendly slap on the back. "It sure is a blessing to have you around."

"No, Pastor," Tom replied sincerely, "it's a blessing to *be* around. You and Katie make me feel like part of your family. Thanks."

"You are a part of our family. You're my brother in Christ and we're all in God's family."

"Right. But it's kind of hard when a guy loses his best friend. Especially around the holidays. I mean, Hal was my best friend *and* my family — except for Matt."

"And what a blessing that your younger brother can take time from his job and college education and visit us at Christmastime too. But I understand your sense of loss," the pastor said, throwing a fraternal arm around Tom's shoulders as the pair walked to the garage, attached to the parsonage. "It's going to be painful for a while."

Tom inhaled deeply as they reached the minivan. "Yeah, painful is right!"

The trip to Tigerton wasn't as hectic as the last time Amie had made it. In fact, it wasn't rushed at all. In the past four days, since her termination from Maxwell Brothers', she'd been able to relax, read through two of her uncle's journals, and now she felt thoroughly rested and all set to celebrate the Savior's birth!

She passed the future site of the hotel, now covered in a thick blanket of snow, and a thrill of expectancy traveled up her spine. The construction company Tom had painstakingly chosen said a crew could probably start excavation as soon as the end of March or early April. But already Amie was ordering catalogues, anxious to select the decor.

Minutes later, she pulled into the Warrens' driveway. Climbing out of the BMW, she opened the back door and withdrew several colorfully wrapped boxes.

"Welcome, Amie!" Katie called from the opened garage. "Want some help?"

"That'd be great. Here . . ." She immediately filled her new friend's arms with boxes.

"What's all this?"

"Presents!" Smiling, Amie shrugged helplessly. "I always go overboard at Christmas."

"Oh no . . . you shouldn't have!"

"Maybe not, but I love to buy gifts. I hope Tom likes his . . . oh! and wait till you see what I got the girls!"

Katie rolled her honey-brown eyes. "You'll spoil them —"

"I bought you and Pastor Jake something too."

"You'll spoil all of us!"

"Good. You deserve it." Amie paused, and the gratitude that filled her being threatened to spill over in the form of sentimental tears. She'd been so certain that she would have to spend Christmas alone. Either that or endure a Florida vacation with her family, listening to her mother, Dottie, and Stephen badger her endlessly about how foolish she was for building a hotel in this hick town. "Thanks for inviting me to share your holiday."

"Oh, you're welcome. This will be so much fun!"

After attempting a no-handed hug, Katie laughed softly while Amie turned to extract the remaining presents from the backseat. With her arms filled, she met Jake near the porch. He took the packages from her and scolded her the same way Katie had only moments ago.

"You shouldn't have done this!"

"But I wanted to! Besides, my mother taught me that guests who show up empty-handed are rude ... and I already disobeyed her at Thanksgiving."

"All we expected you to bring, Amie, was yourself."

"And here I am," she replied lightly, returning to the car and opening her trunk. "Along with a few other things ..."

"You mean there's more?"

"Uh-huh. But I think I can get the rest."

She removed the last three Christmas surprises and then lifted out her luggage. As she followed the pastor into the house, she could hear the girls' excited exclamations, and already, she knew this would be a Christmas she'd never forget.

Chapter 10

After Pastor Warren left the parsonage to prepare for the night's Christmas Eve Vespers Service, the girls managed to coerce their mother into allowing them to open one present. Of course they chose Amie's gifts — the newest under the evergreen tree decorated with handmade ornaments.

Amie watched in delight as eight little hands excitedly tore at the colorful wrapping paper, revealing the clear plastic boxes containing Madame Alexander dolls, each representing one of Louisa May Alcott's *Little Women*.

"Oh, Amie, how generous of you!" Katie exclaimed, looking as impressed as the girls.

"I couldn't help myself," she replied, hunkering beside little Ellen and freeing *Beth* from her plastic restraints. "When I saw these dolls at a boutique in Chicago, I just knew I had to buy them for the girls."

As Katie began explaining to her daughters about the dolls' value and that they weren't toys but keepsakes, Amie wondered if she'd ever have a little girl of her own. At twenty-six years old, she still had plenty of child-bearing years ahead of her —

Suddenly a horrid memory flashed through her mind. An empty sanctuary filled with her uncontrolled weeping. "Please, God, don't let me be pregnant!"

A heavy sadness spread across her chest when she had stood. The Lord had honored her request, yet her heart ached and tears threatened at what she perceived as His punishment. While she had friends who were blessed by their singleness, Amie felt cursed.

No husband.

No children.

"Amie, are you okay?"

She snapped out of her musings to find Katie and the girls staring at her with concerned expressions. She forced a smile and swatted at an errant tear. "Oh, I'm fine. I just . . ." She swallowed. "I'm just so glad the girls like their gifts."

"Oh, we do!" cried Emma, obviously trying to make her feel better.

Amie felt like a fool as she glanced around the living room adorned with the children's drawings and cut-out snowflakes from red and green construction paper. Her new friends were likely to think she was a nut case — and maybe she was. Why else would those haunting remembrances plague her in the midst of a joyous celebration?

"Well," she said, looking back at Katie and shifting uncomfortably, "I guess I'll go change for church."

"You do that. Feel free to lie down if you're tired."

"Thanks. I think I'll do that."

"And, Amie?"

She turned back around. "Yes?"

"Don't be too hard on yourself . . . I mean about whatever's troubling you. You're probably still recovering from working all those long hours."

Amie blinked back an onset of fresh tears but could only manage to nod in agreement.

"You've got so much to look forward to, what with building that hotel. Why, the entire town is buzzing with excitement!"

This time Amie actually smiled.

"And I can't begin to tell you what your partnership has done for Tom. It's like he's a . . . a new man." Katie took a step closer. "What I mean is, he's been a believer for years but he never stepped out in faith before. He was always too afraid of what people might say to give in to God's promptings. But now he's trusting the Lord to direct his paths, instead of letting that old insecurity stifle him. Isn't that wonderful?" She grinned impishly. "Just for the record, I'm not tattling or gossiping. Tom himself stood up and gave that very testimony during the last mid-week worship service. Jake and I were so encouraged. We think God's going to use what Tom said to light some fires in other Christians' souls!"

"How amazing," Amie replied, slightly envious that her partner could experience such inner healing. At the same time, she was happy for him. His melancholy was what she'd liked the least about him when they first met. But lately it seemed to be the very thing she liked the least about herself. Up until now, she'd kept so busy she never had time to think about her past. Oh, she remembered well enough. But she quickly suppressed each awful memory as soon as it took form, locking it tightly inside herself. Perhaps, that secret hiding place had begun to overflow. Perhaps her panic attacks were the result. . . .

If I could just talk to somebody, she thought as desperation tweaked her heart. *Another Christian — but not some indifferent psychologist and not dear, sweet Katie who'd probably faint in horror, or my pastor's wife who'd most likely shun me for being a bad girl in the wrong place at the wrong time.* She sighed inwardly. *I just have to find someone who'll understand.*

"I'll stop foaming at the mouth," Katie announced in her soft voice, penetrating Amie's thoughts. "You rest and change clothes. I'll knock on your door when we're ready to leave."

Amie nodded and resumed walking down the hall.

The bedroom she would occupy during her stay was, in actuality, a nook that served as a sewing room too. Pattern pieces were stacked neatly beside the machine, and portions of material lay in an orderly fashion on half of a long, narrow table. The other half sported Amie's suitcase.

Opening it, she pulled out the clothes on hangers, hoping they hadn't gotten too wrinkled from the trip. She hung them on the brightly colored plastic hooks, mounted on the wall since the room didn't have a closet.

Dear Lord, she prayed silently, lying down on the single bed, intending to take just a short fifteen-minute rest, *I know You are good and everything You do is good. I know You are love and that You love me — enough to die for me. But I have so many questions and so many feelings boxed up inside. I need You to answer them, Lord. Please help me.*

Amie dozed, awaking with a start a half hour later. She swung her legs off the bed and grabbed the long, full black skirt she planned to wear tonight along with a belted red, silk tunic and black vest. After she dressed, she pulled up her blond hair, fastening it on top of her head with a red ribbon and allowing it to spill down in a chic mess of curls. She was just putting the finishing touches on her makeup, using a small hand-held mirror, when Katie knocked.

"Ready to go, Amie?"

She opened the door. "Ready."

"Oh, you look pretty!"

"Pretty . . . what?" she teased. "Pretty ridiculous?"

Katie giggled, putting a hand over her mouth, and Amie noticed her simple red dress with its white lacy collar. "You look pretty *pretty*," she replied, still smiling. "But we'd better leave now if the girls are going to be on time."

The walk to church was a short one since the quaint structure was located just beyond a row of pine trees that separated the cemetery from the Warrens' home. Inside, the place bustled with activity as they hung their winter coats in the cloak room. Excited voices echoed from little children, hustling to the front of the sanctuary to receive last-minute instructions from the music director. In her haste to get out of the kids' way, Amie nearly bypassed Tom, who was standing in the doorway, passing out programs.

"Merry Christmas," he said pointedly, leaning slightly forward.

"Oh!" She felt herself blush. "Merry Christmas. I didn't see you there. . . ."

Katie was right behind her. "Did you save us some seats, Tom?"

He nodded, handing each of them a program. "First pew on the left."

"Thanks." She gave him a grateful smile before looping her elbow around Amie's. "This place is packed on Christmas and Easter," she remarked, as they glided forward, little Lucy in tow. "Jake always wishes he could get the same crowd in every Sunday."

"I'll bet."

Reaching the pew, marked as saved by a row of hymnals, Amie was hard pressed not to turn around and take a second, more appreciative glance at Tom. In his khaki tan slacks, forest green dress shirt and tan, red, and green speckled tie, he looked quite the "new man" as Katie had said earlier.

Meanwhile, the church filled rapidly. Then, at precisely six o'clock, Pastor

Warren stepped up to the pulpit. "Merry Christmas, ladies and gentlemen. Tonight is a special service with special music and readings from our children. But first, let's open in prayer."

Amie bowed her head, eyes closed, and after the last "Amen!" she looked up to find Tom beside her. They exchanged polite smiles before sitting down, Tom positioned on the end. With him next to her, Amie experienced that same awkward feeling she had at Thanksgiving. It almost seemed as if each time she and Tom saw each other, they had to get reacquainted. Phone calls and E-mails just didn't match face-to-face communication.

A group of kindergarten-aged children were lined up on the stairs below the podium. They began to sing "Silent Night," their cherubic voices ringing throughout the small sanctuary. Amie smiled just as Katie nudged her.

"Can you move over?" she whispered. "The Morrisons need a place to sit."

Nodding, Amie scooted down, causing Tom to slide over.

The children finished their song and stepped off the makeshift platform as the next group came up. Amie guessed they were the elementary group.

"Amie, can you move over a little more?" Katie asked softly, pulling Lucy onto her lap. "Here comes Mr. Morrison."

Nodding, but skeptical, since the aisles were filled with people in folding chairs, she inched closer to Tom. He had no place to go but up against the end of the pew. "Sorry," she told him under her breath.

Beneath the dimmed lights, she caught a slight accommodating grin as he shifted his weight to one side and stretched his arm along the top of the pew. She knew it was a necessary gesture if he hoped to obtain any measure of comfort, yet Amie got so flustered, she barely heard the children's chorus of "Away in the Manger." She kept imagining Tom's arm around her in a display of affection, though it was hardly that. She stiffened, then slowly realized it felt rather pleasant to sit so close to him.

The tension in her muscles ebbed as a group of junior- and senior-high kids spread out on the stairs and began reciting select Scripture passages from the second chapter of Luke. "And it came to pass in those days, that there went out a decree from Caesar Augustus that all the world should be taxed . . . and Joseph also went up from Galilee . . . To be taxed with Mary his espoused wife, being great with child . . . And she brought forth her firstborn son, and wrapped him in swaddling clothes, and laid him in a manger . . ."

By the time the young people were ending their segment with an enthusiastic rendition of "God Rest Ye Merry, Gentlemen," she had relaxed against Tom. But it was hardly the romantic setting it might have been since Katie and Lucy were fairly lounging against her too, causing Amie to feel like the middle domino. But at least she was no longer so uptight about the seating arrangement. She only hoped Tom wasn't getting squashed!

Minutes later, Jake stepped forward and gave a brief message, encouraging unbelievers to "repent and be saved."

"Just as our teens sang only moments ago: 'Remember Christ our Savior was born on Christmas Day to save us all from Satan's power when we were gone astray. . . .' " He paused momentarily. "I urge you folks who aren't born again to make this Christmas a celebration to remember for all eternity. Ask the Lord Jesus, Who came to this earth as an infant and died as a man so our sins would be forgiven — ask Him into your hearts today." He smiled at the congregation. "Let's bow for prayer. . . ."

The Christmas vespers service ended and

everyone rose from the pews as the woman at the old pipe organ played "O Come, All Ye Faithful." Amie finally turned to Tom.

"I hope you weren't totally squished for the last half hour."

A little smile curved his lips and his face reddened slightly. "I think I survived. Thanks."

Deciding he'd been as uncomfortable as she in the beginning, Amie dropped the subject. She turned and started making her way toward the center aisle when she bumped into Nancy Simonson.

"I was just coming over to say Merry Christmas to the Warrens," the expectant mother said. Her light brown gaze did a quick assessment of Amie's attire before she smiled. "Nice to see you again."

"Same here." She looked at Nancy's protruding middle, covered by the green maternity sweater. "I never did ask — when's your baby due?"

"The end of May."

"And it better be a boy too!" Al exclaimed, emerging from seemingly nowhere. He now stood blocking half the aisle and staring at Amie through a dark, piercing gaze that sent a shiver of fright up her spine.

Then in one sudden motion he leaned toward her, his right hand extended, and she stepped back anxiously. As she did, her heel landed on someone's foot. Fighting for balance, she felt a pair of strong hands steady her.

"Well, Tomboy, Merry Christmas."

"Same to you."

Amie heard his voice just behind her ear before he leaned forward and shook Al's hand, still dangling out in front of him.

She breathed a sigh of relief.

Just then Katie appeared. Nancy gave her a hug and the two began to chat.

"Sorry I stepped on you," Amie stated over her shoulder.

"Not a problem," Tom replied easily.

Big Al smirked. "Don't worry, he's used to getting stepped on. Whole town used to step on him, till he inherited a lot of money. Now suddenly Tomboy's not such a loser."

Amie stood there, aghast. She'd never met anyone so blatantly rude.

Al laughed. "Aw, I'm just kidding." He moved sideways and rapped Tom on the shoulder. "Me and him's known each other since seventh grade."

Amie opened her mouth to retort but thought better of it. The last time she'd smarted off to "Brutus," Tom hadn't appreciated it.

A few moments of uncomfortable silence

passed and then Al commanded Nancy to the car. He turned and left, allowing his pregnant wife to gather up the children and follow behind, pausing only to get them bundled before heading out into the cold.

Feeling disgusted, Amie turned to gauge Tom's reaction and found him observing Nancy with an intent expression. Were those clouds of compassion in his hazel eyes, or was that something else she saw?

He's still in love with her? Amie thought, wondering why she should even care. Tom had his own life to live. So did she! They were just business partners!

Finally he glanced her way and grinned solemnly. "Guess I'd better help Pastor Jake pick up the folding chairs."

She just nodded, watching him walk away.

Chapter 11

Snow flurries danced crazily in the night air, illuminated only by the church's solitary yard light as Amie and Tom trudged to the Warrens' house. Katie and the children had gone on ahead, but the pastor was still in the sanctuary, counseling a parishioner.

As they walked the short distance, a weighted silence hung between them, and Amie found herself wishing vehemently that she didn't care so much about Tom. Moreover, she wished she didn't enjoy the feeling of sitting so close to him. Then, of course, there was the way he always seemed to understand. He was the first man she could ever remember talking to so candidly about everything — well, *almost* everything.

They reached the gravel driveway of the Warrens' home, and suddenly Tom paused. "Amie, can I ask you something?"

"Sure."

He tarried an instant more, as if collecting his thoughts, while a faint bulb beside the front door cast a shadow across his features. "Amie," he began again, "are you afraid of men?"

The directness of his question stunned her, and she groped for a reply. "Well, it . . . it's not so much that I'm afraid of men per se," she stammered. "It's that I get . . . well, just sort of . . . oh, I don't know . . . I get edgy, I guess . . ."

He rubbed his jaw, and even in the darkness, she saw his thoughtful concern. "So, in a word . . . yes."

She shrugged, unable to disagree. But then, in an effort not to appear the weak, simpering female, she quickly added, "I'm not afraid of *all* men, just some men . . . until I get to know them. A single woman can't be too careful, you know. The world is filled with lunatics!"

"Well," he stated, looking down at his booted feet, "I don't think you're afraid of me — at least not anymore."

"No . . ."

An idea began to form as she watched the snowflakes accumulate in Tom's dark brown hair. Perhaps he would be the one who'd understand . . . about that night. . . .

Tom lifted his gaze. "And I don't think you need to be afraid of Al," he continued. "You heard him tonight. We've known each other since junior high, and I'll admit he gets to me sometimes, but I can tell you firsthand that Big Al's bark is all he's got. There is no bite."

Any hope of confiding in Tom shattered like a piece of fine Baccarat crystal. *Didn't you see that look in his eyes?* Amie wanted to scream at him. But she didn't utter a sound. He'd never understand. No one ever would.

Beneath her red wool, full-length coat, her shoulders sagged in defeat. She turned away from him and began walking toward the Warrens' front door.

"Amie, hold on."

She quickened her pace and managed to enter the house before Tom could stop her. He arrived just an instant later.

"There you two are!" Katie exclaimed. She looked past them. "But where's Jake?"

"He'll be along shortly," Tom said, panting slightly. "Someone at church cornered him after the service."

Katie sucked in her lower lip, looking troubled. "Was it Mr. Tucker?"

Tom nodded.

"Oh, that poor man. His wife is in a nursing home, and he just doesn't know what to do without her. Fortunately, he does have a sister who lives nearby."

Amie hung up her coat, ignoring Tom's

gesture to help, and walked on ahead into the living room.

"By the way, the girls are upstairs, changing into their nighties," Katie informed them. "When Jake gets home, he'll light the fireplace, and then we can open presents. Meanwhile, I'll finish getting supper ready."

Amie was quick to volunteer in the kitchen, and Tom supposed she was angry with him. *Don't have to hit me over the head with a brick,* he thought sardonically, taking a seat on the sofa.

He tried to think of what triggered her "cold shoulder." Defending Al? Why would that be such a major deal? Big Al could be surly, and he rarely had a good word to say about Tom — especially in front of others, but he'd never hurt anybody, at least not physically.

Tom picked up a magazine, flipping through it sightlessly. He thought about Nancy, who had only recently become a Christian. Al's shameless insensitivity was hurting her, no doubt about it. It was painful for their whole congregation to watch, and yet, in seeing the Simonsons' misery, he'd come to realize those feelings of desolation didn't just belong to him. If he trusted God to pull him up by his bootstraps, couldn't he then be used to help others? Like the Simonsons?

Lord, make me a success story, he often prayed these days, *so I can be a blessing to others.*

Now, if he could only figure out what to do about Amie.

Tossing the periodical back onto the coffee table, Tom wondered over their growing friendship. Was it just a friendship? Perhaps, on her part; however, tonight in church he could scarcely concentrate on the Christmas program, what with Amie sitting right up beside him. A few nights ago Jake had teased him about asking her for a date, and since then he'd done little else but imagine doing exactly that. How was he ever going to run a hotel with her around?

Amie entered the room, causing Tom a good measure of trepidation. He hated the thought of any sort of confrontation, yet he longed to set things straight. Sitting forward with forearms on his knees, he watched her settle in the adjacent armchair. As much as he tried to catch her eye, she wouldn't look at him.

He cleared his throat. "Um, Amie . . . look, I'm sorry if I offended you."

She glanced down at her lap, picking at

her black skirt. "You didn't offend me."

"Okay." Tom sat back, puzzled. "Well, could you tell me what happened then? I mean, everything seemed fine until I mentioned Big Al."

Her blue-eyed gaze snapped to his. "I don't *like* him," she said vehemently.

Tom nodded. "Yeah, I sort of got that impression." He rubbed his rough chin contemplatively. "To tell you the truth, he's not exactly one of my favorite people either."

"Then why do you insist on defending him? Personally, I think you ought to punch him in the nose." She sat back with a huff. "Or maybe I will."

He grinned, trying to imagine that. "Listen, Amie, we're supposed to turn the other cheek as Christians, not retaliate. I don't like what Al says about me — I'll admit it's humiliating. But I'm trying to keep the whole picture in mind. Nancy's a new Christian, and she wants Al to get saved too. If I treat him the same way he treats me, what's that going to prove?"

Amie blushed, looking properly chagrined.

Tom shifted self-consciously, having to tell her the next bit of information. "Um . . . I suppose you best be aware that it's Big Al's company I selected for the construction of our hotel."

"What?" At this she stood, fists clenched at her side. "Are you out of your mind? That . . . that *brute* doesn't deserve our business!"

Tom rose from the sofa and swallowed hard. "I didn't deserve God's saving grace, but I got it anyway."

"That's different."

"Maybe. But the Simonsons need the money."

"Oh, so that's it. You're hiring Al for Nancy's sake. Why didn't you just say that in the first place!"

He was momentarily taken aback by her venomous tone — mostly because he didn't know where it came from. "I thought you liked Nancy."

She closed her eyes for a brief instant, then shook her head apologetically. "I'm sorry. I do like Nancy. I don't know what's the matter with me."

Lowering his chin, Tom blindly studied the coffee table as some of the old insecurities and discouragements came prowling back. Should he have consulted her first? She'd only met Al once. She told him to choose the construction company . . . but maybe she was right. Maybe he shouldn't have selected Al's corporation.

"I prayed about it," he stated, looking over at her again. It was the truth, yet it sounded so lame.

She folded her arms. "I don't like him," she said once more. He saw her chin quiver slightly and guessed she was still afraid.

"Al does a good job," he tried to assure her. "And you won't have to see him often. He stays mostly in his office."

She rolled her eyes. "I suppose you've signed the contract."

He nodded. "Right after I had Jim Henderson look it over."

"Well, what's done is done. I'll just have to deal with it."

She crossed the room, glanced out the door, walked back, and stood right in front of him, glaring into his face. Positioned just inches away, Tom decided she was the most beautiful woman he'd ever seen. Her indigo eyes sparkled with unshed fury, and her cheeks were heated to a lovely color that nearly matched her red blouse.

"Tom, I don't like this. I don't like Al! He gives me the creeps! I think you should forget about —"

"You're so pretty when you're angry," he mumbled, barely aware that he'd voiced the thought.

She gave him a quelling look, putting her

hands on her hips. "Don't try to change the subject."

Tom felt entranced. Was there even a remote possibility? No. He didn't have a chance with a woman like Amie Potter.

"Will you listen to me?" She was obviously working hard to stay angry. But a moment later, she burst into a fit of giggles, surprising Tom right out of his catalepsy. "Oh, you nut!" she said between chortles. "You are just like my dad. Every time he gets me upset and I try to give him a piece of my mind, he ends up making me laugh!"

Combing his fingers through his hair, Tom was relieved that she wasn't perturbed anymore, though he was more than a little baffled about this whole thing — his feelings for Amie included.

She sighed, her mirth fading. "We'll work it out, won't we?"

"Yeah . . . sure we will."

The front door suddenly opened, and Pastor Warren stepped into the house, shaking the snow out of his auburn hair and brushing it off the shoulders of his black wool coat. "It's really coming down out there," he said in a robust tone. Then, just as heartily, he added, "I hope supper's ready. I'm starved."

Katie's voice echoed from the dining room. "It's all set. I'll just call the girls, and we can eat."

Supper consisted of homemade vegetable soup and freshly baked bread. The girls barely touched their portions, being so excited about the gifts under the tree. But Jake made them sit politely while the adults finished up, and Amie was impressed by their good behavior.

When at last the meal was finished, everyone ambled into the living room, Emma, Carol, Ellen, and Lucy running on ahead. Katie dispersed the gifts, making piles for her enthused daughters. When her laden arms deposited a couple on Amie's lap, she glanced up in surprise.

"For me?"

Katie nodded, smiling and appearing almost as excited as the children.

Sitting at one end of the sofa, Jake dug right in and ripped open his gift with fervor. "A coffee mug!" he exclaimed, proudly showing it off. "Thank you, Amie. I'll pray for you each time I drink my morning coffee from it."

She smiled. "You're welcome."

Tom opened up his present. It was a thick, quality knit sweater, predominantly green in color but having other shades interwoven throughout. She had selected it with his hazel eyes in mind.

"Thanks," he said, looking over at her from the adjacent arm chair. "Just what I need."

"Good," she replied, feeling a bit embarrassed.

"That, um, top one's from me," he informed her, raising his voice slightly to be heard above the din of the four little girls, squealing with delight.

Amie looked down at the large, square, neatly wrapped box in her lap. "From you?" She carefully lifted the taped edges and then removed the colorful candy cane decorated paper, inhaling sharply when she spied what lay beneath it. "Oh . . . ," she breathed, viewing the darkly stained wooden jewelry box. It was intricately carved on the sides and on top. She opened the lid, discovering the quilted patchwork piece embedded within its depths. "It's beautiful."

Crossing the room, Tom hunkered beside her chair. "I discovered this when I was cleaning out the Laundromat," he explained. "I remembered when Hal found the thing. It was in old Mrs. Thorbjorg's attic. The box was dried out, the bottom of it severely cracked. When she died, her family stuck it in a heap of rubbish on the side of the road, and that's where your uncle picked it up."

Tom fingered the etchings. "You told me when we first met that you wished you'd known your uncle better; well, he was a man who saw beauty in things that other folks had long decided were trash. Like this little jewelry box." He lifted his gaze to hers, his eyes taking on their sorrowful appearance. "Like me."

Amie felt hot tears threatening as she looked back at the now expertly varnished creation.

"You remind me a lot of Hal," he whispered.

That did it. A surge of emotion streamed down her cheeks. She was touched to the heart by his words and, at the same time, riddled with guilt for her earlier fit of temper. Suddenly she saw things in a different light, realizing there were a lot of people like this box, in need of repair and the Master's touch, and a vision of Big Al came to mind.

"Oh, Tom," she sniffed, holding the piece of artistry to her. "You're so thoughtful. I'll treasure this forever."

He gave her a warm smile, rising to his feet, and Amie was suddenly aware that the room had become deathly still. One quick glance around told her the entire Warren family was watching on with tender expressions — even the children.

Wiping her eyes, she gave them each a shy smile.

"I was impressed with Tom's work," Jake said. "I saw the box before and after." He shook his head. "Amazing."

"Mrs. Jensen was kind enough to make the padding inside," Tom said.

"Thank you," Amie told him as gratitude flooded her being once more.

The girls resumed tearing at their gifts. In addition to the dolls, she'd bought them one book each and a video to watch. One by one, they came over to give her a "thank you" kiss on the cheek.

Katie opened her gift, a bottle of perfumed body lotion, and then Amie unwrapped the present from the Warrens. It was a wall hanging that Katie had made with the words THE HAVEN OF REST embroidered along the top, and beneath it, Matthew 11:28: "Come unto me, all ye that labour and are heavy laden, and I will give you rest."

"This is wonderful! I'll hang it in the lobby of our hotel!" She flashed the fabric mounting at Tom, who smiled and nodded approvingly.

"Well," Katie said, getting up from the sofa, "it's time for all little girls under the age of ten to go to bed."

"Awwww . . . ," the four children replied in unison, sounding utterly disappointed. But after a pointed look from their father, they readily complied and marched off in the direction of their bedrooms.

Tom rose from his chair. "I'd better leave too. Matthew's supposed to arrive bright and early tomorrow morning."

"Matthew?" Amie asked curiously.

"My younger brother," he explained. "He's driving up from Madison. He's attending the university there — a junior this year."

Jake slung a friendly arm around his shoulders. "Spoken like a proud papa," he teased. Turning to Amie, he added, "Tom has been like a second father to Matthew."

Nodding, she recalled her uncle mentioning the young man in the beginning of his third journal.

"Jake," Katie called from down the hallway, "can you give me a hand?"

"Coming, hon." He turned to Tom. "See you tomorrow for . . . brunch?"

He grinned sheepishly. "I'll be here. And hopefully Matt will too."

The pastor left the room to help his wife,

and Tom walked to the front door, pulling his coat out of the hall closet.

"See you tomorrow, huh?"

Amie nodded, leaning against the half-wall that divided the rooms. "Sorry about before . . . losing my temper. I hope you don't think I'm some kind of shrew."

"No, I don't think that at all," he said with a little chuckle.

"I see what you mean now . . . about trying to help the Simonsons."

A tiny smile curved his lips. "All's forgiven."

Their gazes locked briefly before Amie looked away. He wasn't in love with Nancy. That was apparent. She'd jumped to a false conclusion earlier tonight. One she regretted. Tom was an empathetic man with a deep understanding of the human heart. She briefly wondered if he would understand her . . . if she trusted him enough to tell him her whole story.

"Well, I'd better go," he said, opening the front door. "Merry Christmas."

"Merry Christmas, Tom."

Once he'd gone, she stared out the window after him until the falling snow covered his footprints.

Chapter 12

When Matthew Anderson arrived, he livened up Christmas Day with his quick wit and hearty laughter. It was obvious that Tom felt proud of his younger brother's achievements, and likewise, it appeared Matthew had the utmost respect for his eldest sibling.

With the men gathered in the living room, Matt talked animatedly about his latest college experiences while Amie helped Katie in the kitchen. Once the pork roast was cooked to perfection, everyone took a seat around the expanded dining room table, and Jake prayed over the food.

"This looks great!" Matt exclaimed, shoveling a fork full of mashed potatoes and gravy into his mouth. "Mmm . . . tastes even better."

Katie blushed pleasingly. "Well, thank you."

"The stuff at the university is like cardboard." Then, very suddenly, he set down his fork. "Okay, okay, you guys, something's driving me nuts. I've been waiting all afternoon for you to tell me, Tom, but since it doesn't look like that's going to happen, I'll just have to ask."

"What's that?" Tom replied, munching on his salad.

Matt smirked. "We–ell," he drawled, "I stopped by the Kelsigs' on my way into town to say hello to Laura, and what do you suppose her dad tells me?"

Tom shrugged. "What?"

"What? What, you say?" Matt threw his hands in the air in mock exasperation, causing Emma and Carol to giggle at his theatrics. "He tells me you two are getting married!" he replied, looking first at Tom, then at Amie, and back at his brother. "You don't even tell me yourself, you goon! I gotta hear it through the Tigerton grapevine! What kind of brother are you?"

Sitting across the table from him, Amie did her best to hide a smile. Tom groaned, and Jake chuckled openly from the far end.

"It's a rumor, little bro."

The younger man's face fell. "Yeah? I thought maybe you were going to tell me . . . you know, sort of my Christmas present. . . ." Matt turned to Amie. "He hasn't proposed yet?"

"Will you knock it off!" Tom told him,

sounding genuinely agitated. "The Warrens might understand your warped sense of humor but Amie doesn't, and you're making her feel uncomfortable."

"Oh, sorry." Matt gave her a penitent grin. "But, um, seriously . . . Ron Kelsig really did tell me that." He looked back at Tom and resumed eating. "I figured it was just talk since you hadn't said anything to me. I mean, you've told me about your plans for the hotel and all."

Amie watched Tom nod as his gaze met hers. She noted the apology pooled in his eyes and sent him back a reassuring smile. The talk didn't bother her. In fact, she wished there was a fraction of truth to it — perhaps even more than a fraction — and the silent admission surprised her.

"I think Amie's getting used to this particular piece of gossip," Jake inferred.

Her smile grew, as did her embarrassment. It was as if the dear pastor had discerned her very thoughts.

"As for the hotel," he continued, "it's been one miracle after the other, what with all the red tape that goes along with trying to build a new establishment. But there hasn't been a single snag."

Tom agreed. "It really has been amazing."

"And while there are those in town who'll

always be critical of somebody trying to do something new," Jake stated, "most everyone else is excited about Tom and Amie's new business venture."

"My father calls it our *adventure*," Amie said, chuckling lightly. "But I have to admit that Tom has done all the work so far." She turned to Matthew. "He's been absolutely wonderful. He's managed everything." She stabbed a few green beans with her fork. "Frankly, I don't know what I would have done without him."

Matthew eyed her for a moment, then turned to his brother. "You sure you haven't proposed to her yet?"

Tom scowled at him.

"I mean, if you don't want her, *I'll* marry her!"

Amie nearly choked on her dinner.

"Oh, I can just hear the gossip mill grinding on this new tidbit," Jake moaned, a sound that ran contrary to the amused twinkle in his Irish-blue eyes. "Quick, Tom, let's send this hooligan back to Madison where he belongs!"

A sudden outburst of laughter spouted from the men while the two eldest Warren girls gazed on, wide-eyed, and Amie wondered if her incredulous expression mirrored theirs.

"All right, that's enough," Katie scolded. "Poor Amie — I wouldn't blame her if she never wanted to have dinner with us again!"

"It's okay," she murmured, somewhat astonished at her soft-spoken friend's spurt of gumption.

But Katie wasn't through with her reprimands. "Now, girls, you will *not* repeat this to anyone, understand? Matthew was just joking."

"Yes, Mama," they said, their honey blond heads bobbing in unison.

The men seemed properly put in their places and, after that, no more wisecracks ensued around the children — or Amie.

A good portion of the remaining evening was spent around the piano, Katie at the keys, singing Christmas carols and favorite hymns. Amie sat on the couch with Ellen and Lucy curled up beside her. From her vantage point, she observed the Anderson brothers undetected.

She'd heard a lot about Matthew from Tom and decided the two resembled each other in many ways — the well-defined jawline and slight cleft in the chin, the tear-shaped, hazel eyes, and dark brown hair. But where Tom's features looked almost worn beyond his twenty-nine years, Matt's features appeared rather juvenile for twenty.

Amie then remembered her uncle's journal. *Tom's the fall guy in his family*, he'd written. *Makes me sick. His childhood is gone. The boy's only seventeen years old, but he looks and acts twice his age!*

Uncle Hal hadn't given any specifics, but Amie guessed there had been physical abuse in the home. Tom openly admitted his father's alcoholism, and the diary confirmed it. Still, Tom's background didn't lessen her opinion of him. It was just as Hal had penned: *Tom isn't responsible for his father's bad decisions. Just because old Norb goes and gets drunk every night of the week, doesn't mean his oldest kid'll do the same. Tom knows the Lord now. He's got a lot of character for one so young, and I'm convinced God will guide his path. The boy knows right from wrong. He's seen the effects of his father's sin, and I don't believe Tom'll touch a drop of booze in his entire life. But there are a few strong voices in this town that go around slandering less fortunate folks who don't meet up to their hypocritical standards. It's a crying shame that Tom believes what comes out of their mouths.*

A sad chord plucked Amie's heartstrings when she thought of all Tom must have suffered. Conversely, she was grateful her uncle had been his advocate and his mentor. No wonder Tom missed his fatherly friend so much. She wondered if this Christmas holiday was especially difficult for him, then berated herself for being so insensitive that she'd never asked.

The two girls rose from the couch to play with their new toys, and Tom strolled over from where he stood near the piano.

"You look deep in thought," he said observantly, sinking into the sofa.

She sighed, unable to deny it. "Ever since I got fired, I've been so introspective."

"That's not always a bad thing."

"Maybe not, but I'm getting myself depressed."

Tom turned toward her. "About what?"

She shrugged, still unwilling to share.

"I suppose getting canned from any job is a major letdown. But you had a career, Amie. Can't really blame you for feeling bummed out about losing it."

"Thanks . . ."

"But, like we talked about before, the upside is now you can concentrate on . . . what does your dad call it? Our 'hotel adventure'?"

She smiled. "Yes, and my father also got me another job in the meantime."

Tom furrowed his brows, eyeing her curiously. "I thought you were moving up here."

"I am . . . eventually. But until construction on our hotel begins, I've got to do something with myself."

He nodded. "Yeah, I suppose . . ." After momentarily studying his folded hands, dangling off his knees, he shot her a teasing grin. "Just don't get too comfy at this new job, huh? I've gotten rather used to the idea of having my partner around."

"Don't worry," Amie replied on a slight note of sarcasm, "it's a secretarial position. You'd realize that was funny, Tom, if you had any inkling as to how disorganized I am. Besides, the job only pays eight dollars and fifty cents an hour. I'm practically working for free!"

"Eight-fifty an hour?" He shook his head, smiling slightly. "That's a better-than-average wage up here."

"Well, I don't know. Maybe it's a better-than-average wage in Chicago too . . . for a secretarial job. But it's a far cry from the salary I used to earn."

"Welcome to the real world," Tom replied facetiously.

Amie bristled, but was then reminded of the chasm between her world and his. She'd grown up with money, a stately home in a posh neighborhood, and two sophisticated parents who had handed her their elite social status. He'd grown up with nothing and no one . . . save her uncle. And yet, she couldn't say that she was any better off, or any happier. Besides, couldn't their faith bridge that social gap?

"Better rethink this partnership," Tom said, gazing at her intently, "before it's too late."

"What?" Amie felt confused.

He seemed pensive for a few long moments as he peered over at the Warrens and Matthew still singing around the piano. "I mean, Tigerton is a whole lot different than Chicago. Might even be backwards to a woman like you. Maybe you won't like living up here."

"Maybe," she replied carefully. "But I don't like living in Chicago all that much anymore. There's nothing for me in that city, and I think I've sensed it for a long time." She paused, considering him and concluding that the look on his face was one of worry. "I'm tired of living my life at such a break-neck speed, Tom. I'm looking forward to the change up here. But, I will admit, it'll probably take some getting used to."

"What about me?" he asked challengingly. "I've got a GED and in a few months I'll have three managerial courses under my belt. But that's it. I'm not exactly your typical Harvard graduate."

"And praise the Lord for that!" she exclaimed, smiling at the comment. "Just remember, you've got a lot of wisdom gleaned from life experiences. You're also honest, forthright, and a Christian . . . as well as one of the best friends I've ever known. Who else would put up with my babbling?"

He chuckled and sat back, appearing more at ease and . . . even confident. "Okay, then, Amie. Seems your fate is sealed."

"I hope so."

He paused. "Yeah, me too."

His gaze met hers, searching her face intently, and a tiny breath caught in her throat as she slowly comprehended the meaning in his expression, the desire shining plainly in his hazel eyes. *He wants to be more than just my friend,* she realized. Oddly, she didn't feel panicked in the least but filled with a wondrous sense of anticipation.

"I'm telling you, she's interested," Matt said, his voice carrying in the darkness from a few feet away where he lay on the double bed.

Stretched out on his back on the inflatable mattress, hands behind his head and gazing at a ceiling of nothingness, Tom couldn't believe what his brother was saying — and yet he'd detected it as well.

"I mean, there you two were, sitting on the sofa tonight and giving each other calf eyes." Matt sighed dramatically. "If that ain't love . . ."

"We were not giving each other . . . *calf eyes.*"

"Oh yes, you were. We all saw it."

Embarrassment stabbed at Tom's gut.

"You've got it bad, dude," his younger brother continued. "I've never seen you so taken with a woman before — not unless you include Nancy Chesterfield."

"It's Nancy *Simonson* — and has been for the last nine years."

"Yeah, but who's counting, right?" Matt laughed.

Tom rolled his eyes. "I got over Nancy before dropping out my senior year."

"I know. I'm just giving you the business." The younger man hesitated momentarily. "So . . . are you really interested in Amie? I mean, romantically? I don't hear you denying it."

"Oh, I'm interested, all right. More than I should be." Tom heard the bed springs creak as Matt shifted his weight, and he imagined his brother had rolled onto his side.

"Seems she's good for you — you look a lot better than the last time I saw you."

Tom knew that much was true. "You saw me right after Hal's funeral when I was down in the dumps."

"Down in the dumps? Try clinically depressed. I was worried about you."

Tom couldn't help but grin. "I was worried about me too."

"And then Amie comes along . . ."

Tom's grin broadened. "When she first showed up at the filling station, I assumed she was going to be like her greedy siblings and take everything of value. I figured she'd be one of those high-society snobs, but instead she . . . she wasn't." Tom chuckled reflectively. "She talked me into taking her to dinner, and that night we ran into Big Al. He started up with his usual slams, but Amie put him in his place."

"You were down and out, so God sent an angel to cheer you up."

Tom laughed again. "Yeah, something like that." He went on to relay the story of how he came into the partnership, and how he and Amie had been corresponding for months, with the exception of Thanksgiving, when they'd actually seen each other. And now Christmas. "I guess that's where we're at."

"So, you gonna ask her out? I mean, *officially?*"

"Been thinking about it."

"Take her to the bowling alley, why don't you?"

"Yeah, right," he said, amusedly. "Somehow I don't think my Chicago angel would appreciate the place."

"Well, okay, how 'bout a concert? Laura told me about one in Wausau tomorrow night. It's a four-man ensemble that plays classical music — guitar, two violins, and a flute, I think. You know, kind of boring, but the stuff females think is romantic. I can't go because I'm due back in Madison tomorrow night for work. But I could get the details for you."

"A concert, huh?" Tom's mind went into a tailspin. They'd be in Wausau anyway to see Jim Henderson . . . maybe they could just stay for dinner . . . a concert . . . their first date . . .

"Tom? You dreaming before you even fall asleep?"

"Very funny." He rolled over and plumped his pillow. "Yeah, find out the specifics for me."

"Sure." A moment of silence passed between the brothers. "Hey, Tom? About your wardrobe —"

"I'm working on it."

"Okay . . ." Matt paused. "Uh, well, if you're not above taking some advice from your little bro, I could share what I learned in that business class I had last semester. We spent weeks on the subject of dressing for success. We were even assigned partners and had to go shopping for the best deals on clothes."

"Sure. I'm open to hearing whatever you've got to say on the subject." Tom grinned into the darkness of his makeshift apartment. "As long as you passed the class, that is."

An unseen, hurled pillow suddenly landed on Tom's chest, and he chuckled.

"I'll have you know I aced it!"

"Well, that's a relief," Tom replied, tossing the thing back at Matt. "But how 'bout you play professor tomorrow morning? I'm beat."

"No problem," he quipped. "Gives me time to plan my lessons."

Tom gave his brother a derisive snort and turned onto his stomach. A hush fell over the room, and soon he heard Matt's light snoring. Still, sleep eluded him as he imagined scenario after scenario of his possible date with Amie. Then, grimacing, he wondered how he'd ever ask her out.

Chapter 13

Tom's palms were sweaty, his stomach rolling, and his mouth felt as dry as an old soda cracker. Was asking Amie out really worth all this? As if in divine reply, Amie strolled into the Warrens' living room and gave him a sunny smile that melted his trepidation. It was worth it, all right.

"Believe it or not, I'm finally ready," she stated brightly. "Are you all set to go?"

Nodding, Tom rose from the couch where he'd been waiting for her. "Say, um . . ." He glanced around to be sure everyone was out of earshot. "Would you, um, well, what I'd like to know is . . . would you go out with me tonight?"

Her blond brows shot up in surprise. "You mean like . . . on a date?"

He hesitated. Maybe mixing business with pleasure wasn't such a good idea after all.

"Sure," she said, before he could reply. "That'd be fun. What do you want to do?"

Relief flooded his being. Then, feeling

more surefooted, he said, "I thought we could go to dinner and a concert in Wausau. We'll be there anyway for our meeting with Jim Henderson this afternoon."

"Am I dressed okay for the concert?"

Tom felt himself flush as he gave her attire the once-over. In a denim skirt, multi-colored sweater, and cream-colored turtle-neck underneath it, she looked perfect. "You look great," he finally replied.

"So do you."

He could feel his color deepening and decided to thank Matt for lending him the navy dress slacks and gray corduroy jacket. He'd never paid much attention to his wardrobe and only bought new blue jeans, underwear, socks, and shoes when the old ones wore out. His sweatshirts, T-shirts, few dress shirts, and the one suit he owned, he'd acquired. But since the end of October, he had become more aware of the way professional men dressed, and as he told his brother last night, he was working on upscaling his apparel. If he was going to be manager and half-owner of a hotel, he figured he'd better look the part.

Amie pulled her coat out of the hall closet, and Tom politely helped her into it. Then they left the house for his pickup truck.

"When did you buy this vehicle?" she asked, strapping herself in the seat. "It looks rather new."

"I try to take care of it." Tom started the engine and backed down the gravel drive. "A couple of years ago, after my dad died, I sold our property," he explained, heading for the highway. "I put some money away for my sisters, whom I haven't seen in years, gave my brothers a portion, and put down a chunk on this truck." He smiled wistfully. "Hal was the one who insisted I buy something with my share of the sale, even though I had intended on giving it all to Matt for college."

"Hmm . . . so you have two brothers and two sisters?"

Tom nodded, wishing she wouldn't ask too much about his less than admirable family background. But he knew, if she did, he'd tell her.

"And Phillip was always the trouble-maker, huh?"

He turned toward her in a quick, jerking motion. "How'd you know that?"

"Well, ah, my uncle told me."

"He did, huh?" Tom returned his gaze to the road ahead and submitted to the informal interrogation. As much as he disliked talking about it, he didn't want any of the past ever coming between Amie and him — even if their relationship didn't develop into anything beyond a strong friendship. "Yeah, Phil always had a knack for getting himself into all sorts of predicaments. Wound up in jail and still has a couple more years to serve. I try to visit him a couple times a month."

"That's so sad," she lamented. "That he's in jail, I mean. But perhaps his life will be much different once he's released."

"It better be. Now that he knows the Lord, I guess he's got a fighting chance at a decent life after he gets out."

From the corner of his eye, he saw her nod in agreement.

"And your sisters, Lois and Jeanne, they got married awfully young, didn't they?"

"I guess you could say that . . . yeah." Discomfort mounted in his chest. Had Hal really told her all this? When? More importantly . . . *why?*

Silence filled the truck's cab.

"Am I asking too many questions, Tom?" Amie queried.

"No, it's okay."

More silence.

"My family background is different from yours," she began in her typical sweet, babbling way. "But there are similarities. For

177

example, we're both the eldest of our brothers and sisters, and I suppose a good measure of responsibility goes along with that rank."

"I suppose," he conceded cautiously.

"I was always the black sheep of my family, since I got saved in junior high. It was Uncle Hal who found a church for me to attend outside of Chicago, and he'd check on me every so often to make sure I was really going." She chuckled lightly. "And there's another similarity between you and me, Tom — my uncle called us his 'son and daughter in the faith.' "

He grinned. "That's right."

"Did he ever talk about me?"

"Uh-huh. All the time."

"What did he say?"

Tom had to think about it for several long moments. "It's hard to remember the specifics," he said at last, "but I can recall the time you were in a high school play, and Hal got all worried you'd be so wonderful on stage you'd run off to Hollywood and ruin your life. He wanted me to pray you'd be a flop."

Amie giggled. "Did you?"

"Sure."

"Well, it worked." She laughed again. "When it came time to say my lines, my mind went totally blank. Right in front of a packed auditorium! I was so humiliated that I never tried out for another production." Leaning toward him, she gave his shoulder a playful swat. "So you see, your prayers probably saved me from becoming another Marilyn Monroe, complete with tragic ending and all."

"Whew! That's good." Tom grinned, feeling more at ease now that the topic was off of him. "Tell me some more about your family."

"No way!" she replied teasingly. "I don't want to scare you off before we even have our first date."

"Yeah, right." His grin broadened. "I don't scare that easily, Amie. Besides, I already met your brother and sister."

"Oh yes . . . Dottie and Stephen. They can be difficult. They're not easily impressed with anyone — unless you're, like, some top exec of a Fortune 500 company. But I think you'd like my dad. I've told you about him."

"A practical joker?"

"I guess that sums him up, yes." Amie smiled broadly. "I'm sure you'll meet him eventually; after all, we are business partners."

Tom nodded.

"Now, my mother . . . she's another story."

"Hal mentioned her. What did he used to call her again? The socialite?"

"That's her." Amie paused. "I love her dearly and I pray for her soul, but she and I rarely get along. My dad sort of plays mediator." She sighed. "Mom's very different from Uncle Hal. You'd never guess they were even related."

Tom pondered the remark. "Kind of funny how people turn out like that . . . so different, given the fact they've got the same parents."

His own words convicted him. If Hal and Amie could be different from their siblings, couldn't he also be dissimilar from his family — all except Matt, anyway? It occurred to him then that he judged himself unfairly. The measuring stick he used on others was long and marked with understanding, while his was short and scored by self-condemnation based upon who his father had been: the town drunk.

Shaking himself mentally, Tom tuned in to Amie's congenial prattling. He smiled, thinking he'd never known a woman who could talk as much as she did and still be coherent. But it didn't annoy him. Rather, he found it endearing somehow.

Lord, is she the one? he silently asked. *Is she the woman You would have me marry someday?* The questions sounded incredible to his own soul; however, he couldn't help wondering as his feelings for Amie grew beyond their business association and friendship.

Nearly an hour later, they arrived in Wausau, a city of some thirty-eight thousand people. Tom parked his truck, and then he and Amie ambled into the building that housed Henderson's Law Office. They took the elevator to the fourth floor and only had to wait a few minutes for Jim to finish up with another client.

The meeting went well. Several loose ends were tied, their limited liability company established, and some unfinished financial predicaments solved. Jim proved infinitely helpful when it came to several confusing forms and permits that Tom had been unsure of how to handle. As it happened, with the money Hal left his "children in the faith," there was a good chance they wouldn't have to take out a building loan.

"Watch your pennies," the attorney advised. "It's doable."

At the end of the conference, Jim stood and wished them a Happy New Year.

181

"We've got a couple of hours to kill before dinner," Tom announced once they'd left the office building. A chilling gust of December wind blew against Amie's face, causing her eyes to tear.

"Is there a shopping mall around?" she asked, as they walked back to his truck. "I can easily pass the time away in there."

Tom nodded slightly. "Okay."

Upon arriving at the mall, it soon became apparent that December twenty-sixth was *not* a good shopping day, at least not in Tom's opinion. The stores were crowded with customers returning gifts and hastening to purchase sale items. Amie, however, was hardly intimidated, being accustomed to competing with other Chicagoans, and she managed to coax him into a few shops. But after a while, they sat down in the middle of a thoroughfare, conversed, and watched people pass by.

When at last it came time to leave the mall for the restaurant, a comfortable, easy ambience had settled between them.

"It's strange," Amie began, "but I feel like I've known you my whole life."

He nodded. "I can relate to that."

"You can?" she asked as the cold winter wind took her breath away.

"Sure. Except for Hal, I can't ever remember telling anybody the things I've told you."

Amie smiled. "I'm flattered."

Flashing her a look of chagrin, Tom shrugged, and she felt guilty for bringing up things she'd read in her uncle's journal. It really hadn't been any of her business, and Amie was grateful that she hadn't offended him. In truth, his candidness amazed her.

Leaving the truck parked near the mall, they walked down Third Street, heading for the old Wausau hotel and the Chinese restaurant located inside. Once they arrived, Amie curiously surveyed the high-vaulted ceilings, accentuated with thick, polished wooden beams.

"This used to be a hotel," Tom informed her, "but now it's more of a rooming house. The lobby is still intact; it's on the other side."

Amie nodded as she continued to take in her surroundings with fascination. The walls were decorated with rococo C-and-S scrolls and shells in gilt gesso, framing panels of photographs of China. White linen cloths covered the tables, and a large marble fireplace stood in the center of the far wall. "This restaurant is so . . . charming," she stated at last.

Tom looked pleased as the hostess

showed them to a table. "Just don't get any ideas," he stated jokingly as they sat down.

"What do you mean?"

"I mean, like our café." His hazel eyes scanned the room. "It sure won't look like this."

Amie grinned. "No, I suppose it won't. I'll just have to wait to expand our full-scale restaurant after we're wealthy entrepreneurs, selling franchises all over the world."

Tom let out a soft, slow whistle. "Amie, you're a big dreamer, you know that?"

"Dreaming is fun."

He paused, looking over the dinner selections. "And what if your dreams never come true? Then what?"

"They're just dreams."

"You're not going to get disappointed, are you?"

"Probably."

He looked at her askance. "You really want to be a wealthy entrepreneur?"

She considered the question while taking a sip of water from the long-stemmed glass goblet. "Actually, Tom, I don't care a whole lot about money. Perhaps that's because I've never been without it. But, no, I'm not aspiring to earn some great fortune. I just want to do something fulfilling — something that's mine. God gives all His children *something* . . . a ministry of sorts." She paused reflectively. "Maybe it's our partnership and building the hotel, but I think that's really only the first step — to what, though, I'm not sure."

"A dreamer and a deep thinker." Tom shook his head. "You are so much like Hal it's spooky!"

She smiled. "Except he needed a level-headed business partner."

"He sure did."

"Someone who could have helped him develop that gas station and Laundromat into a profitable business," she murmured, trying to decide on either the sweet-and-sour chicken or the shrimp and snow peas. "He had such visions for the place when he first purchased it, after his wife died."

Tom sat back, and immediately Amie knew she'd said too much. She could feel his penetrating stare.

"You told me the day we first met that you never really knew your uncle."

"And that's true. But I've been finding out more and more about him." She cleared her throat uncomfortably and then took another sip of water.

"Where are you getting your information, if you don't mind me asking?"

"From my uncle." She almost laughed,

realizing how ridiculous that sounded, but she knew she'd backed herself into a corner by giving her tongue free rein. While her predicament was somewhat amusing, she prayed Tom wouldn't hate her for what he might perceive as snooping.

He sat forward once more, hands folded over his menu. His countenance was a mask of disbelief. "Your uncle?"

Amie gave him an apologetic look and confessed. "I've been reading Uncle Hal's journals."

His green eyes lit up with understanding. "Ahh . . . I wondered where those went."

"Please don't be angry, Tom. I wasn't prying into anyone's past . . . except, perhaps, my uncle's. But that's only because I wanted to know who he was and what he was like."

"And that's how you found out about my family."

"Yes," she admitted, feeling like a naughty child. "But it's only been in this third diary that he's talked about you. I won't read any more, if you don't want me to. I'm not even halfway through."

"I never read them," Tom mumbled as he gazed off in the distance. "But I saw him writing from time to time. He said it helped him sort things out." He glanced back at her. "I thought I'd accidentally pitched his journals in the trash when I emptied the apartment."

Amie shook her head. "No, I packed them up with his other books and the photographs that were on his dresser." She fretted over her lower lip. "Tom?"

"I'm not angry, and I guess I don't care if you read the rest or not." His features softened, and Amie sighed audibly with the relief she felt. Then he took her hand, holding it between the two of his, and the mantle of warmth that suddenly enveloped her was startling. "I've got no secrets from you," he told her, wearing a tender expression. "You're my business partner and my friend and my . . . well, I guess there comes a point in every relationship where you either trust the other person or you don't. And, Amie . . . I trust you."

"Oh, Tom." That was about the sweetest thing she'd ever heard, because she knew the words came straight from his heart. Her lips parted to speak the same thing back to him — *I trust you*. And yet the utterance refused to take shape.

Finally the blond waitress who'd introduced herself as Tracy approached their table, ready to take their orders, and Amie realized she had more of a decision to make than simply which entree to select.

Did she dare share it? Her dark secret?

Tom's words reverberated within her soul: *I guess there comes a point in every relationship where you either trust the other person or you don't.*

It seemed she'd arrived at that very crossroad.

Chapter 14

Dinner was delicious and the musicians, playing with heart and soul, wooed the couple with their romantic serenades. During the ride back to Tigerton, Amie and Tom fell into an easy conversation.

"I'll send you Uncle Hal's journals," she promised, "just as soon as I finish reading the last one. But I have to warn you, I'm a slow reader. Might take me a good week or two."

"No problem. Send them when you're ready."

"I've really enjoyed reading them. I feel like I've gotten to know what kind of man my uncle was and . . . I'm proud to be his niece."

"I'm glad. He was a good man."

At last Tom pulled into the Warrens' driveway, and an awkward hush filled the inside of the truck's cab.

"I had a really nice time tonight . . . today. All day," Amie said, breaking the silence.

"Yeah, me too." He cleared his throat. "Um . . . I'll walk you up to the house."

Smiling in reply, Amie opened the door and jumped down out of the pickup. Tom met her halfway around, and in the still and frosty night, they walked side-by-side to the small front porch. Little flutters of nervousness welled up in Amie, and she decided that the end of any first date always seemed uncomfortable. Except the one three years ago. That finale was a nightmare! But tonight, she shoved aside those horrible memories and focused on her present companion. The thought of Tom's embrace was not at all unpleasant, and the idea of his mouth lingering on hers in a sweet kiss sent shivers of excitement through her. Somehow he'd captured her heart in a very special way.

They stopped by the front door, and she watched as indecision flittered across his face. She guessed he was debating whether to kiss her good night. It felt like eons before he decided. Finally he leaned forward. She lifted her chin and pursed her lips ever so slightly. Her eyelids drifted shut in dreamy anticipation.

"Amie . . ."

She blinked. "Yes?"

"I . . . I'm falling in love with you," he

stammered. Beneath the porch light, his face shone with a boyish innocence.

"Tom, you're so sweet . . ." She smiled. "But aren't you supposed to kiss me and *then* tell me you're falling in love with me?"

"I don't need to kiss you to know that."

His expression was one of adoration, and Amie knew he meant every word. Suddenly she longed to throw her arms around his neck and smother him with the unshed emotion building within her.

"But, I hope you'll understand . . ." He stuck his hands into his jacket pockets. "About eight years ago, I made a decision not to kiss a woman until she was my wife. I probably sound like some dumb country hick," he said, shuffling his feet nervously, "but I know that conviction came from God, and I can't break my vow to Him."

"I wouldn't want you to," Amie stated sincerely, and given her past, she could see the wisdom in that resolution. She wished she'd been a stronger Christian a few years ago.

Tom momentarily looked down before returning his gaze to hers. "It's not that I don't want to kiss you —"

"It's all right. Really."

He nodded. "I've watched so many of my peers, Christians included, date and kiss women, only to break up and move on to someone new. Then I got to thinking that what they were doing was the same as . . . well, kissing somebody else's wife, since a lot of those ladies wound up marrying other guys." He paused and cleared his throat. "I made a decision to keep myself pure until marriage."

Something deep within Amie began to wither.

He shrugged, looking chagrined. "I guess I just wanted to share my heart with you on this . . ."

"Oh, I'm glad you did," she replied readily, although it lacked genuine enthusiasm. Inside, that old familiar ache of sheer and utter discouragement quickly choked any hopeful feelings of love she might have begun to entertain.

"You're a fine Christian man, Tom," she said matter-of-factly, opening the door to the Warrens' house. "You made a godly decision. I pray you will never go back on it." A flash of confusion crossed his features, but Amie didn't bother to explain. "Good night, and thanks . . ."

Entering the house, she closed the door on his murmured " 'Night" and stood in the little foyer. Everything was dark and quiet; obviously the Warrens were already sleeping. In the silence, she stood there pondering the events of the last few minutes. How ironic that on the way back from Wausau tonight she'd determined to share her hurtful past, certain that Tom would be the one who'd understand. And he would, no doubt about it. But he wouldn't want her after learning about her shameful secret. If he considered kissing "impure," what would he think of . . .

Amie put her face in her hands, feeling the need to weep until she could no more. And once her tears had dried, she'd begin her life again. Single. Forever on her own. The curse.

I can't stay here, she hastily concluded. *How can I ever face him again? I can't lead him on. Nothing good will come of it.* Moving away from the front door, she crept down the hall to the little sewing room where she quietly packed her things.

Tom couldn't believe it.

"She must have left some time during the night," Katie told him once the worship service had ended. She opened her purse and pulled out a slip of paper. "This is what I found just before I made breakfast."

He took the proffered note on which a simple *Thank you for the memorable*

Christmas! was penned, signed by Amie at the bottom. Looking back at Katie, he was speechless.

"Why don't you come over for lunch today," she suggested. "We can talk about it then."

"Thanks . . . sure, I'll do that. But I think I'll go downstairs and give her a call first."

"That's a good idea." The look on Katie's face mirrored the confusion in his heart.

Leaving the sanctuary, Tom's puzzlement over Amie's swift departure mounted. *Did I offend her? But how?*

In his makeshift apartment, he picked up the extension in the kitchen area and dialed her phone number, only to get her answering machine. "Hi, Amie, it's me," he began, leaving a message. "Give me a call back when you can."

Hanging up the receiver, he decided to try her parents' home. He knew that number from memory too. But again, only a machine answered and he chose not to leave a message there.

Concern and frustration plagued him as he walked back into his bedroom/living room area. He glanced at his computer and decided to check his E-mail. Much to his relief, Amie had left a message; however, it was short and revealed nothing about why she left. *Don't worry. I got home all right. I'm sorry, Tom. It's not you. It's me.*

"What does *that* mean?" he asked aloud, staring in utter confusion at the words on the screen.

Clicking on the REPLY TO AUTHOR button, he responded with: *Glad you made it back to Chicago okay, but would you mind telling me why you left?* He thought about asking more, but settled on one question at a time. He only hoped she'd respond. Soon.

Shutting down his computer, Tom made his way over to the Warrens', where, after lunch and out of the children's earshot, he divulged to Jake and Katie the entire conversation he and Amie had on the porch last night.

"She said I was sweet," he relayed. "I don't get it."

"Perhaps she's a person who fears commitment," Jake suggested.

"I don't know; she agreed to our partnership readily enough."

"Yes, that's true," Katie said, looking at her husband as though he possessed the answers.

"But you know," Tom began, "she does have a curious fear of men. I've seen it. She panics — at least she does until she gets to know them. But she's not afraid of me, and I don't think I did anything last night to change her opinion of me."

"Hmm . . . a fear of men?" Jake inhaled deeply, then stood and strolled to the coffeepot, pouring himself another cup. "I hate to even speculate as to what that could mean." He returned to the table and sat down. "We'll, of course, keep her in our prayers."

Katie agreed, her soft brown eyes looking sad. "She's a special young woman, Tom. The girls and I enjoyed her company. I'm so sorry she left."

He nodded. "Me too."

"Maybe I could give her pastor a call tomorrow and try to get some insight from him," Jake offered.

"Naw, don't bother. I'd rather hear about whatever's bothering Amie straight from her," Tom said, pushing his chair from the table. He looked at Katie. "Thanks for the lunch. I don't know what I'd do if you decided not to feed me."

She waved a hand at him as though it were nothing.

"See you guys later."

" 'Bye, Tom," Jake called as he made his way to the door.

Lord, Tom prayed on the way home, *You're gonna have to close the door with a bang and build a cement wall so high I'll never get over, if You want me to forget about Amie. But I don't think You do. Besides, what would I have done if Hal hadn't taken a chance on me?* Tom walked into the church building and went downstairs. *But You'll sure have to give me the smarts to deal with this thing — whatever it is — because I have no idea where to even start.*

Chapter 15

One of the first things Amie did after she arrived home was pack up her uncle's journals and ship them off to Tom. She didn't think she could bear reading any more about his life. The mere thought of him caused her heart to ache. She felt as though she were mourning the death of something that hadn't had the chance to even be born.

The days passed, and Amie managed to skirt Tom's phone calls and refused to reply to his E-mail messages, deleting them before she even read them. She knew his questions and words of concern would break her heart all the more, and she prayed that in avoiding him altogether, he'd change his mind about falling in love with her and lose interest in her romantically. Then perhaps by spring, they could resume a platonic business partnership during the construction process; however, she doubted her plans to move up to Tigerton now . . . which meant she couldn't sell her condo . . .

which meant they'd most likely have to take out a mortgage on the hotel. Suddenly everything seemed highly complicated.

New Year's Eve came and went with Amie choosing to stay home. Friends tried to coax her to church and New Year's parties, but she didn't feel up to it. Then, the following Monday, she began her new job.

"Okay, let me get this straight — all you want me to do is answer this phone?"

"That's it. For now." Buzz chuckled. "Don't want to overwhelm you on your first day."

Buzz Felton, her new boss, was a short, squat, jolly man who laughed at just about anything. Amie wondered if he'd been moonlighting as Santa Claus during the holidays.

"Go ahead. Have a seat," he told her. "Just answer the phone. The other girls will answer your questions."

Amie made herself comfortable at the end of a large U-shaped desk. It was part of what the company called The Information Center, and two other secretaries worked side-by-side as they greeted customers and answered calls.

The phone began to ring, and Amie soon discovered her job consisted largely of taking messages and listening to Buzz's customers complain. Her only reprieve came at noon when her father invited her to lunch.

"You'll love working here, Princess," he said as they dined in the company's cafeteria.

"Dad, I can't afford to love working here." Amie poked at the salad she'd ordered, pushing the lettuce around her plate. "I'm going to have to find a job that pays as much as MBMD did."

Her father's whitened brows went up in surprise. "What about your hotel?"

She shrugged. "I don't know."

"Hmm . . ." He munched hungrily on his hamburger.

Amie chafed at her father's ambivalent attitude, although she told herself she ought to be used to it. While he was the only one in the family who encouraged her, she sometimes wondered if he only did so to escape dealing with her feelings, not to mention her "religion."

Even so, she made an attempt. "Tom and I . . . well, our relationship started to develop beyond a mere partnership."

"Oh, really?" He took a drink of his coffee. "Pass me the ketchup, will you?"

Amie nodded and handed him the round red bottle at the end of the table.

"Well, you know the old saying," he said,

pouring the condiment onto his burger, "don't mix business with pleasure."

"Yeah . . ." She sighed woefully. "I kinda wish I hadn't."

His blue-eyed gaze met hers, and she hoped he'd inquire further. She needed to talk so badly. However, her hopes were soon dashed when her father changed the subject.

"Say, would you like some dessert? The cheesecake down here is out of this world. But don't tell your mother. She thinks her cheesecake is the best . . . and it's close. Real close."

But Amie had long since lost her appetite. "No . . . no, thanks, Dad."

Tom's business management and accounting courses began in mid-January. After a few weeks, he found a job at a motel in Shawano, working a split shift, six o'clock in the evening until two A.M. He didn't plan on keeping the position long, but determined to learn everything possible about running the place. And even with his busy schedule, he faithfully e-mailed Amie once, sometimes twice, a day. He wasn't sure if she read his messages, even though he tried to keep them light and friendly. She never wrote back.

Lord, he prayed early one morning before falling into bed exhausted, *only You know a woman's mind, that's for sure! But I'm not giving up.*

Valentine's Day decorations cluttered The Information Center where Amie worked, causing her to hate the job all the more. She'd sent out at least a dozen resumés but hadn't gotten a single response.

"Say, Amie, are you doing anything special this weekend?" Nora Craig, another secretary, asked. "I mean, Valentine's Day *is* Sunday, you know."

"How could I forget?" she quipped, glancing at the cardboard cupid dangling from the ceiling, close to her head. She sighed. "No, I'm not doing anything special."

Lifting her gaze from the fingernail file she held and raising her penciled eyebrows, Nora frowned. "Your boyfriend isn't taking you someplace romantic? Why, my Ronald is taking me away for the weekend, except he won't tell me where." She laughed gaily. "He's such a Casanova — even after twelve years of marriage!"

"That's really special," Amie replied in an apathetic tone. She glanced at her wristwatch. Two more hours to go. Could she last till five o'clock? The afternoon had dragged on until she couldn't stand this place anymore. No way was she coming back Monday. Not a chance. Her father and Buzz could beg her blue, but she'd refuse to step a foot into this office again!

At that moment, Amie looked up to see a delivery man walking into the building carrying a large bouquet of red roses.

Casanova strikes again.

"Ooh! Who are these for?" Charis, the main receptionist, asked.

The delivery man read the name on the attached envelope. "Amie Potter."

Her two associates gasped with pleasure.

"She's right here!" Nora grabbed the boxed blossoms and brought them to Amie.

"They're probably from my dad," she said facetiously, as her face warmed with embarrassment.

The ladies "oohed" and "ahhed" as they took charge of setting the flowers aright in their accompanying cut-glass vase. With a roll of her eyes, Amie opened the card. Liquid numbness spread through her veins as she read the words: *I love you, Amie. Tom.* For several moments, she stared at the note in her hand, feeling as though she couldn't breathe.

How can he still love me? she wondered. *I've given him the cold shoulder for nearly two months.*

"Well, now, honey," Nora crooned, "are you sure you're not doing something special this weekend?"

Amie finally conceded a laugh.

The last couple of hours passed quickly that afternoon, and Amie found herself actually enjoying the conversation between herself and her coworkers. Since her first day on the job, she'd been cool to the ladies, ignoring their attempts at friendship. But somehow today her icy facade cracked, and it wasn't long before she told them about her hotel "adventure" in Tigerton, Wisconsin, and gave them a vague rundown on Tom.

"Marry him quick, Amie," Charis advised, her eyes a too-bright shade of green from her colored contact lenses. Shaking her bottle-blond head, she continued, "There's not many of those kind of guys left these days. And I should know! I think I've dated every eligible bachelor in the Chicago area under fifty years old."

"Well, try frequenting the senior citizen centers," Nora shot back jokingly. "You're no spring chicken anymore."

The ladies, both twenty-plus years older

than Amie, cackled and teased each other, making her giggle until her sides ached.

That night, as she made her way through the front door of her condo, her arms filled with fragrant roses, she wondered what to do about Tom. She supposed she could be blatantly honest with him regarding her past so he'd change his mind about her once and for all. Get it over with. Quickly. Or she could break his heart and lie, telling him she didn't love him and that she never would.

With her winter coat hung up and the flowers on the coffee table, Amie walked to her office and booted up her computer. She sat down in front of the monitor and decided she couldn't hurt Tom for the world nor could she lie and hurt her Savior. She'd rather hurt herself. But if he rejected her, once he knew the truth, could she ever face him again? And yet, what did she have to lose? Could she really feel any more miserable?

Oh, Lord, she prayed, *I'm so scared . . .*

It was then the Lord spoke to her heart from 1 John 4:18. "Perfect love casts out fear."

Jesus Christ loved her so much that He died for her. In these past several weeks, she'd felt as though she'd grown closer to the Savior. It was His love that kept getting her out of bed every morning and His love that gave her hope for the future — with or without Tom.

"Perfect love . . . all right, Lord. With Your help, I'll tell him. I don't know how or when, but I'll share my past with him. You'll have to orchestrate it all and prepare Tom's heart. But I won't be afraid of his reaction anymore, I'll just think about You . . . and how much You'll still love me. . . ." She wiped an errant tear from her eye. "Even if Tom changes his mind about his feelings for me."

It was as if that Still Small Voice replied to her soul, "One day at a time, beloved. One day at a time."

Taking a deep, cleansing breath, Amie accessed her server and downloaded seven E-mail messages — two of them from Tom.

The first message from Tom gave his work phone number, "in case you misplaced it."

Amie frowned, confused. Work number? Where was he working?

She read the second message. *And just in case you forgot, I don't get to work until six o'clock. Dinner break at eight. Call then.*

Her frown increased until she figured out that somehow Tom knew she hadn't read any of his E-mails for the last seven weeks.

He obviously hoped she'd read these, no doubt since he'd sent her the roses and the simple, yet poignant, Valentine's Day card.

He knows me too well, she mused with a slip of a smile.

Then she replied to his last message on a lark he'd get it before he left for work. *Thanks for the roses, Tom. I'll call you around eight.*

Chapter 16

Tom glanced at the octagonal wall clock stationed behind the check-in desk. Seven fifty-five. Would she really call?

Before coming to work, he'd checked his E-mail just to see if Amie had sent him a message. Much to his immense elation, she had. Would she keep her word?

At eight, Tom turned to his coworker Rosa. "I'm going on my break. Will you watch the desk?"

She bobbed her graying curls and smiled easily.

"Oh, and I'm expecting a phone call . . ."

"I'll patch it through to the lounge," she finished for him.

"Great."

Down the hallway, Tom entered the small break room. Opening the slim refrigerator he extracted the sack with the supper Katie graciously prepared for him, then he moved to the round veneer-topped table and plunked down in a swivel chair. Physically, he felt exhausted. Emotionally, he could run the Olympic mile. He glanced at his wristwatch. *Eight-o-three. Anytime now, Amie.*

He reminded himself that she always ran late. Ten minutes ticked by. *No, she's not going to call.* Filled with a huge sense of disappointment, he started picking at his sandwich, ham and cheese on a hard roll. He popped the top off a soda can and took a swig.

The phone rang and he nearly choked in his haste to answer it. "Staff lounge," he said, the receiver to his ear.

"Tom?"

His heart sped up in the most peculiar way. "Yeah, hi, Amie." He pulled the long, coiled phone cord across the table and sat down again. "It's nice to hear your voice."

He heard her soft exhalation. "I guess it's been a long time coming, huh? I'm sorry, Tom, for being so . . . so . . ."

"Forget it. I'm just glad you're okay." He paused, feeling a twinge of concern. "You are okay, aren't you?"

"Actually, no. I've been miserable. I hate my job. I'm not exactly multi-task oriented. But who in their right mind can answer five incoming phone calls at once? And my father certainly doesn't help matters. He taunts me with his dumb-blond jokes. So, I'm not secretary material," she huffed. "Excuse me!"

She's nervous, he realized. Still, he wasn't about to dismiss matters. He'd waited too long for some answers.

"Is that all you've been miserable about?" he queried gently. "A job that you never intended to stay at anyway?"

"No." She took a ragged breath. "I guess you and I need to talk, Tom . . . but not tonight. Not over the phone."

"All right," he agreed, curiously . . . warily.

"Thank you for the roses," Amie said quietly. "And the card. Actually, it was the card that touched my heart. You're really sweet."

"Last time you told me I was sweet you didn't talk to me for two months."

Silence. "I'm sorry, Tom. It's me —"

"What does that mean, Amie? *It's you?*" He fought to control his mounting frustration. "Are you trying to tell me that you don't share my feelings? Is that it? You know, I think I could handle point-blank honesty better than all of this."

"No . . . no, in fact . . ." She paused, her voice wavering slightly, and Tom instantly regretted his impatience with her. "In fact," she began again, "I feel very much the same way you do, Tom. But, see, that's why this whole thing started."

"I don't get it," he stated flatly, sipping his soda. "I love you . . . you share my feelings . . . shouldn't we be . . . *rejoicing?*"

"Yes." There was a smile in her voice now. "And I hope we will be . . . rejoicing . . . soon."

"You hope?"

"Uh-huh. That's why we've got to talk. Except, until today, I haven't been ready to discuss anything. Maybe I've been feeling sorry for myself on top of being so frightened, I don't know."

"Frightened? Of what?"

She hesitated. "Do you remember when you said that you were afraid I'd change my mind about our partnership once I heard the gossip regarding your family?"

"Yeah," he replied cautiously.

"Okay, well, that's sort of how I'm feeling now. I'm afraid you're going to change your mind about . . . about me . . . after I share something from my past."

That's it? Tom shook his head in wonder. "Amie, there's nothing you could ever say to change the way I feel about you. I'm hopeless. The only cure is . . ." He balked, not wishing to broach the subject of marriage over the phone. "I guess we'll have to talk about that too."

"Are you working this weekend?" she asked. "And what in the world are you doing at the Best Rest Motel?"

"On-the-job training."

"Oh."

"You would know that, if you read all the E-mails I sent you."

"Sorry . . ."

She sounded satisfactorily remorseful, so Tom didn't rub it in further. "And, yeah, I'm on this weekend. I'm working a double shift tomorrow, filling in for the manager."

"Good going. As soon as you figure out how to run a hotel, you can teach me."

He laughed. "You bet. Well, my break's just about over so I'd better hang up. But, Amie?" He softened his tone. "Don't stop talking to me. Whatever's bothering you, we'll work it out."

"All right." She still sounded skeptical.

"Promise me."

A moment's pause — or was it reluctance? "I promise."

"Can I call you early Sunday afternoon before I go to work?"

"Yes. I'd like that." Her voice returned to its honeyed tone.

Neither spoke for several seconds.

"I love you," Tom said at last, cringing slightly at how trite his admission might sound to the average hearer. He figured those three words were probably the most overused and misused in the English language, yet the most profound when spoken earnestly, as he'd intended.

For most of his teenage years, he'd longed to say them to that "special someone." But, shortly after his twenty-fifth birthday, he all but convinced himself he'd never fall in love — that he was unlovable. And then Amie babbled her way into his heart.

He grinned.

Fleetingly, Tom wondered if he ever told his father he loved him. He hoped so. It was true — he'd loved his father enough to stick with him year after year, hangover after hangover, until finally the booze he cherished more than his family killed him. Still, Tom had refused to give up, praying his dad would trust the Lord with his soul. And he might have.

Even so, Tom saw more suffering than he cared to remember while living with his father. He'd survived horror stories that would intimidate Hollywood film makers.

No, whatever the secret Amie harbored, it could neither shock him nor change his feelings for her a mite. He *loved* her.

"Tom . . . ?" Like a healing balm, her soft voice penetrated each scabbed wound. "I love you, too."

Within a week, Tom and Amie had more than made up for the past two months of not communicating. However, because of his classes and work schedule, it soon became apparent that the earliest they'd be able to spend time together was Easter weekend.

And so it was planned. Tom would come to Chicago and meet Amie's family, and they'd talk — face to face. Despite the forty days she had to wait to see him, Amie didn't feel anxious in the least over sharing her three-year secret. Not anymore. It almost seemed as if it didn't matter if she told Tom or not; he insisted his feelings for her were unconditional. But she'd tell him anyway. He had to know, and she needed to confide in the man she loved.

However, there was another matter causing her mild apprehension, and that was telling her family about Tom and his upcoming visit.

Two weeks before Easter, on a sunny March afternoon, Amie finally found the nerve to address the subject at the family dinner table.

Upon hearing the news, Dottie dropped

her fork. It clanged loudly against the expensive Haviland dinnerware. "The gas station geek! You're kidding!"

"Tom is *not* a geek," Amie stated, giving her younger sister a furious look.

Beside her, Dottie's fiancé shifted uncomfortably. "He works at a . . . *gas station?*" He said the last two words in a manner of distaste with a perfectly wrinkled nose.

"No, Gregory," Amie corrected him, "Tom is my business partner."

"Amie, dear," her mother crooned from one end of the long, polished dining room table, "what happened to that charming young man . . . Wanda Carter's son?"

"He wasn't all that charming," Amie quipped. The truth was, she'd met Kevin Carter only once, very briefly — and she hadn't been impressed.

Besides, she loved Tom.

"Now, listen everyone," John Potter told his family from where he sat at the head of the table, "we owe it to Amie to at least *meet* this fellow before we pass judgment on him."

"Thanks, Dad," she muttered, picking at her veal cordon bleu.

"After all," he continued, "Tom did inherit quite a bit of money from Hal. Let's not forget that."

Amie groaned inwardly, wondering how she happened to be born into this money-minded family. Except she knew God never made mistakes.

"I met him," Dottie stated flatly, "when Stephen and I drove to northern Wisconsin to claim our inheritances. He was . . . a dirty-fingernailed car mechanic with long hair and a stubbled face." Her brown-eyed gaze zeroed in on Amie. "Are you out of your mind?"

Amie shot a quick glance across the table at Gregory, his soft, shiny baby-face grinning amusedly, and thought she might ask Dottie the same thing. Of course, Amie hadn't judged her sister's fiancé on appearance alone. It was his bad temperament, moodiness, and sickening habit of whining that made her dislike him. Dottie's attraction, however, seemed to stem from the fact that marrying Gregory ensured her a position within the wealthy Bradford family.

Lillian cleared her throat. "Just how . . . serious are you about this man, Amie?" Her mother's white-winged brows were knitted together in concern.

The room fell deathly quiet and all eyes turned on Amie. She took a deep breath, feeling overshadowed by her family's expectations. They'd never understand. They never did.

Gazing back at her mother, who looked as she always did, very dignified, very regal, Amie began. "I'm quite serious about him. Tom is probably the best friend I have on earth and I . . . I'm in love with him."

Dottie shook her head, looking disgusted. "You have flipped your wig! You're going to ruin your reputation. What are people going to say when they find out you're involved with a . . . a grease monkey?"

"He is not a 'grease monkey,' and I couldn't care less what anybody says," Amie replied sharply, scooting her chair back and rising from the table. "Tom is a warm, caring person with a good head for business. He's a hard worker and . . . oh! never mind. I don't want him to meet you . . . any of you!" Tears of humiliation filled her eyes. "I would be ashamed for him to discover how shallow my family really is!"

With that, she tossed her linen napkin onto her barely touched plate, ignoring the gasp from her mother and the appalled expression on Dottie's face. Leaving the room, she grabbed her purse and walked into the wide foyer, her heels clicking smartly on the Spanish tile. There she opened the closet and pulled out her coat.

"Amie, don't leave the house like this," her father warned, coming up behind her.

Casting a look of disappointment his way, she yanked open the front door and marched out to her car parked in the circular drive.

By the time she arrived back at her condominium, Amie felt ashamed at her outburst of temper. It was one of the things she couldn't stand about Gregory, yet she'd behaved the same way.

"Lord, I don't think my actions glorified You to my un-saved family, did they?" she muttered, kicking off her shoes with more force than necessary. She walked to the answering machine and checked for messages.

"Hello, Miss Potter, this is Dennis Templeton of Templeton Realty. Good news. I believe I've sold your condo this afternoon. I told you it wouldn't take long . . ."

Good grief! Amie thought, smacking her palm against her forehead. *Now I'll be forced to actually live with my parents!*

The telephone rang and she checked the Caller ID. Seeing it was her parents' number, she decided against answering it.

"Amie, darling," her mother's smooth voice lilted through the machine. "I'm so sorry we hurt your feelings this evening. Of course we want to meet Tim."

"*Tom,*" she grumbled, rolling her eyes in aggravation.

"Now, you just tell me when he's coming, and we'll all be on our best behavior." A pause. "Honey, I want you to be happy, it's just that . . . well, you know, I grew up near Tigerton, and I've always wanted better for my children. People are so . . . so *backwards* up there, and . . . oooh!" she moaned, "my worst fears have been realized. My daughter . . . romantically involved with someone from the small town I endeavored to escape." She sighed dramatically before her voice took on a steely tone. "It's a good thing Hal's already dead because if he were here, I'd wring his neck for starting all this trouble! I knew it was a mistake for him to leave you that gas station!"

A decisive click, and then Amie collapsed into a nearby armchair. She couldn't allow Tom to come to Chicago. There was no way. She wouldn't put him through it!

"All right, people, listen up." Amie watched her father trying to get his family's attention. They were all gathered in the living room, including Stephen, who'd come home from college on spring break. "We've promised Amie we would be polite, and I will not tolerate any rude remarks or condescending comments about her . . . friend. Got it?"

Dottie clucked her tongue and cozied up next to Gregory on the love seat. "Oh, Dad, you make us sound like naughty children."

If the shoe fits, Amie thought wryly, folding her arms.

For the past week, she had pleaded with Tom, begging him not to come for Easter weekend. However, he seemed bound and determined no matter what she said. Amie even phoned Pastor Warren and explained the circumstances, only to have him side with Tom.

"He's going to have to meet them eventually, Amie. Trust God to work in the hearts of your family members, and let Tom face the challenge. It'll be good for him — for both of you."

But she had her doubts. And, now, as she gazed around at the faces here in the living room of her parents' home, she felt so sorry for Tom. Her siblings and Gregory looked like felines ready to pounce. Her mother, situated comfortably in one of the two matching powder blue wingbacked chairs, filed her fingernails indifferently. Only her father appeared to be making any sort of attempt.

A car door slammed outside and Amie startled. Dottie peaked out the side of the off-white pleated drapes covering the large picture window. "He's he–ere," she crooned.

"Be nice," John Potter cautioned her.

"I'm always nice," Dottie replied irritably, while Stephen and Gregory snickered.

Oh, Lord, help! Amie prayed silently as the front doorbell sounded. "I'll get it," she said quickly.

Hurrying into the foyer, she checked her reflection in the antique wall mirror. With a deep breath, she pulled open the large front door.

Tom smiled a greeting.

"Hi," she said. "Come on in."

As he stepped into the house, she impulsively threw her arms around his neck in a hug of welcome. "I've missed you so much," she murmured. His cheek felt cool against hers as a rush of nippy spring air blew into the house.

"I've missed you too."

Amie pulled out of the embrace and shut the door. Turning back to Tom, she asked, "May I hang up your coat?"

He nodded, shrugging out of the handsome camel's hair coat and handing it to

221

her. After tucking it in the closet, she gazed at him, taking in his every feature. Four months apart had certainly dulled her memory of him and how incredibly handsome he was. His dark brown hair was neatly cropped, although, for the moment, it looked windblown. As if divining her thoughts, he quickly combed his fingers through it. Their gazes met, and Amie decided his hazel eyes no longer seemed sad, as they stared back at her with adoration sparkling in their depths, leaving no doubt in her mind as to how he felt about her. She noticed, too, that he wore the sweater she'd given him at Christmas and a pair of khaki trousers. He looked terrific. He might even impress Dottie!

Amie smiled almost apologetically. "Can I introduce you to my family?"

He nodded. "Lead the way."

Chapter 17

"So, what line of work is your father in?"

Amie cringed at the barrage of questions being hurled at Tom, although he seemed to be holding his own.

"My father's dead, Mr. Potter," he replied politely. "But he worked for the railroad for almost fifteen years."

"The railroad? Hmm . . . I had a cousin who worked for Union Pacific."

Tom nodded, looking interested.

"Anderson . . . I'm trying to think if I went to school with any Andersons," Lillian stated, drumming a well-sculpted fingernail against her chin pensively. "You wouldn't happen to be related to Margaret Anderson, would you?"

Tom smiled patiently. "Not that I know."

"So, um," Stephen began, sitting forward on the sofa, "like where are you working now that my uncle's filling station is gone?"

"I'm the assistant manager of a motel in Shawano."

"Assistant manager, huh?" John Potter looked mildly impressed.

Amie was aware of the promotion and felt proud of him. The national motel chain knew Tom planned to move on but advanced him anyway, citing his outstanding work ethic. Within just a few months of his employment! She wished he'd tell her family that piece of information, but figured he'd probably consider it bragging, which wasn't at all Tom's nature.

The interrogation continued; however, it wasn't long before Dottie and her fiancé grew bored and left, claiming they had dinner reservations. Stephen, too, made his excuses and exited the house.

"Our dinner will be ready shortly," Amie announced.

"She's making lasagna for us," her father added, looking at Tom. "Took over our kitchen so she could impress you with her culinary skills."

John Potter laughed, and Amie shot him a dubious glance, while Tom's face reddened slightly.

"Amie could make peanut butter and jelly sandwiches, and I wouldn't care."

She was touched by Tom's kind remark — and even her parents looked a bit taken by it.

"So, how's this hotel adventure coming along?" her father asked, clearing his throat.

"Excavation has already begun," he replied. "And if the mild weather keeps up, the foundation could be poured as early as next month."

"Don't count on it," Lillian said. "I can remember snow storms up there occurring as late as May."

Tom agreed courteously.

John drew his brows together. "How'd those architectural drawings work out for you?"

"Would you like to see the plans, Mr. Potter? I've got a set out in my truck."

"Sure!" he boomed on an enthusiastic note.

Tom fetched the drawings, and while he explained the layout for the hotel, café, and antique shop, Amie made the final preparations for their dinner. At last they sat down to eat, and although her parents' questions persisted, the focus now centered on the business adventure instead of Tom's personal life.

Amazingly, the evening progressed at a comfortable pace, and by the time her father turned on the late edition of the news, Amie was sure he liked Tom. Even her mother behaved sweetly toward him now.

"Tom, dear, the guest bedroom is all ready for you."

"Thanks, Mrs. Potter."

She yawned, placing a delicate hand over her mouth. "Gracious! I'm tired. See you all in the morning. Amie, you will be here for breakfast, won't you?"

"Yes." She planned to drive home tonight but return bright and early tomorrow. "Good night, Mother."

Lillian blew her a kiss as she left the family room.

The night wore on and Amie began to wonder if her father would ever get sleepy and allow her some time alone with Tom. But when Stephen arrived home and settled down in front of the television, she gave up.

"Guess I'll go home," she finally announced. Glancing at Tom, she added, "I hope you don't mind me abandoning you this way."

"Not at all," he replied graciously. "I'm in good company."

"G'night, Princess," her father called from his recliner.

"See ya, sis," Stephen mumbled in between a fist full of corn chips.

Tom offered to walk her to the door.

"Will you be all right here?" she asked feeling uneasy.

"I'll be fine. I like your family."

Amie smiled. "They like you too. I can tell."

He grinned.

"I thought we could eat lunch over at my place tomorrow," she said, praying they'd have time to talk then. "Later we've been invited to some of my friends' house for fellowship and board games." Amie shrugged into her coat with his mannerly assistance. "Does that sound okay?"

"Sounds great."

She paused, longing to kiss him but remembering his vow to God. Somehow that special promise made her feel secure, evidencing that Tom was a man of his word.

"Well, good night."

His expression softened. " 'Night, Amie."

For lunch the following day, Amie created peanut butter and jelly sandwiches *extraordinaire*. While eating, they laughed together about Tom's first racquetball experience. Her father had insisted he come to the club that morning, along with Stephen and Gregory, and a highly competitive game ensued between the four men.

"I still can't believe your dad and I won," Tom remarked as they moved to the living room after their meal. "I mean, I never played before!"

"You must be a natural."

He laughed. "Right."

Amie watched him walk to the grandfather clock and appraise the piece with admiration.

"Nice," he said. "You've got a really nice place."

"Thanks."

He pursed his lips, looking momentarily thoughtful. "Do you think you'll be happy living in a small country town like Tigerton after . . ." He waved his arm, indicating their surroundings, "after living like this? Plush carpet, expensive furniture, fine paintings, knickknacks . . ."

She shrugged. "Sure? Why not? Can't I take this stuff with me?"

Tom grinned wryly. "Why do I have visions of Zsa Zsa Gabor on that TV show 'Green Acres' when I think of you living in Tigerton?"

Laughing, Amie picked up a throw pillow from the colorful floral-printed sofa and threw it at him. "So, you've been watching those old late-night reruns at work again, huh?"

His grin broadened.

"Well, I'll have you know, Tom Anderson, that I don't need any of these *things* to be happy."

"No?"

"No." She stepped closer, feeling as though her now-sober expression matched Tom's. "I'm a single woman who, up until recently, made a lot of money. I bought what I wanted, but I never needed any of this." She cast one quick glance around the well-decorated living room before her eyes came back to his. "I've learned that it's the Lord who puts joy in my heart, but Tom . . . just being with you makes me happy."

"You're sure about that?"

She tipped her head, puzzled over all the questions. "Yes, I'm sure."

"Well, in that case . . ." Tom reached into his blue jeans pocket and pulled out a diamond solitaire, set in sterling. Slipping the ring onto her left-hand finger, he got down on one knee. "Will you marry me, Amie?"

Gazing at him, she didn't know whether to laugh or cry — so she conceded to both. The most she could do was nod a reply.

Standing to his feet, he chuckled lightly. "Does that mean yes?"

"Yes," she fairly choked, throwing her arms around his neck.

He pulled them back, then held both her hands in his. The expression on his face was of a sorrowful apology. "I don't think it'd be a good idea to have a . . . a real long engagement."

"Oh, but, Tom," she pleaded, "wouldn't it be wonderful to have our wedding reception at our new hotel?"

He looked skeptical. "We're talking September, October . . . ?"

She nodded, adding, thoughtfully, "Otherwise, we'll both be living in the church basement."

"Not necessarily. There's an apartment for rent above the funeral home."

Dropping her hands to her side, Amie lifted an incredulous brow. "Funeral home?"

"It's spacious," Tom continued, wearing a sheepish smile. "And it'd be . . . quiet."

She winced. "It'd be creepy. No. No way! We wait till fall."

Smiling, he walked to the sofa and sat down. "I figured you'd say that."

She seated herself on the other end, leaving a generous amount of space between them. In that moment, she wanted his convictions to be her convictions, and she made her own vow to God.

Heavenly Father, I will not tempt this man to break his promise to You. She'd love to kiss him and knew herself to be somewhat impetuous at times. Like now, when passion overruled her common sense. *Lord, help me keep my feelings for Tom in check until after the wedding.*

In that same, prayerful state of mind, Amie realized it was time to share her heart.

"Tom, before we start seriously discussing our future, there's something you need to know about my past."

"It doesn't matter, Amie," he insisted. "I read Hal's journals. You never finished them, did you?"

She shook her head.

"Well, I'm not completely done myself, but I got far enough along to have figured out that something pretty soul-shattering happened to you about . . . four years ago."

"How could that be in my uncle's diary?" she asked, frowning heavily. "He never knew. No one did . . . or does."

"He knew *something* happened. He wrote about his visit with your family over Easter. He'd looked forward to it because the holiday always reminded him of your spiritual birthday, and we both know Hal felt like a proud papa in that respect."

Amie smiled slightly at the comment, trying to recall that particular time in her life, yet wishing vehemently she could wipe away the event from her mind forever.

"Hal wrote that he saw you at supper and everything seemed fine," Tom relayed. "You talked about going to a company party later in the evening. You were smiling and happy, but the next day you'd completely changed. You appeared . . . 'skittish,' and he caught you crying your heart out a couple of times. Hal stated your mind was a million miles away. He asked you if something was wrong and if you wanted to talk, but you refused and pretty much stayed in your room the rest of the weekend. Hal said in his journal that it appalled him none of your family members acted concerned about you. But, to use his words, 'something happened . . . something bad.' "

Listening to Tom's recitation hurt more than Amie imagined anything in life ever could. His words were like a searing brand upon her memory, so hot and horrid that she wanted to scream from the pain. She rose from the sofa and walked over to the front windows and stared out over the soggy spring lawn.

"Look, Amie, you don't have to tell me any more than what I learned from Hal's writings."

"But I want you to know," she said tearfully. "I *need* for you to know everything because I need to share this . . . with somebody. With you."

Tom sat back. "Okay, I'm all ears."

She brushed away a tear. "I did go to that party," she stated with a sniff. "I had the afternoon off but went back to work because everyone at Maxwell Brothers was celebrating the acquisition of a large account and I didn't want to miss out on the . . . fun. Besides," she added, fighting against the all-consuming humiliation, "there was a business consultant there whom I'd been flirting with for months, and it was his last night with our company so, of course, I wanted to say . . . good-bye."

Avoiding Tom's probing gaze, she folded her arms tightly, peered at her cream-colored carpeting, and continued. "I was such a little fool. I don't know what I was thinking . . . well, that's just it: I wasn't thinking. I never bothered to find out if he was a Christian, and I had allowed my co-workers to delude me into believing coquettish behavior was an acceptable part of having a good time. I know how wrong they were . . . how wrong I was."

She sighed ruefully. "But that night, I accepted a couple glasses of champagne against my better judgment. Then when he asked me to drive him back to where he was staying since he'd relinquished the keys to his company car, I jumped at the opportunity.

"After we arrived, he asked me up to his place, and I willingly followed him inside. It was very romantic at first." Amie swallowed painfully, urging herself to go on. "He put on some soft music and I let him kiss me. Th–then everything happened so fa–fast," she stammered. "It was like he turned into a different person, so rough and demanding. I tried to stop him. I said no, but —"

She choked on a sob and squeezed her eyes closed. Every muscle in her body felt taut as the rest of the horror washed over her. When she looked up again, Tom was standing in front of her, his face a mask of pity, coupled with something indefinable.

"Did he rape you, Amie?" he asked in a tone filled with such incredulity that it sent a chill right through her.

Nevertheless, she managed a nod as the familiar trembling began.

"Did you report the incident? Tell police?"

She shook her head. "He said I deserved it . . . and I did."

"What are you talking about?" He gave her a mild shake. "No one *deserves* to be raped."

"I was hardly the innocent victim. I led

him on." Scalding tears of shame streamed from her eyes.

"You were naive. But, even if you weren't, it still doesn't excuse the guy's actions. What he did to you was criminal!"

Amie couldn't reply, so overcome by emotion was she. Tom gathered her into a comforting embrace.

"You know," he said, after a few long moments passed, "I thought I'd prepared myself for everything. But I didn't prepare myself for this."

Pulling back, she saw an angry muscle working in his jaw, and his hazel eyes glistened sharply.

"Do you want your engagement ring back?" she sniffed.

He blinked, the dark clouds of wrath dissipating. "No . . . no, I love you, and nothing will ever change that."

However, the truth about her past changed his heart about something, and for the remainder of the weekend, Amie sensed a barrier between them. While Tom had been two hundred and fifty miles away, he'd never seemed so distant as he did now.

It was the very thing she'd feared the most.

Chapter 18

Amie drove fast along the last stretch of highway, the windows of her BMW open to let in the early summer air. She'd given the situation six weeks to change, and she wasn't about to wait any longer. Oh, Tom had maintained a terrific facade — too bad she could see right through it. But after today, it'd be all over. She fully intended to break their engagement. As for their business partnership — she'd have to decide what to do about that later.

One hand on the steering wheel, Amie finger-combed her wind-blown blond hair back off her face with the other. Making the turn onto County J, she saw that the hotel's construction was well under way — its foundation poured, the wooden skeleton of its walls erected. Tom had kept her posted on the progress — and he'd even recently inquired about starting wedding plans, but Amie sensed his heart wasn't in the latter.

"And I'm not playing any more games!"

she declared to an empty car. She'd had four hours of solitary driving to get herself worked up into a fitful state that would not be abated until she had had her say.

She turned onto the gravel road and sped toward the church. At three-thirty on a Friday afternoon, she'd been hoping to catch him, and thankfully she spotted Tom walking from his truck. Curiously, she watched his expression as he saw her car. His eyes lit up in surprise and he smiled broadly.

Amie's resolve wavered.

"What are you doing here?" he asked, walking up to her car as she parked. His grin hadn't lessened.

Opening the door, she climbed out. "I want to talk to you."

He looked amused. "You couldn't phone or e-mail?"

She shook her head stoically. "Not for this."

"Okay." Tom's expression changed to one more earnest. "Something wrong?"

Amie took a deep breath and glanced around her. The tops of the tall pine trees swayed gently on the tepid June breeze. Beyond them, she could hear laughter from the Warren girls at play in their yard. In that very moment, she almost wished she could pretend, like Tom.

Steeling herself against those expressive hazel eyes, she slipped off her engagement ring. "I'm letting you off the hook." She took his hand and set the ring in his palm, ignoring the look of shock on his face. "You're a fine Christian man, Tom, and I know you'd never go back on a promise. So, I'm doing it for you."

"Amie —"

"You don't have to say a word," she prattled, feeling impotent. "I know you changed your mind when I told you about . . . my past. I can't blame you, and if you'll remember, I expected it. But, you know, you could have saved us both some heartache if you would have left things alone back in December."

"It's that obvious, huh?"

His admission startled her and all she could do was nod.

"Here," he gently admonished her, "put this back on . . . and don't you dare take it off again." He slipped the ring back in place. "It's not what you think, Amie. I haven't changed my mind about marrying you." He paused and she watched his Adam's apple bob with emotion. "I love you. It's just that . . . I'm so angry. Not with you. With . . . well, let's just say I'm glad you didn't mention any names, because I'd probably kill the guy who hurt you!"

Amie felt taken aback by the severity of his statement, yet, in some strange way, it consoled her too. "You're the most chivalrous man I've ever met," she finally whispered. "You'd fight for my honor? How sweet!"

"It's not *sweet*, Amie. I never get angry," he announced. "That's why this has been so hard on me. I watched anger destroy my father. He was furious with God for taking Mom, and he vented his wrath on us kids. Afterwards, he comforted himself with a bottle of whiskey. I vowed when I was thirteen that I'd never get mad — at anything. I swore I'd let nothing and no one push me to commit an act of violence against another human being. But here I am. Right where I vowed never to be."

Amie empathized with his inner struggle. "But, Tom, I'm glad you told me."

He shrugged. "I s'pose I should have been up-front with you from the start. It's just that I felt so . . . ashamed." After giving her a long look, he glanced at his wristwatch. "Listen, Amie, we'll have to finish this discussion later. I'm sorry. But I'm meeting a building inspector at the construction site." He shook his dark brown head ruefully.

"Something's not right. I can tell — except I don't know enough about building to pin-point the problem. Then, again, maybe this is all my imagination."

"*What* is all your imagination?" Amie asked, puzzled.

He grinned sardonically and looped an arm around her shoulders. "Well, as long as you're here, *business partner*, you might as well come along and find out."

When they arrived, the construction crew was packing up for the day. The men cast curious glances at them, especially after they met up with the building inspector. Amie noticed ominous stares from two in particular.

"Who are those guys, Tom?" she whispered as they walked into the site.

"Keith Reider and Tyler Johnson. They're Al's buddies. We all went to high school together."

"They look mean."

"They're probably hot and tired from working all day."

Amie was tempted to argue but decided against it and turned her attention to the inspector. He had a very round head, and his dark gray hair was buzzed, except for the very top where he'd gone completely bald.

Wearing tan trousers and an off-white short-sleeve dress shirt and brown-striped tie, he possessed a military-like appearance, even though he barely stood five feet five inches tall.

He poked at pipes and rattled wooden beams, scrutinized the cement foundation, asking minimal questions. Then every so often he'd pause to consider Amie, who was growing increasingly uncomfortable.

Finally, he said, "Don't I know you?"

She shrugged.

"I'm Ed Holm," he stated, even though introductions had already been made.

"My mother's maiden name was Holm," she replied, "but I really didn't think anything of the similarity, since it's a common last name around here."

He snapped his fingers. "Lillian's daughter — Halvor's niece."

She smiled, somewhat relieved to know the reason behind his earlier observations of her. "That's me."

"I'm Lil and Hal's cousin."

"Oh." She gave him a polite smile.

"Sure. But I'll bet it's been at least ten years since I last saw you."

She nodded. "I'll tell Mom I ran into you."

"Do that." Cousin Ed began studying Tom.

"This is my fiancé," Amie told him.

"I worked for Hal at the filling station."

"Right." Ed chuckled. "I thought you looked familiar too. Small world, eh? You request a building inspector and you get me!" He glanced around the construction site. "So, you two are going to get hitched and then run a hotel together, huh?"

They nodded.

"Be good to have more family up here." Ed gave Amie a look of approval. "Well, listen, kids," he said more soberly now. "There's nothing here that's in any code violation, but the workmanship stinks. Who's the contractor?"

"Simonson's Building and Lumber."

"Big Al? Well, he usually does an okay job," Ed stated, pulling up the front of his trousers by the belt buckle. "Maybe he's got a new crew this year."

"Don't think so. I recognize most of them."

"Then money must be tight; he's using seconds. Look here. The quality of wood isn't the greatest; pipes are cheap; foundation looks sloppy."

"I noticed the foundation," Tom muttered and Amie stifled a surprised gasp.

"But, believe it or not, it's up to code." Ed grinned wryly. "The big bad wolf'll just be able to huff and puff and blow the place down."

"Great," Tom replied sarcastically.

Ed crossed his arms and looked at them earnestly. "You two are family. Normally, I don't do this, but I'm going to give you some advice." He tapered his stare. "Hire a different builder."

Later, sitting beside Tom in the pickup truck, Amie guarded her tongue against any "I told you so" remarks. He seemed miserable enough without her adding to it.

"Do you have to work at the motel tonight?" she asked.

"Yeah," he replied flatly, turning onto the church road.

Feeling a case of nerves on the rise, she decided to change the subject. "I quit my job this morning," she announced. "Poor Buzz. I thought he was going to have heart failure. The other secretaries actually started to cry because I was leaving." She shook her head, still amazed. "They knew I wasn't going to stay forever. But these past few months we kind of got to be friends. The ladies even came to church with me one Sunday."

Tom reached across the truck's cab and took her hand. "Amie, I can tell you're upset. But don't worry, all right?"

She took a deep breath and chastened herself for babbling. "Are you going to terminate Al's contract?"

He dropped her hand. "I don't have a choice, do I? I gave him a chance, but . . ." He paused, looking almost hurt. "I don't get it. What did I ever do to make him hate me so much that he'd try to ruin our hotel?"

"Do you think this is a personal thing, Tom? Maybe Al's funds are just low and he's cutting corners."

"His funds *are* low, but it's personal."

"You're sure."

"I'm positive."

Amie wanted to inquire further, but they'd reached the Warrens' drive.

"I'll let you off here 'cause I've got to get to work. I know Katie will be happy to see you. She and Pastor Jake can fill you in on everything else."

"Everything else?"

Tom gave her a guilty nod.

"You mentioned your run-ins with Al, but you haven't told me the whole story, have you?"

"No. I didn't want to worry you."

"Worry me? It's that bad?"

"Katie can explain, and I'll call you on my break."

His hazel eyes pleaded with her until finally she acquiesced. Opening the door, she jumped down from the truck.

After the four young Warren girls were tucked snugly into bed, Katie and Jake were able to join Amie in the small living room of their home where they could talk uninterrupted.

"Thanks for putting me up tonight," Amie stated, "although I suppose I could have stayed at the Best Rest in Shawano and bothered Tom all night by calling him at the front desk every fifteen minutes." She laughed impishly.

"Oh, you could never *bother* Tom. I'm sure he would have enjoyed your staying there," Katie said, smiling. "But we're a lot cheaper than the Best Rest, not to mention the fact that we love your company too."

Amie felt herself blush at the kind sentiment. "Okay, tell me," she began, putting all humor aside for the time being, "what's going on with Big Al?"

The Warrens gave each other a quick look, and then Jake spoke up. "We don't have any evidence that anything's going on with Big Al. It's just that things have happened —"

"What *things?*"

"Well, a few weeks ago, Tom was on his

way home from work. It was about two-thirty A.M. and the highway was pretty much deserted. But then he noticed an old rusty pickup truck tailing him. Finally, it passed him and Tom noticed there were three men inside, but he didn't get a look at their faces. All he can swear to is that they wore ball caps of some sort." Jake paused thoughtfully. "After the truck got ahead of him, it slowed down, and when Tom tried to pass, the other driver sped up — even crossed lanes so Tom couldn't get ahead of him. That lasted all the way until Tom turned onto the church road out here."

"Intimidation," Amie muttered.

"Exactly."

"But then there was an accident at the site last week which really started to concern us."

"First tell Amie about Nancy," Katie interjected.

"Oh, yes, Nancy gave birth to another girl. Did Tom tell you?"

Amie nodded. He'd e-mailed her about a month ago with the news.

"Well, that sent Big Al into apoplexy. He'd had his heart set on a boy, and I don't know . . . Nancy told us he thinks fathering all females is some kind of insult to his manhood." Jake spread his arms wide. "I've got four daughters, and I feel blessed! I tried to share as much with Al, but he refused to listen, and finally he became so hostile toward Nancy that this past weekend she packed up the girls, moved out of their home and in with her parents for safety reasons."

"Right around the time the accident at the site occurred," Katie said.

Amie raised an inquiring brow. "Accident?"

"Tom got the notion things weren't going exactly right with the construction of the hotel," Jake informed her. "As you said, it's just what the building inspector confirmed this afternoon. But last Saturday morning, Tom was nosing around, thinking he was alone at the site, when suddenly a generator fell from a crane where it'd been strung up for safekeeping. It nearly hit him. In fact, he got a gash that needed a couple stitches on his elbow from flying debris. But God, in His infinite mercy, protected him from real harm."

Amie folded her arms, feeling slighted. "Tom never said a word about it."

"He didn't want you to worry," Katie said. "But he planned to tell you eventually."

"And no one saw anything?" Amie's question sounded more like a retort.

"Not so. Big Al saw the whole thing. In fact, he took Tom to the hospital."

"Big Al?" Amie replied incredulously.

Jake nodded. "He said he was driving down Highway 45 when he saw the generator crash. That's why he stopped. Told Tom it was one of his most expensive pieces of equipment. Couldn't understand how it fell from its perch."

"But Tom doesn't believe him?"

"No, Amie. And, unfortunately, neither do I. There are too many questions unanswered. Such as, why was Al's minivan near the crane? If, indeed, he'd seen the accident and pulled into the site off of 45, he would have been out in front, not around back."

"Are the police involved?"

Jake shook his auburn head.

"They're not?" Amie was shocked.

"There's no proof and, for Nancy and the girls' sakes, we're keeping quiet until more evidence surfaces . . . if it ever does."

Rising from the comfortable armchair, Amie strode to the bay window where she viewed the eastern sky's reflection of the setting sun. She shuddered inwardly, suddenly fearing for the life of the man she loved.

Chapter 19

Amie pensively tap-tap-tapped the end of a pencil on the dining room table until Tom's hand covered hers, putting a stop to her fidgeting.

"Yes or no, Amie? We're all waiting."

"Yes!" she declared at last, smiling into his eyes. "Yes, yes, yes! This'll be great!" She glanced at Katie and Jake who were all smiles now also. "If I move in here until the wedding, I won't have to live with my folks!"

"Is that the only reason?" Tom asked with an injured expression.

"Of course not," she replied, thinking he was about the most sensitive man on earth. "If I move in with the Warrens, I'll get to see you everyday — that's the biggest blessing of all!"

He grinned.

"Well, Amie, you handled that just right," Katie teased. "We, ladies, must always be mindful of our men's fragile egos."

She and Katie shared a good-natured

chuckle, while Tom and Jake gave each other leveled looks.

"All right, all right," the pastor said, his hands up as if in surrender, "our fragile egos aside for now, the best reason for Amie moving in is so that the four of us can begin discipleship classes twice a week." He narrowed his gaze in earnest. "From what you've both shared, I sense you'll be bringing a lot of baggage to this marriage unless certain issues get settled before the wedding. Delving into God's Word will help you give your pasts over to Him."

"I agree," said Tom.

"Me too." Amie looked over at him, glad they'd confided in Jake. It became apparent during the weekend that they both needed to learn how to communicate and better address their insecurities.

Jake scooted his chair back from the table and stood. "I'm whipped. Good night, people."

Katie rose as well. "Am I a terrible hostess if I turn in before you, Amie?"

She laughed. "Not at all. Besides, I won't be a 'guest' for long."

"True enough."

The Warrens ambled off for the night, and Amie considered the pad of paper before her. Picking up the pencil again, she jotted down several more notes about the hotel. After the worship service that evening and just before the conversation had turned so personal, they'd been discussing the business and how to handle their current predicament.

"Do you want me to call these other construction companies in the morning?"

Tom nodded. "We'll need estimates." Looking weary, he combed a hand through his hair. "And I've got to tell Al I'm backing out of our contract."

"Did you get a hold of Jim Henderson?"

"Yeah, and he's taking care of the legalities, but now it's back to square one."

Amie nibbled her lower lip in consternation. "Do you think the hotel will still be ready to open before the wedding in October?"

"I hope so." He gave her a smirk. "Those invitations go out yet?"

"No," she replied guiltily. "They're printed, but . . . well, I was holding off mailing them until I talked to you this weekend."

Tom shook his head. "You thought I'd change my mind." He reached out his hand to her. She took it before he continued. "In reality, I was just too afraid to confess my angry feelings."

"But that's all over with now. We're taking measures to correct things." She smiled. "I'm relieved. We've really got a chance, Tom. Our whole future is filled with promise. If God is for us, who can be against us?"

"Amen."

Amie giggled. She hadn't meant to preach. It was just that a bright sense of hope had been renewed in her — a far different feeling than the one she'd had on Friday, or the past few months for that matter. As far as the situation with Big Al, she felt encouraged about taking steps to rectify it too. She only prayed that once they canceled their contract with him, he'd stay out of their way for good. Perhaps he'd concentrate on reuniting himself with Nancy and their children.

"But you know what I wish?" Tom said, standing and stretching with arms behind his head. He sighed, suddenly sounding as tired as he looked, light shadows lining his lower lids. Amie was glad he didn't have to go in to work tonight.

"What do you wish?" she replied to his question.

"I wish our wedding was a lot sooner than October." He grinned sheepishly. "How am I supposed to stand firm on my convictions with you around all the time?"

"Need a chaperone out there, Tom?" Jake called from the other end of the hallway.

Amie swallowed a laugh.

Looking thoroughly abashed, he shook his head. "No, sir, I'm just on my way out."

"Good. I want to get some sleep."

Tom chuckled. Then, after gazing at her for a few long moments, a pining light in his eyes, he told her good night and departed, leaving Amie wishing their wedding was sooner too.

Monday morning, God sent a thunderstorm, so none of Al's crew showed up at the construction site. By the end of the day, Jim Henderson had terminated The Haven of Rest, LLC's contractual agreement with Simonson's Building and Lumber Company. However, Tom still felt he owed Al an explanation or, at the very least, a phone call. Getting the big man on the line, he got five words in — "Hi, Al, it's Tom Anderson" — before the profanity began. Finally Tom hung up on him.

"You did what you could," Jake told him. "Now it's up to the Lord."

Tom nodded his agreement but couldn't seem to rid himself of a nagging fear that something would happen to destroy his new-found joy with Amie before they even made it to the altar. *Heavenly Father, help me trust You more,* he prayed. *Strengthen my faith.*

With her condominium sold and most of her belongings moved into a large storage facility in Shawano, Amie began to relax and enjoy the summer. After just a few weeks, she adjusted to country living and learned to perform amazing feats, such as weeding Katie's vegetable garden and hanging clean laundry on the clothesline to dry. Such simplicity, yet so foreign to Amie, who had lived her whole life in a bustling city. Her mother had never hung clothes out to dry, neither had she cared for gardening, thus Amie hadn't given such chores much thought. But, lately, when she lay in bed, preparing for sleep, she could smell the sunshine in her linens and feel a healthy freshness in her skin that tanning booths couldn't ever achieve.

"You look . . . happy, Amie," Katie remarked one evening as they stood at the kitchen sink, washing dishes.

"I am. I'm very happy."

Katie smiled. "I've been meaning to ask if you've met more people. I feel bad that the neighborhood Bible programs have been keeping me so busy. I've neglected introducing you around."

"In this town, introductions aren't necessary," Amie replied with a little laugh. "Even Judy at the grocery store knew who I was. She said, 'Aren't you the one marrying Tom Anderson?' And I said, 'Yep. I'm the luckiest girl in the whole world.' Then Judy told me she'd marry Tom, too, since he inherited all that money." Amie chuckled lightheartedly. "But I set her straight by informing her that Tom is flat broke — and so am I. Our hotel is taking every cent and then some!"

Katie laughed. "What did Judy say to that?"

"She asked if we were hiring . . . and we are. Eventually." Amie sighed. "It's one of the million things still left to do."

"Did Nancy Simonson talk to you about a job?"

Amie nodded, recalling the conversation vividly. Al's company had taken a financial nosedive. He was barely supporting himself, let alone his wife and four kids. Nancy's parents were picking up the slack while she was living with them. Meanwhile, the Simonsons' house was pending foreclosure.

Tom had mentioned seeing Al stumbling out of the local tavern on more than one occasion — and in the middle of the afternoon. But, where Tom continued to feel bad for backing out of their deal, Amie felt justified. Big Al's problems were consequences of his own actions. No one else's fault.

However, she didn't have a problem with offering Nancy a position at their hotel — specifically in the café. In dealing with her insecurities, Amie had stopped speculating over Tom's teenage crush on the other woman, and as a result, her friendship with Nancy was blossoming.

Once the dinner dishes were dried and put back into the long, wooden cupboards, Amie gathered her catalogues and sat down on the front porch steps, while Katie and Jake put their girls to bed. As she leafed through the pages of motel room decor, sounds of animated voices and girlish giggles floated to her through the screen door. She marveled at how bedtime was such a family affair in the Warren household, and she vowed to make it the same in hers, should she and Tom be blessed with children.

Momentarily forgetting the colorful, thick books in her lap, she gazed out over the emerald green cornfield across the gravel road and got lost in a daydream about life after marriage. Tom would make a wonderful husband. He'd be gentle, passionate. Oddly, the latter didn't scare her in the least, as it used to when she thought about marriage. Tom had already proved his love for children. Amie prayed they'd have their own brood of Andersons some day, each with their daddy's hazel eyes.

The sound of tires on the dusty road drew Amie out of her reverie. Tom was at work, and not many cars passed by this way, unless they had business with the pastor. Curiously, she watched as a black minivan with a red pinstripe running along its side came into view.

Big Al . . . what does he want? she wondered as her stomach did a nervous flip.

The van slowed to a crawl in front of the Warrens' house, and Amie inhaled sharply when she saw Al's expression. Pure, unadulterated hatred emanated from his dark, burly features. Standing, she slowly backed up to the front door, then he sped off, the wheels of his vehicle spitting gravel in their wake.

Amie clutched the catalogues to her chest, her heart still pounding fearfully.

"What was that all about?" Jake asked from behind her, his voice wafting through the screen door.

She shook her head. "I don't know."

Later, in the wee hours of the morning, Amie awakened to a loud bang and a shout.

The front door?

Tom's voice?

Definitely.

"Jake?" She heard Tom calling in the hallway. There was no mistaking the urgency in his tone.

Fully roused now, Amie sat up and swung her legs off the bed. She grabbed her robe, tied it about her waist, and then opened her bedroom door where she collided with Tom, who was obviously on his way in.

"Are you okay?" he asked almost breathlessly.

"I'm fine. What's going on?"

"Good question," Jake said from behind Tom.

He pivoted. "Are you guys all right? The girls?"

The pastor didn't waste any time in checking on his children, Katie right beside him. When they discovered them unharmed, they turned back to Tom who sighed audibly with relief and sagged against the door frame of Amie's room.

"Something happen tonight?" Jake inquired, flipping on the hall light. Amie saw the concern etched upon the pastor's freckled countenance.

Tom nodded, his eyes suddenly looking so sad and mournful that Amie took his hand. She gave it a little squeeze as a sense of dread filled her being.

"I just got home from work and . . . well, you'd better come back to the church with me, Pastor." With reluctance, he added, "Have Katie call 911."

Chapter 20

Amie was still seething as she took the last of Tom's clothes out of the dryer at Brown's Laundromat in town. The horrid vision of white, spray-painted swastikas on wooden pews, walls, and outside on the church's front doors caused Amie's muscles to tense in anger. Several stained-glass windows had been cracked, and Tom's living quarters . . . totally ransacked, his computer smashed on the floor, and his clothes strewn about and trampled upon with soiled boots. There was no doubt in her mind who was responsible for the desecration of the sanctuary and the destruction in Tom's apartment. Big Al, although it'd be hard to prove it. The sheriffs who had answered their early morning call tried in vain to obtain fingerprints.

At least it was only Tuesday, and they'd have most of the week to repaint and repair before Sunday services. Pastor Warren was already making alternate plans for tomorrow's Wednesday night worship service.

Folding Tom's things neatly into a large plastic laundry basket, Amie was glad that she could help him in this small way. She'd taken his shirts and miscellaneous other items to the dry cleaners in Shawano, and it looked as though his washables had scrubbed up nicely.

She slung her purse over her shoulder and lifted the basket, carrying it out to her car on one hip. Walking down the nearly deserted street, she stopped short, spying Al Simonson perched on the hood of her BMW. On the edge of the sidewalk stood two men whom Amie recognized as his mean-looking friends from the construction site.

Lord, help me, she silently prayed, grappling for composure as she approached.

Al just sat there, watching her with an amused grin.

"Get off my car," she said tersely.

He put his hands out as if to forestall her. "Hey, no problem." Sliding one tree-trunk-like thigh off the hood, he smirked. "Me and the boys're just wondering how that hotel's coming along?"

After checking for scratches on the hood, Amie unlocked the driver's side door, wishing she would have activated the alarm. Setting the basket into the backseat, she bit

261

back a snide reply and prayed for control over her mounting temper.

"Guess she's too good to talk to the likes of us," Al remarked to his friends. He grabbed her elbow and spun her around. "Miss High 'n' Mighty."

"Let go of me!" she said, wrenching her arm free. "Why don't you guys start acting like men instead of delinquents?"

Al hooted at the retort. "Like you know real men, eh? What a laugh! You wouldn't be marrying Tom Anderson if that was true."

Something inside Amie snapped, and she all but forgot her fear of the large man looming above her. Before she knew it, her palm connected soundly with his cheek. "Tom is more of a man than you'll ever be!"

Al scowled, unable to mask the animosity blazing from his dark, beady eyes. He was as poised as a rattlesnake, and Amie fleetingly wondered if he'd strike her back. She braced herself but couldn't back down.

One of his friends suddenly stepped between them. "Forget her, Man. She ain't worth it." Turning to Amie, his gaze signaled an unspoken warning: *Get in your car and get out of here!*

Amie didn't wait for a second urging. Climbing inside, she started the engine and peeled away from the curb.

When she arrived back at the church, she was trembling. She couldn't imagine what had come over her. She'd slapped Big Al so hard, her arm now ached. By the time she entered the sanctuary where Tom and Pastor Warren were busily painting walls and revarnishing wood, hot tears were streaming from her eyes and hysteria was welling in her chest.

Tom glanced up from between two pews and dropped his brush. "Amie, what in the world . . . ?"

With an expression of concern, Jake scampered down the ladder on which he'd been working and jogged over to them.

It took Amie several long minutes to get her emotions in check and relay the story. "Am I going to get arrested for assault and battery?" she cried, feeling miserable hanging onto Tom.

"I doubt it," he replied, attempting to comfort her.

"Amie, I am very proud of you," Jake told her. "Not for losing your temper, even though Al might have deserved the whack upside his noggin, but . . . I sense God is at work here."

"What do you mean?" she sniffed.

"Well, don't you think the Lord has just

proved that you don't have to be afraid of men . . . or anything else? Of course, bad things can happen to all Christians, but we're not to live in fear, Amie. This is exactly what I've tried to explain during our discipleship classes, although I haven't felt very successful. I've been asking the Lord to help me describe trust to you." Jake chuckled softly. "But He had to show you Himself — just now with Big Al."

She thought it over, then looked up at Tom. "God protected me," she murmured.

He nodded, widening his hazel eyes emphatically. "I'll say!"

Later, that evening, just after supper, Amie spotted one of Al's buddies pulling into the Warrens' driveway.

"Pastor Jake? Tom? I think we might have problems."

Katie ran into the living room, looking alarmed. "I'll send the girls to the basement playroom for a while."

Tom squinted as he peered out the window. "That's Keith Reider."

"He's the one who fended off Al so I could drive away this morning," Amie informed him.

Pastor Warren stepped outside and met the man on the lawn. After a few minutes of conversing, they both entered the house.

"Mr. Reider has something to tell us," Jake announced.

The man nodded a brief greeting to Tom, although his expression was one of chagrin.

"Have a seat," the pastor said. "Everyone."

Reider seemed to grow uncomfortable with all eyes on him. "Listen," he began, "I don't want any trouble. My wife is expecting our second kid, and I've got a good chance at steady work in New London. That's why I came over here tonight." Leaning forward in the armchair, he folded his hands and allowed them to dangle between his knees. "It's Al. I don't know what's happened to him. It's like he's gone berserk. I think it started back when you, Tom, bought that pickup truck. Al got real jealous, said no Anderson ought to be allowed to drive something that nice. So he went out and bought himself that Chevy minivan, which put him and Nancy into debt."

Tom shook his head as if he couldn't fathom it. "Al's got no cause to be envious of me."

"Oh, it don't stop there," Reider continued. "A year ago, when you inherited Halvor Holm's money, Al saw red. He kept saying that no Anderson deserved to have that kind of loot. And then, of course, we all heard you were getting married." He nodded toward Amie. "Al figured she was just marrying you for your money, but then Nancy said it was love, all right. She'd seen it with her own eyes on Thanksgiving Day."

Amie blushed, and one glance at Tom told her that he felt equally embarrassed.

"For some odd reason," Reider went on, "that was a real kick in the head for Al. He couldn't get over it. He brought it up all the time. Tom Anderson, a guy from a no-account family, marrying a high-class babe from Chicago . . ." A look of concern crossed his lean, chiseled features. "The fact is, Al was jealous of you — or at least that's what it seemed like to the rest of us. Then he started taking it out on Nancy, and their marriage started really going down the tubes."

Amie groaned inwardly, feeling nauseated. Suddenly she knew why Al Simonson had given her the creeps from the first day she met him.

"And then . . . about the church and your place, Tom," Reider continued, looking apologetic. "We all left the tavern together . . . I was there, but I swear I didn't do any of the damage. Big Al did it . . . and Tyler Johnson helped him some. He didn't want to. He's just more afraid of Al than I ever was." The man shook his sandy blond head and a disbelieving look crossed his features. "But then when this little lady over here gave Al what-for . . . I'll tell you," he added, looking right at Amie, "I was ashamed of myself after that. If a woman can stand up to Al, I should be able to."

Amie lowered her gaze, feeling very much aware of God's handiwork. She found it incredible that Keith would make this confession as a result of her earlier altercation with Big Al. Jake had been right: God was at work — in more ways than one.

"And, Tom," Reider added, "I don't have anything against you. Never did. Not even when we were in high school. The only reason I sided with Al is because he's my friend, and he hated your guts — just like his dad hated your father. But, see, that's the kind of men those Simonsons are. They're like politicians. They can make a whole host of people see things their way. I'm not trying to excuse my wrongdoings." Shaking his head, he added, "If my boy ever did something like this, I'd switch him. But . . . well, I'll bet there's lots of folks in town who can't stand the sight of an Anderson, only they don't know why. They just heard the talk for too long and now they believe it."

Amie found herself fairly gaping at his statement. Such ignorance boggled her mind.

Keith stood. "I told the pastor that I'm willing to talk to the police and help with the cleanup. Like I said, I don't want to bring any trouble down on my family." Then to Amie he added, "I'm real sorry and . . . well, I wish you guys the best."

Everyone rose almost simultaneously, and Tom stuck out his right hand. "I appreciate your honesty."

Reider shook it. "About time, huh?" With a rueful smile, he left the house, and Jake followed him out.

Amie looked over at Katie who lifted her hands helplessly. "I don't know what to say. I'm . . . stunned."

"I'm not," Tom replied thoughtfully. "I don't claim to understand Al's hatred, but having lived with it practically all my life, it's nice to hear somebody acknowledge it. Up until tonight, the prejudice in this town against my family has been something undefined and ignored . . . and accepted."

Amie stepped close to him, slipping her arm around his elbow. "Well, I don't care about any of it. I love you with all my heart."

"I love you too," he said, tweaking her nose affectionately. "Truth is, I can't imagine where I'd be today if God hadn't brought you into my life."

The October sunshine shone through a clear blue sky and warmed the day to a pleasant seventy-five degrees. Down in the church basement, where Tom's living quarters had been up until a week ago, Amie gazed into the large bathroom mirror and smoothed down the lace on the full-length skirt of her antique-white wedding dress.

"Will you stop fidgeting?" Dottie, her only bridesmaid, told her. She stood behind Amie, clad in a burgundy satin gown. "You look fine."

"What about my hair?"

"The French twist is gorgeous. Don't touch it — there's not a strand out of place."

"Better not be," she quipped, "after all the hair spray you put on it."

Hearing high-heeled footfalls descending the wooden steps, they both turned and exited the tiny restroom. Nancy Simonson appeared, her frosted hair falling to her shoulders in permanent waves. "The church is packed," she announced. "It's like Christmas or something!" She grinned. "But I wanted to give you a hug, Amie . . . before you walk down the aisle."

They embraced, and Nancy placed a kiss

on her cheek. "I'm so happy for you."

"Thanks, Nance." Considering her friend's weary countenance, she frowned slightly. "Are you holding up all right?"

"Yes. God has really been looking out for me. I thought that after Al spent thirty days in jail for defacing property, he'd want to get his life back together. I'd been praying he'd want to give his heart to Christ. But nothing's changed. These past few weeks have been awful."

Amie gave her a knowing nod. She had employed Nancy's help in decorating the café and preparing it for the Grand Opening. Nancy had often brought her children with her to their meetings or on shopping trips when they went to pick the perfect decor. Subsequently, Amie had grown close to Nancy and her daughters and understood the stress they'd all been under because of Al's behavior.

"I keep trying to remember him as he was on our wedding day," Nancy said with a sad smile. "Believe it or not, Al was quite handsome and charming."

"There's still hope."

"Yes and I'm not giving up." She hugged Amie once more. "I'm just glad you and Tom are building the foundation of your marriage on your faith. Al and I didn't have that start." She suddenly chuckled. "And Tom's so funny . . . I just saw him. He just cannot wait until you're Mrs. Thomas Anderson." Leaning forward conspiratorially, she added, "He'd probably like to skip the reception altogether and get right to the honeymoon."

"Oh no!" Amie exclaimed, ignoring her sister's chortles over the remark. "My mother and I practically killed ourselves — and each other — getting that banquet room ready for this evening." She sighed. "It's such a shame the entire hotel won't be completed for another month or so — which is not entirely Al's doing."

"I know, I know . . . I'm just glad your apartment is finished."

The old pipe organ began the first strains of the wedding march, and Nancy made a hasty departure back to the sanctuary. Following her up the stairs, Amie and Dottie paused in the tiny vestibule where they were met by their father and Matthew.

"You're lucky, you know?" Dottie whispered, just before taking Matt's arm. "You're marrying a guy who really loves you."

Amie agreed, feeling as though she could start bawling already . . . and the wedding hadn't even begun! It wasn't the first time her sister had made such a comment, and she sensed Dottie's heart was softening.

"You look like a million bucks, Princess!" John Potter declared, taking her hand and wrapping it around his elbow.

She smiled. "Thanks, Dad."

The procession began. The wedding party consisted of a maid of honor and a best man, so Amie didn't have long to wait for her turn to walk up the aisle. As she made her way on her father's arm, she paid little heed to the many well-wishers crowded into the tiny country church. All she could see was Tom waiting for her expectantly, his eyes captivated by her every step. At last her father gave her away, and she linked arms with Tom, feeling his nervous warmth radiating from beneath the black tuxedo.

The ceremony proceeded, and the vows were pledged, Amie choking on her emotion when it came her turn to speak, then crying softly as Tom promised to "love, honor, and cherish." Time had no bearing on Amie, and it seemed only moments passed before Pastor Warren looked at Tom, and said, "You may kiss your bride."

She turned to her new husband, suppressing the urge to giggle like a schoolgirl at his eager expression. Tom gently cupped her face with his hands and lowered his mouth to hers, touching her lips lightly at first, then steadily deepening the kiss until Jake cleared his throat. Chuckles and "Amens!" emanated from the congregation. Amie felt herself blushing profusely before deciding Tom's kiss was the best she'd ever experienced. *Pretty good,* she thought, *for a guy who's never done that before!* She glanced at him in mild amazement as they walked back down the aisle, sporting the new title of Mr. and Mrs. Thomas Richard Anderson.

The remainder of the afternoon was spent taking pictures. Then Amie and Tom changed clothes in their apartment above the hotel in preparation for the evening's reception, and later, their escape. They planned to catch a midnight flight out of Green Bay, heading to Key West, Florida, for their honeymoon. The trip was a gift from Amie's parents, and both she and Tom were looking forward to it.

Tom cornered her as she made her way from the large master bedroom to the bathroom where she intended to perfect her makeup. He pulled her into a close embrace and kissed her thoroughly. "I love you so much," he whispered next to her ear, sending delicious shivers down her spine.

But just as they thought they'd found scant precious time alone, curious friends and relatives filed into the apartment, begging for a tour of the hotel.

"It's a couple of months from being completely finished," Tom explained; however, no one seemed to mind.

Amie smiled wistfully as she watched him lead the way out. Tom was so proud of their endeavor — so was she! The place still smelled of new wood and fresh paint and much of the cabinetry and decorating hadn't been completed, but it was definitely a hotel.

And it was theirs.

Chapter 21

"Well, darling, I had my doubts," Lillian Potter said as her gaze wandered around the banquet room. "But it's turned out to be quite a lovely reception."

Amie smiled. "Thanks, Mom. I couldn't have done it without you. You're the best interior decorator ever!"

"Oh, go on with you!" Her mother appeared embarrassed, but Amie could tell she was pleased with the final result.

The room's motif was Early American, intermingling Colonial-blue wainscoting and dark brown and blue patchwork papered walls. All the woodwork had been painted in the same blue trim, and the drapes, hanging on the multi-paned windows, matched the wallpaper. The carpet was a durable, stain-resistant woven fabric of taupe and seemed to pull all the colors together.

"I love you," Amie said, leaning over and placing a kiss on her mother's press-powdered cheek.

"I love you too. I just hope you'll be . . . happy up here." She cleared her throat, indicating she still found the whole idea quite distasteful. Then, painting a smile on her face, she left to mingle with the guests, most of whom were relatives.

After her mother waltzed away, Amie scanned the reception for Tom. She spotted him standing in the corner near the windows, pointing toward the little creek that ran through the middle of their property. No doubt he was explaining to Ernie Huffman and Russ Thorbjorg that he'd promised to build Amie a gazebo out there next year. The two elderly men nodded their gray heads, looking interested.

From a small platform on the other side of the room, an all-female musical ensemble began to play their next piece. They were local talent, referred to Amie by the Warrens. One of the musicians, Katie said, was a teacher at the grade school. She'd had Emma in her class last year.

Smiling contentedly, Amie made her way toward Tom who had now been waylaid by her mother's cousin Ed, the building inspector. It had become apparent of late that the older gentleman loved to tell stories about "the good ole days," and Amie had a hunch that unless she rescued Tom soon, he'd be listening to Cousin Ed the rest of the night. She got about four steps into the middle of the banquet room when Matthew burst through the side entrance that led into the hotel's still unfinished lobby.

"Fire!" he yelled. "Everyone out the back way. Fire!"

Initially, Amie sent a scolding frown at her brother-in-law, thinking this was his idea of a joke. But then the instantaneous mayhem that broke out, coupled with the steadily increasing smell of smoke, forced the harsh reality upon her. The hotel was on fire!

"Tom!" she called, but he was nowhere in sight.

The alarm system sounded, heightening the panic in the room, which had suddenly grown much too small. Amie guessed the sprinkler system had already been activated. The fire would be extinguished in no time . . . wouldn't it? If everyone would just stay calm —

Her brother, Stephen, caught her around the waist. "C'mon, Amie, we gotta get outta here."

"I can't leave without Tom."

He ignored the argument and fairly dragged her outside. The October night air had grown cold and Amie shivered. Her view from the side of the building revealed a sickening orangish-gold reflection.

"Get out there with everyone else and stay put," Stephen commanded. "I'm going back in to make sure all those old folks get out okay."

"Stephen, wait!" Amie felt icy fingers of terror grip her heart.

"Go on!" he yelled.

Someone grabbed her arm and propelled her forward. Meanwhile, the hotel's alarm continued to ring out into the chilly darkness, resounding within Amie's very soul. Reaching the front of the structure, she turned and beheld a nightmarish vision. Hot flames shot out of the front doors and windows and licked upward greedily, pursued by billows of black smoke. Why wasn't the sprinkler system working? How did the fire get so out of control? And where was Tom?

Tom!

"He's in there!" she shrieked. "Tom's inside!" Mindlessly bolting for the hotel, Amie was swiftly overtaken by three concerned men who hung onto her despite her attempts to break out of their grasps. "Let me go!" she cried. "He's in there. I know it!"

"Tom's not in there," one of them said,

pointing toward the side of the building from where she'd just come. "Look."

Sure enough — it was Tom, along with Stephen, Matt, and her parents. A quick survey of the parking lot told her everyone had exited the burning building unscathed.

Amie sighed with relief. *Thank You, Lord . . . thank You . . .*

In the next moment, she was turned loose and ran to Tom, throwing her arms around his neck.

"I thought you were inside," she said, trembling with a mixture of terror and joy. "I . . . I thought you were . . . inside."

She clung to him, inhaling the acrid smell of smoke from the flames he'd tried in vain to subdue.

"It's okay, Amie. It's okay."

The fire department seemed to take forever in coming, and then it felt like another eternity until the blaze was finally extinguished. The damage looked so extensive that it made Amie sick with grief.

"Our hotel, Tom. Look at it. It took so long to build, and now our plans, our future . . . it's gone."

Taking a hold of her shoulders, he gave her a mild shake. "It's just a hotel, Amie," he said tightly. "It's wood, hay, and stubble in comparison to you and me and what *really* got built this last year. Look at us. Look what we've got — something nobody, nowhere can ever burn down. We've got Christ. We've got each other!"

She gulped down a reply as Tom's lips gently touched hers. He was right. She knew it, and yet . . .

Stepping back, he took her hand. "Come on. We're leaving."

"Leaving? We can't go anywhere now!"

Amie saw his terse expression beneath the red and white revolving lights of a fire engine. "May I remind you, *Mrs. Anderson,* that this is our wedding night?"

"But —"

Tom wouldn't hear another word and, after voicing instructions to Matt, he led Amie over to where her BMW sat parked in the far corner of the hotel's lot. "Good thing I stuck our luggage in the trunk earlier this afternoon."

"Tom, I don't think —"

He pressed his forefinger against her mouth and silenced her protests. Then he gathered her in his arms and held her, laying his cheek against her forehead. As the moments passed, Amie somehow sensed he was praying. Very slowly, her anguished spirit quieted within her.

At last Tom inhaled deeply, kissed her,

then opened the car door. Amie crawled in, waiting only seconds until he unlocked the other side and climbed behind the wheel. She had to smile, remembering how much he enjoyed driving her car — her *hot rod*.

"Think we'll make it?" he asked, starting the engine. "Our flight's in three hours."

"We'll make it," she replied, forcing enthusiasm into her voice.

He sped down the highway, heading for the Green Bay airport, and Amie compelled herself not to look back.

Ten days later, Amie peered out the window of the airplane as it flew the last stretch of sky back to Wisconsin. Beside her, Tom stirred and she glanced over at his snoozing form. No matter how many times she'd flown in the past, she'd never relaxed enough to fall asleep — how did Tom manage it? This was only his second time in the air!

Shifting in her first-class seat, she thought back on her honeymoon. Her parents had purchased their airfare and rented a room for them at a hotel on the ocean in Key West. The weather had been gorgeous — perfect — and each passing day, she'd fallen even more deeply in love with Tom.

On occasion, she wondered whether

she'd gained a husband or a playmate. He would tackle her in the ocean or tickle her until she couldn't breathe. Each time she was tempted to admonish him for his roughhousing, she'd recall the words her uncle had penned: *Makes me sick. His childhood is gone.*

Amie grinned reflectively, deciding Tom had certainly made up for lost time. And yet, when the situation lent itself to intimacy, all rowdiness ceased. Moreover, his tenderness vanquished the horrid memories from her past.

"What are you smiling about?" he asked lazily, startling Amie out of her reverie.

"I was thinking of how much I love you," she replied in a soft voice.

"Well, I love you too." He sat up a little straighter and stretched. "You know what Pastor Jake said? He said he loves Katie a hundred times more than he did on their honeymoon." Taking her hand and weaving his fingers through hers, he added, "Think about us . . . can you even begin to imagine loving each other more than we do right now?"

"It is hard to fathom," she agreed. Then, with a teasing smirk, she added, "But I'll definitely remind you of those words in about five years when the kids are screaming and the bills need to be paid."

He grinned, looking chagrined. "Okay, Amie, you do that."

The plane landed and they gathered their luggage, packing it into the trunk of the BMW. On the drive back to Tigerton, their lightheartedness grew suddenly heavy, and Amie knew it was because of what awaited them. A burned-out hotel. Damaged dreams.

Then, just after they crossed the little bridge over the Embarrass River, Tom pulled the car onto the shoulder of the road and stopped.

"Let's promise each other something," he said, his arm across the back of her seat, his hazel eyes searching her face. "Let's promise not to let any circumstances at home kill the joy that's in our hearts right now, all right?"

Amie nodded timidly, wondering if she could really own up to such a vow.

"I've never been happier in my life than I have been in the past ten days."

His candidness touched her very soul, causing her to remember what was really important in this life — the eternal.

She smiled. "I promise, Tom."

Satisfied with her reply, he maneuvered the car back onto Highway 45, and within

the next mile, the hotel came into view —
along with the hundreds of people milling
about like ants on a sugar cube.

"Tom, look at that!" Amie gasped and sat
forward in her seat. "What's going on?"

"I don't know." There was a wary note in
his tone.

Pulling into the lot, the sound of buzzing
electrical saws and drills made melody with
the many banging hammers. As Amie and
Tom climbed out of the car, they stared in
wonder at the sight.

"Hey, Tom, welcome back," someone
called from the roof.

He looked up. "Thanks."

"Who's that?" Amie whispered.

"Don Satner — a guy I went to high
school with."

"Oh . . ." She frowned. "What's he doing
on our roof?"

"Fixing it, looks like." Tom glanced
around at all the commotion, looking as
confused as Amie felt.

Just then, old Mrs. Jensen approached
them. "Did you two have a nice time in
Tahiti?"

"We were in Key West, Florida," Tom
shouted into her deaf ears. "What are you
doing here? What's going on?"

The woman produced a silent laugh. "All

284

of us in Tigerton decided to rebuild your hotel. We took up a collection and bought some supplies, figuring the insurance company will come through for the rest, and the lumber company in town donated the wood. And the Ladies Aid from Immanuel Bible Church," she added proudly, "fixed up lunch here everyday for the past week."

"The whole town?"

"Pretty near."

Tom's face was a mask of incredulousness. Combing fingers through his hair, he gazed at the old lady before him. "Thanks, Mrs. Jensen," he said loudly once more. "I'm grateful."

"Oh, I know you are, Tommy," she said, patting his cheek affectionately as if he were five years old again and in her kindergarten class. Then she ambled off.

Chuckling softly, Tom took Amie's hand and together they walked toward the hotel, waving back at those who called greetings.

"Well, well," John Potter said, exiting the building. The burned wood had been torn away from the main entrance and new bare wood replaced it. "I see you two finally decided to come home."

Amie couldn't suppress a little giggle. "Hi, Dad. What are you doing here? I thought you'd be back in Chicago by now."

"Took some vacation time and . . . hey! Would you believe we've just about got your apartment shipshape? And your mother and Dottie are just about finished up with the café."

Amie's heart swelled with love for her family. "Thanks," she replied, unable to find the words to adequately express her feelings.

"The second floor didn't suffer too badly. Mostly smoke and water damage. But the lobby and Tom's antique shop were completely destroyed." He shook his head. "What a shame."

"Any news on what caused the fire?" Tom asked. Amie felt him tense at her side.

He nodded. "A man's in custody. Seems he got burned pretty badly on his face and hands when he lit the blaze. After he gets out of the hospital, he'll go right to jail. Your brother knows who he is — said he's been undermining the hotel's construction since day one."

Tom grimaced. "Al Simonson?"

John snapped his fingers. "That's him." He frowned. "Must have some mental problems, huh?"

"Yeah . . . and some spiritual ones too," Tom muttered.

"Well, good thing your pastor is on the

ball. He's been with him at the hospital for the last couple of days, from what I heard."

"That's good," Tom replied, his expression teetering somewhere between disgust and sorrow.

Amie squeezed his hand supportively, feeling grateful that no one else had been hurt.

At that moment, she caught sight of a pile of rubbish, heaped at the far end of the lot. It made her sick to see all the beautiful new items she'd purchased for the hotel and their apartment lying there in utter ruin.

Suddenly a flash of red, poking out from beneath the mound, caught her eye and she gasped. "Uncle Hal's journals!"

"Sorry, Princess, all your books got wrecked."

She ran over to the garbage and pulled out the diary. It was badly warped and the pages were smeared beyond recognition, but she managed to identify it as the final log. "I never finished reading it," she lamented, doing her best to swallow down a lump of emotion.

Tom gently took it from her fingers and assessed the damage. Then he flipped to the back page, took several long moments to read it over, before throwing his head back in a laugh. "I don't believe it! Here," he said, amusedly, "finish it right now."

The last paragraph was amazingly legible and Amie noticed it was dated three months before her uncle's death. *When I look at the photographs on my chest of drawers, I can't help but think Tom and my niece Amie would make a nice match. Her bouncy personality alone would give him hope, and Tom, being so kind, would help Amie forget whatever happened to her a few years back. Oh, those two are worlds apart, all right, and I don't know how God will ever manage it, but I just can't get the notion out of my head and I pray about it everyday. But, like I told the boys at the bowling league Tuesday night, God always answers my prayers. I told them they best expect a wedding in the near future . . .*

"Uncle Hal, you stinker!" Amie said, gazing down at the journal. "So he's the one who started the rumor!"

She chuckled softly before looking back at Tom. A little tear had formed in the corner of his eye.

"God answers prayer," he stated simply.

"He sure does." Wrapping her arms around his neck, she kissed the sadness from his face before fastening her mouth to his.

"Hey, Tom," a voice boomed from the balcony above the hotel's front entrance.

Parting, albeit reluctantly, they glanced up to see Keith Reider grinning at them. "Honeymoon's over, pal." His wave beckoned them. "Come and take a look at this new carpet."

With a sigh, Tom turned to Amie. "Shall we?"

She nodded, and as they walked hand-in-hand toward the hotel, a feeling of excited anticipation surged through her veins. "You know," she said, as he opened the new front door for her, "I'm going to like living in Tigerton. Look at how this community pulled together for us. You just wouldn't find that anywhere else in the whole world. I think we've really found our Haven of Rest, Tom — in more ways than one."

He smiled broadly. "Very well stated, Mrs. Anderson."

September Sonata

Prologue

Milwaukee, WI — May 2000

Icy fear gripped Kristin Robinson's heart as she raced down the emergency room's stark corridor.

A dark-haired woman in blue scrubs stepped into her path. "Can I help you?"

"I . . . I'm looking for my husband," Krissy panted, halting in midstride. "His name is Blaine Robinson. He's a fireman, and he was injured —"

"Yes, I know who you mean. Follow me."

The nurse led her into a bustling area where doctors, nurses, and secretaries conducted business matters around an island containing desks and computers. Reaching the last room in a row of six, the woman opened a sliding glass door. There, right before Krissy's eyes, lay her husband, stretched out on a hospital gurney. His face had been blackened with soot and his hair and skin smelled singed by the hungry flames that had obviously sought to devour him.

"Blaine," she choked, rushing to his bedside. She noticed the blue and white hospital gown he wore, and the lightweight blanket covering him from the waist down. "Are you all right? I came as soon as I could."

"I'm okay, Honey." He peeked at her through one open eye. "I fell through the roof and injured my back. Looks like I might have cracked a couple of vertebrae."

"Oh, Blaine, no!"

"Now, don't worry. It's not as bad as it sounds. Could have been worse. I'm praising the Lord that my spinal cord is intact. I can move my feet, wiggle my toes . . . sure hurts though." He winced as if to prove his point.

"Blaine . . ."

With tears pricking the backs of her eyes, Krissy lifted his hand and held it between both of hers. In all their twenty years of marriage, this is what she'd feared the most: An injury in the line of duty. How many endless nights had she lain awake worrying that he'd never come home again to her and their two daughters? She knew too well that firefighters faced the possibility of death each and every time they responded to a call and by now, Krissy thought she'd have become accustomed to the ever-present threat. Today, however, when she'd received the phone call informing her that Blaine had been hurt, it was like living the nightmare.

"Hon, I'm going to make a full recovery," Blaine assured her, his eyelids looking heavy with whatever the nurses had given him for pain. "The ER doc said the orthopedic surgeon on call is coming to speak with us. I'll probably have to have surgery to help my back heal, and after a few months of recuperation, I'll be as good as new." He paused, grinning beneath the filmy soot covering his mouth. "Maybe even better . . ."

Chapter 1

Three months later

"Are you sure you're up to driving?" Krissy asked Blaine as they headed north in their minivan. They'd dropped their twin daughters off at a Christian college in Florida and had been traveling most of the day. According to Krissy's calculations, they had another seventeen hours to go before they reached Wisconsin. Since Blaine was still recovering from his back surgery, she didn't want him to overdo it. "Would you like me to take the wheel for awhile?"

"I'm fine," he replied, "but I think we'll stop at a motel in Knoxville."

Krissy nodded, knowing her husband wasn't all that "fine" if he intended to stop for the night. Not Mr. Drive-'til-we-get-there Blaine Robinson. His back was most likely aching from all the activity last week. He'd loaded and unloaded the girls' belongings in and out of the van and carried items into their dormitory that he probably shouldn't have lifted.

Krissy glanced over at the profile that, in the past two decades, had become as familiar as her own face. Blaine's chestnut-brown hair was tinged with just a hint of gray above the ears, and in the last five years, he'd developed a bald spot at the crown of his head that the girls liked to kiss just to irritate him. His skin was tanned from the summer sunshine since he took advantage of convalescing outdoors. His neck and shoulders were thick with muscles he'd developed lifting heavy fire hoses and other equipment while he'd been on the job, although his midsection was getting awfully thick these days. Krissy didn't want to mention it, but she figured he'd put on about twenty pounds in the past three months. Worse, it seemed to her that he'd gotten lazy and slack when it came to his appearance. All these years, they had both tried to take care of themselves and keep fit, but lately Blaine seemed to have let himself go. It was rather disappointing.

Still, she loved him. He was the man with whom she would spend the remainder of her life . . . but why did that suddenly sound like such a long time?

"It's kind of weird without Mandy and Laina around," Krissy stated on a rueful note.

"Yeah, I think the girls chattered the entire way to Florida."

Krissy grinned. "They did . . . and now it's too quiet in here."

Blaine apparently decided to remedy the matter by turning the radio on to a syndicated talk show.

"Must you really subject me to this?" Krissy complained. "You listen to this guy every day."

"Yeah, so?" Blaine took his eyes off the road for a moment and looked over at her through his fashionable sunglasses.

"I don't care for some of his views."

"Well, I do, and with the presidential election coming up in November, I want to stay informed."

Krissy gritted her teeth and leaned back in the seat, closing her eyes and trying not to listen to the male voice booming conservative credos through the stereo speakers. While she considered herself a conservative Christian, she simply found the popular radio talk show host, in a word, annoying. In the last twelve weeks, while Blaine recuperated, Krissy had tolerated his penchant for the program. But now, as a captive audience, she felt resentful. Trapped.

She opened her eyes and leaned forward abruptly. "Blaine, can't we compromise?

Surely there's another news station we could listen to."

"Relax. This show is only on for another hour and then I'll change the channel if you want."

Won't be any reason to change the channel then, she silently fumed.

Krissy turned her head toward the window and watched the scenery go by. It was only late August, but already some tree-tops were turning gold, orange, and russet. Autumn had begun in the Smoky and Appalachian Mountains. And next week Krissy would be back at school, teaching third graders. She mulled over everything she had to do in preparation. This year would be much different than the past twelve since Grace Christian School, the elementary school in which she'd taught, had merged with a larger institution due to financial constraints. Krissy expected changes, but she tried not to worry about them. Monday would come soon enough.

The minutes ticked by and finally the ragging on the liberals ceased. Blaine pressed the radio buttons until he found classical music. Krissy's taut nerves began to relax.

"Better?" Blaine asked, a slight smirk curving his well-shaped mouth.

"Much. Thanks." Krissy couldn't seem

to help the note of cynicism in her reply. Then she paused, listening. "I don't recognize this piece."

Blaine gave it a moment's deliberation. "I believe it's one of Mozart's sonatas, obviously for the violin and piano."

"Obviously," Krissy quipped, smiling. She had acquired a taste for classical music over the years but hadn't ever learned to discern the various artists' styles, let alone the titles. "And tell me again how a sonata differs from, say, a waltz or serenade."

"A waltz is basically dance music written in triple time with the accent on the first beat."

"Ah, yes, that's right."

"A sonata is written in three or four movements."

"It's coming back to me now," Krissy said.

Blaine chuckled. "After hearing this music for twenty years, you should be an expert."

"Yes, I suppose I should."

"Well, after another twenty," Blaine stated in jest, "you're bound to be a fine critic of classic music."

An odd, sinking feeling enveloped Krissy. Symphonies and overtures were Blaine's forte, not hers. He was an accomplished musician himself and played the piano, although he hadn't practiced in years. Regardless, she had developed knowledge and respect for the art because of him and had to admit that Brahms, Beethoven, and Mozart did have a way of soothing her jangled nerves after a long day at school. Nevertheless, she enjoyed other types of music as much or more. In fact, she and the girls liked to attend musicals, both in Chicago and Milwaukee. They had seen *Show Boat* and *Phantom of the Opera . . .*

But the girls are eighteen years old and in college now, Krissy thought. *Blaine and I have the rest of our lives . . . together. Alone.*

The reality of her situation suddenly struck with full force. There were no more children to care for, fret over, shop with, or cook for. No more parent-teacher conferences to attend, basketball and football games to watch as her lovely daughters cheered on their high school's team. Although Amanda and Alaina were twins, they weren't identical, and each had her own fun personality that Krissy now realized she would sorely miss.

Tears began to well in her eyes and spill down her cheeks. She sniffed and then reached for her purse to find a tissue.

"What's the matter?"

"Oh, nothing."

"What?" Blaine pursued. "It's not the talk radio show . . . ? It's over now."

"No, no . . . it's the girls. They're gone." Krissy's tears flowed all the harder now. Her babies. Grown up. Living far away from home. Why, she'd been so preoccupied with helping them prepare and pack for college, not to mention nursing Blaine back to health, that she hadn't realized the impact the girls' departure would have. "They grew up so fast," Krissy said, blowing hard into the tissue. "Where did the years go?"

"Oh, for pity's sake . . ." Krissy heard the exasperation in her husband's voice. But then he reached across the built-in plastic console in the center of the two front seats and stroked the back of her hair. "Sweetheart, the girls'll be back. In just a few months it's Christmas. A few months after that, they'll be home for summer vacation . . . and you'll never have the telephone to yourself again."

Krissy managed a smile. "You're right," she said with a little sniffle. "I'm being silly." She thought it over, then sighed. "I just wish we would have had more children."

"That's a ridiculous wish, and you know it," Blaine said, removing his hand and placing both palms on the steering wheel.

"We tried, but God didn't see fit to give us any more kids. Instead, Mandy and Laina were a double blessing. Still are. Always will be."

Krissy couldn't argue. Their twin daughters were a special gift from God.

"Think of it this way," Blaine continued, a smile in his deep voice, "we're still young. You and I have the rest of our lives together."

Krissy winced, and fresh tears filled her eyes. How could she tell Blaine that the very words he just spoke to cheer her up depressed her? She wasn't exactly feeling like the godly, submissive wife of which the Bible speaks, yet her feelings were real, and she didn't know how to handle them. True, she and Blaine had the rest of their lives, but what would they do with all those years together? She loved him, but somehow that didn't seem like enough. In the past twenty years, Blaine had been gone more than he'd been home, and Krissy had been a busy mother and schoolteacher. Of course, she and Blaine would continue to have their work. But was that all their lives together amounted to? Separate occupations? Separate lives, joined together by a vow to have and to hold, for better or for worse . . . 'til death do us part . . . ?

"What's eating you?" Blaine asked later as he lay on one of the double beds in the motel room. He was clad in a white T-shirt and navy-printed boxers, and beneath his knees, Krissy had placed three pillows to ease his back discomfort. Unfortunately, she couldn't do anything about the atmosphere. Coupled with her melancholy, the air-conditioning unit wasn't working well, and the room felt hot and stuffy on this sweltering August night in Knoxville, Tennessee. "You haven't said more than five words since we stopped for supper."

"Oh, I'm just tired." Krissy decided that had to be it. Exhaustion. Sitting in a nearby floral-upholstered armchair, she stared blindly at the newscast on television. Maybe once she got back home and fell into a routine, teaching during the day, correcting homework in the evenings, she wouldn't miss the girls so much.

"Go take a cold shower," Blaine suggested. "That made me feel better."

"Yeah, maybe I will."

She looked over at him again, noticing for the first time that his brawny frame took up most of the bed. They slept on a king-size mattress at home. Last night, they'd rented a motel room with the same size bed. But tonight, this room with two doubles was all the desk clerk could offer them if they preferred a nonsmoking environment — which they did. If Blaine weren't healing from back surgery, Krissy wouldn't hesitate to tell him to move over, but it appeared as though tonight she'd sleep alone.

Separate lives. Separate beds. What a way to start the rest of their lives together.

Chapter 2

Blaine watched Krissy back the minivan out of the driveway, then accelerate down the street. He couldn't figure out what had gotten into her. She'd been glum for the past few days. He'd first concluded that it was because the girls were gone, but after listening to her talking on the telephone with them yesterday afternoon, hearing her encourage their daughters, Blaine had to assume there was more to Krissy's doldrums.

So he questioned her.

In reply she had merely shrugged and admitted she didn't know what was wrong.

Maybe after today she'll feel more like her old self, he thought, moving away from the living room windows. After today Krissy would be teaching school again.

Walking into the kitchen, Blaine smiled at the red apples on green vines that Krissy and the girls had papered onto the walls not even a month ago. They had urged him to stay out of their way while they pasted and hung the wallpaper, giggling and chattering all the while, and Blaine had no problem finding something else to do.

Females. After living with three of them for nearly two decades, Blaine still couldn't figure them out half the time.

He continued grinning as he poured himself a cup of coffee. Taking a sip, he thought over Krissy's odd mood swing, then recalled what she'd said about her new school, its principal, and the other teachers. He figured she was most likely suffering from a case of nerves. Or maybe it was getting to be that time of month. Well, whatever bothered her, she'd snap out of it.

Blaine glanced at the clock and realized he had to hurry and shower in order to make it to his physical therapy appointment. Pushing thoughts of Krissy from his mind, he set down his coffee mug and headed for the bathroom.

Krissy glanced around at all the enthusiastic faces in the conference room of Wellsprings Academy and realized she was one of the older teachers here. Surrounding her were five other women, all appearing to have just graduated from college, and three men, who couldn't be any older than the academy's principal, Bruce Sawyer, who looked about thirty-something. As Mr. Sawyer detailed his plans for the upcoming year, Krissy wondered if she really belonged at this place.

"I'd like every teacher to get personally involved with his or her students' education this year," the principal said, and when his gaze came her way, Krissy noticed how blue his eyes were, how strong his jawline seemed, how tall he stood, and how broad his shoulders looked beneath the crisp, white dress shirt he wore.

I wonder if he's married. In the next moment, she berated herself for even allowing the question to take form in her mind. *I'm married and I love my husband,* she silently reaffirmed. However, it was disheartening that she found another man attractive.

Oh, Lord, what's wrong with me? Nothing has seemed right since Blaine's accident.

Krissy sighed. When no divine reply was forthcoming, she gave herself a mental shake and forced her thoughts back to the meeting.

At the midmorning break, Krissy helped herself to a cup of steaming coffee from the long, narrow refreshment table which had been set up in the hallway. She looked over the delectable treats which were also on display and chose a small cinnamon muffin.

"Those are my favorite."

Krissy turned to find Bruce Sawyer standing directly behind her. Then he reached around her and plucked a muffin from the plastic plate.

"Well, what do you think so far?" he asked.

She smiled. "I think your staff is very young."

He grinned and took a bite of his muffin. Chewing, he looked around at the other teachers congregating on either side of them. "They're all qualified educators, believe me."

"Oh, I'm sure they are. It's just that . . . well, I don't see any of the teachers I worked with last year."

"They seemed competent and experienced. I read each one's resume. Unfortunately, we only had need for one third grade teacher since Leslie Comings got married this past summer."

Krissy couldn't believe her ears. "You mean to tell me I'm the only teacher who didn't lose her job?"

"Combining two schools isn't as simple as it might appear, I'm afraid. There were no easy decisions for the board members. The truth of the matter is, the merger didn't warrant extra teachers — even with the addition of Grace Christian School's populace."

"I see." She suddenly felt very badly for all her former colleagues.

"But we're glad you're here . . . Kristin, isn't it?"

She nodded.

"I've always been partial to the name. If I'd have had a daughter, I would have liked to name her Kristin."

She smiled nervously, unsure of how to respond. "Well, thank you, Mr. Sawyer."

He grinned. "Call me Bruce. We're all in this together, and I think we should be on a first name basis, don't you?"

"Sure." She'd been on a first name basis with the principal of Grace Christian School. The solidly built, gray-headed man had been a father figure to her when situations arose in the classroom and Krissy wanted advice. But somehow she couldn't imagine herself running to Bruce Sawyer's office for morsels of wisdom and seasoned counsel. The guy was too charming. Too . . . threatening.

"So you, um, have no daughters?" Krissy ventured, thinking that bringing up his family life would deter her attraction to him. "You and your wife have sons?"

"I have neither a wife nor children,"

Bruce said as a rueful expression crossed his handsome features. "My wife is dead. She died very suddenly about three years ago."

Krissy sucked in a horrified gasp.

"It's no secret around here," Bruce continued, "and I find being open about the tragedy has helped me recover."

"I'm so sorry . . ."

"Thank you." He paused and took another bite of his muffin. "My wife suffered with severe stomach problems. The medicine she took caused her to feel tired and depressed much of the time. Finally, she conceded to have surgery to fix the problem but something went horribly wrong and she never regained consciousness despite the doctors' best efforts."

"How tragic," Krissy said.

Bruce nodded and finished the rest of his baked treat. "Yes, but I'm comforted to know that my wife was a believer. I like to imagine that when she met the Savior, He put His loving arms around her and . . . and wiped away all tears from her eyes. He probably assured her that there would be no more death, neither sorrow, nor crying, and no more pain."

Krissy recognized the paraphrase from the book of Revelation, saw the faraway, mournful look in Bruce's gaze, and marveled at the depth of his sensitivity.

"Well, I hope you'll enjoy your year at Wellsprings Academy," he said, snapping from his reverie and pulling Krissy from hers also.

"Thanks." She gave him a smile.

"And I'll look forward to getting to know you better," he added with a light in his blue eyes.

"Same here." The words were out of her mouth before Krissy even realized she'd spoken them.

Blaine groaned in pain as he lowered himself onto the padded lawn chair in the backyard. His physical therapy session had taken a toll on him today; he'd used muscles in his back he hadn't realized he possessed. Unfortunately, instead of feeling better, he felt more disabled than ever. Glancing around the yard, he wished he could pull out the weed-whacker and get rid of some of the growth inching upward through the patio blocks. He wished he could mow the lawn. This summer Krissy and the girls had taken turns and, while they did an adequate job, they didn't mow it the way Blaine liked. But he didn't complain. How could he? He'd been little more than vegetation, supervising from the lawn chair.

"Hi, Blaine." The cool feminine voice wafted over the wooden fence from the yard next door. "It sure is hot this afternoon."

Lifting an eyelid, he saw his neighbor, Jill, wearing nothing but a little halter top and a skimpy pair of shorts. He closed his eyes again. "Hi yourself. Pardon me for not being a gentleman and getting up. The truth is, I can't move."

He heard his neighbor's soft laugh. "Give me a break. Even flat on your back you're a gentleman."

Stretched out in the shady part of the yard, Blaine grinned at the remark. He felt complimented.

"I wish Ryan was as much a gentleman as you."

Hearing the anguish in her voice, Blaine's heart filled with sympathy. His neighbors weren't exactly the happily married couple that he and Krissy were. During the summer months with the windows open, sounds of their feuding drifted over the property line nearly every night. Blaine and Krissy had shared the Good News with the couple, inviting them out to attend a Bible study and church, but Ryan and Jill had vehemently stated they weren't "into religion." Regardless, prayers continued on their behalf.

"Did the girls get off to college all right?" Jill wanted to know.

"Yep. They called this weekend and seem to be doing fine. They like their room-mates."

"Think they'll get homesick?"

"Probably."

Jill laughed and Blaine prayed she'd quit her chatting and tend to the toddler he could hear yelping inside the house. Nothing grated on his nerves more than a bawling child. Krissy said the neighbors' bickering bothered her more than listening to their kids throwing temper tantrums. Blaine, on the other hand, had no problem tuning out the arguing, but the kids' fussing made him edgy.

"I'll sure miss Mandy and Laina," Jill said. "They were such handy baby-sitters."

"They'll be back."

"Yeah, but my sanity might be gone by then." The child's wailing increased. "Well, I'd better go. See ya later."

"Sure, Jill. See ya."

Blaine opened his eyes in time to see his neighbor stoop near the sandbox and re-trieve two small navy-blue sneakers. She shook the sand off of them, then entered the house.

Left alone to relax once more, Blaine suddenly felt glad those days of sandboxes, diapers, and crying children were behind him. He recalled how he had enjoyed leaving the house for work just because he knew he wouldn't be back for thirty-six hours. Thirty-six hours without listening to kids cry. Krissy, of course, handled things much better than he; she never complained. Not once. She never seemed to get upset or impatient with the twins. They turned out to be sweet young ladies largely because of her, although Blaine had made it a point to be part of their lives as much as possible. He'd enjoyed his daughters from the time they were about six years old on up. He coached their girls' softball team in the summertime and gymnastics team during the winter months. He involved himself with the youth group at church and chaperoned outings and events whenever his schedule permitted. He had fond memories of his daughters' growing up years. But he felt glad they were over.

Off in the direction of the garage, a car door slammed shut and Blaine realized Krissy had arrived home from work. He heard her enter the house and wondered how long it would take before she found him languishing in the yard. She'd have to help him out of the lawn chair. He hadn't been lying to Jill when he said he couldn't move. Minutes later, much to his relief, Krissy appeared.

"Must be nice to lounge around all day," she quipped, her hands on her slender hips. The tepid autumn breeze tousled her blond hair, causing it to brush lightly against the tops of her shoulders.

"Hey, you're a sight for sore eyes. Can you help me out of this chair?"

Krissy wagged her head, obviously over his pathetic state, and walked toward him. When she reached the edge of the lawn chair, she held out her hand. Blaine took it, but instead of allowing her to pull him up, he tugged, causing her to fall against him. Then he kissed her soundly, albeit awkwardly.

"You're real funny," she said, working herself into a sitting position on the side of the chair near Blaine's knees. "The two of us are liable to break this flimsy thing and then you'll really have back problems."

Blaine sighed. "I suppose you're right."

"As always." Krissy discreetly tucked her denim dress beneath her.

"How was your day?" he asked.

"Not too bad. And yours?"

"In a word . . . painful."

"Sorry to hear that." Krissy stood and

helped Blaine to his feet. Lightning-hot pain bolted down his lower spine and thighs, blinding him for about ten seconds.

"Are you all right?"

"Yeah." He forced a smile, not wanting to worry his wife. "What's for supper?"

"I don't know. What are you hungry for?"

"Not sure."

"We're a decisive team."

Blaine grinned, then looped his arm around Krissy's shoulders, leaning on her as they walked toward the house. He didn't inquire further about her day. Didn't need to. His wife seemed to be her old self again.

Chapter 3

"Mind if I use you for a pillow?"

"Do I look like a pillow?"

Blaine grinned. "You're soft and curvy. You'll do."

Unable to help a grin, Krissy scooted over and made room for Blaine on the couch. He stretched out, his head at the far end, while he lifted his legs onto her lap.

"I've got to have something under my knees when I lie down," he explained. "I think that's why I couldn't get myself out of the lawn chair earlier."

"I'm honored that you've selected me as your cushion," Krissy replied on a note of sarcasm. "Nice to know I'm good for something around here other than cooking, cleaning, and playing nurse and taxicab driver to a convalescing husband."

"Playing nurse is my favorite," Blaine shot back with a mischievous gleam in his eyes. "I only wish I could enjoy it more."

Shaking her head at him, Krissy lifted her

feet onto the coffee table and set aside her now-empty paper plate. She and Blaine had decided to order out tonight. He wanted Italian and she wanted Chinese and neither would compromise, so Krissy ended up making two stops.

"How was your supper?"

"Great," Blaine replied. "Yours?"

"Marvelous. Sweet and sour chicken is my ultimate favorite."

"The stuff gives me gas. Are you sure it's chicken that Chinese place uses? Hard to tell with all the breading and sauce."

"Oh, quiet. Of course it's chicken."

Blaine chuckled, and Krissy rested her hands on his navy wind-pants. "One of the guys at work told me this joke about a Chinese Restaurant."

"I don't want to hear it."

"Something about a cat in the kettle at the Peking Room."

"Blaine, I said I don't want to hear it!"

He laughed while she bristled. Why did he always have to poke fun at the food she ate? She would never do such a thing to him . . . not that he'd let an unsavory joke spoil his appetite.

Still fuming, she tried to squelch her irritation by allowing her gaze to wander around their lower-level family room. The walls were paneled with knotty pine and decorated with various family snapshots that ranged from Blaine and Krissy's wedding to the twins' first steps to their graduating from high school last May. As she recalled each special event, a wave of nostalgia crashed over her.

Her exasperation forgotten for the moment, she turned to Blaine. She'd intended to engage him in a match of "remember when" but noticed that he'd begun to doze. Disappointed, Krissy looked back at the television set. As she watched the handsome, syndicated talk show host, she decided he had the same strong jawline as Bruce Sawyer and a little smile tugged at the corners of her mouth.

Yes, the principal of Wellsprings Academy could certainly dub for a celebrity with his good looks and charming manner. Krissy couldn't help but wonder why he didn't remarry. She imagined Bruce would most likely say it was because he hadn't "found the right one." That seemed to be a standard line among single people these days. However, Krissy noticed that there were a number of unattached, pretty females teaching at the academy and she guessed it wouldn't be long before the "right one" walked into Bruce's life.

Within moments, her musings took flight and she speculated on the sort of woman it would take to win Bruce's heart. Obviously, he'd been devastated when his first wife died, so the next woman to enter his life would have to somehow dispel all the hurts and fears born from such a tragedy. Krissy thought she knew what she'd do if she weren't married. She'd cultivate a friendship with the man, learning all his likes and dislikes, and she would be quick to point out the interests they shared. Like reading for instance. This afternoon while Krissy acquainted herself with her new classroom, Bruce had stopped by with a novel in his hands.

"Have you by any chance read this book?"

Spying the cover, Krissy recognized it, nodded, and rambled off an impromptu quote that could have come straight from the book jacket.

"Yes, that's the one." Bruce grinned. "I'm enjoying it very much."

"I recall it was a very touching story."

"Quite. And this entire series . . . have you read it?"

"Every book."

"What's your take on the novels?"

For nearly an hour, they had discussed books and shared their perspectives on various authors, styles, and story lines. Krissy found the conversation refreshing, since she'd been trying for two decades to get Blaine interested in books. But he only liked to read if the topics pertained to sports or firefighting, and he couldn't appreciate anything longer than a feature article.

She glanced over at him now, expecting to find him snoozing. But to her outright chagrin, she discovered Blaine staring back at her.

"What are you thinking about?" he asked softly. His eyes seemed to scrutinize her every feature.

Krissy felt her cheeks redden with embarrassment. "Books. I was thinking about books."

"Mmm . . ."

Blaine's gaze was like a weighty probe, searching into her heart, her soul. Suddenly she felt like the wickedest woman ever to roam Wisconsin. Here she ought to be enjoying her husband's company, but instead she was dreaming of capturing another man's heart.

Forgive me, Lord, she silently prayed. *What's wrong with me?*

Krissy crawled out from under Blaine's knees, then placed a large throw pillow beneath them in her stead.

"I'm tired. I think I'll turn in."

"Sure. Good night, Hon."

" 'Night."

Heavyhearted and feeling more than just a tad guilty, Krissy made her way upstairs to the master bedroom.

That was weird, Blaine thought, watching Krissy's departure. He'd never seen such an odd expression on his wife's face. She'd been daydreaming, that was obvious. But about books? No way. If she would have said she'd been thinking about the girls and remembering some silly thing the three of them had done together, Blaine would have bought it, lock, stock, and barrel. Unfortunately, he didn't buy it at all, and a slight foreboding sent a chill up his already aching spine. What was with Krissy these days?

Time to find out.

With a determined set to his jaw, he roused himself from the couch and made his way upstairs. He walked down the hallway, heading for their room. When he reached the doorway, however, he stopped short, seeing Krissy on her knees at the side of the bed, her Bible open on the floral spread in front of her. Silently, Blaine stepped backward, retracing his steps to the living room where he decided to put off any discussion until she finished her devotions.

Nearly twenty minutes later, he heard the bathroom door close followed by sounds of the shower spray.

Great, he thought, *she'll be in there all night.*

Well, fine, he would just wait for Krissy in the bedroom. Once more he ambled upstairs and down the hallway and entered their room. Lowering himself onto the bed, Blaine threw a pillow under his knees, turned on the small television, and began his vigil.

Krissy heard him before she ever saw him. Blaine. Snoring loudly. On top of their bed. And with her pillow under his knees, no less. Had he worn those wind-pants all day? To physical therapy with a lot of sick people around? Wonderful. Like she really wanted to place her head on it now!

Irritation coursed through her veins as she slipped into her nightie. Did Blaine ever once think of her? Couldn't he respect her feelings on anything, be it carry-out food or books or her own, personal pillow?

With a huff, she grabbed the remote from where it lay on Blaine's T-shirt encased stomach and turned off the TV. Next, she switched off the lamp and stomped out of the room, intending to sleep in one of the girls' beds tonight. She wanted to slam the door but refrained from doing so. Still, she wasn't quiet about putting clean sheets on Mandy's bed.

Regardless, Blaine never awoke.

Chapter 4

Blaine yawned and stumbled into the kitchen. "How come you slept in Mandy's room last night?"

Krissy threw him an annoyed glance, then whirled around and finished preparing a pot of coffee. She had already dressed for school and Blaine thought she looked quite attractive in the blue and green plaid cotton skirt and hunter-green T-shirt. The outfit complemented her blond hair and tanned skin.

"All right, Krissy, spit it out. What's up with you these days?"

She flipped on the coffeemaker and it began to brew. Turning to face him again, she folded her arms in front of her.

"Well?" Blaine demanded.

"Nothing is 'up with me.' "

"Nothing? It's hardly nothing, Kris," he said, easing himself into a chair at the kitchen table. "You've been acting so strange . . . ever since the girls went off to school. I mean . . ." He searched his mind for the right words. "Sometimes I feel like I don't even know you anymore. Like last night. I've got a feeling you weren't daydreaming about books. So what was going through your head?"

He watched as she blushed slightly before lifting her chin. She appeared almost defiant — another trait unlike the Krissy he'd married.

"I think you said it all," she stated softly, "when you said you don't know me anymore. In all honesty, you don't."

"What in the world are you talking about?"

"It's true," she said, avoiding his gaze, her voice wavering. "We never talk like we used to and when I try to discuss a topic of importance to me, you never listen. You don't even know what's going on in my life these days. You think you do, but really you don't."

Minutes ticked by as they regarded each other in silence. Then, once the coffee finished brewing, Krissy turned and poured two mugs. She crossed the room and placed one in front of Blaine.

Sipping it, he tried to think how he should handle this situation. Maybe hormones were to blame. Sometimes when she got this way it was just a matter of riding out the storm.

As if she'd read his mind, she spat, "And don't think this is just a PMS thing. It's not. This is something I've been aware of for a long time now. An intricate part of our marriage is gone, and it's never been more prevalent than it has since your accident. You and I, Blaine, have nothing in common. We're two people who are married and live under one roof, but we're not one flesh. Not anymore."

Blaine narrowed his gaze, feeling more than just a little disturbed by what he'd just heard. "Krissy, are you . . . are you thinking . . . ?"

He couldn't get himself to say the word "divorce." Thinking about it caused his gut to knot up.

"Krissy," he began again, "you and I made vows to each other —"

"I'm not about to break my wedding vows," she shot back.

"Well, that's good."

"We're just stuck with each other . . . for the rest of our lives."

Blaine felt his jaw drop slightly. "Stuck with each other?"

Krissy had the good grace to look chagrined.

"Stuck? Is that how you see it?"

"I'm going to be late." She marched

quickly past him and grabbed her bagged lunch and purse.

Blaine rose from the chair. "Wait."

She didn't. "See you tonight."

She fled out the side door before he could stop her. As a feeling of disbelief enveloped him, Blaine listened to the van door slam, the engine roar to life, and the sounds of Krissy backing the vehicle out of the garage and down the driveway.

"Stuck with each other," Blaine whispered incredulously. Next came the tidal wave of hurt that threatened to submerge him in a mixture of sorrow and rage. He didn't feel "stuck" with her. He loved Krissy — loved her with all his heart. He'd do anything for her. But she felt "stuck" with him.

First the rage. *How can she be so selfish, thinking only of herself and what she wants? And what does she want anyhow? She's got everything. A house, a job she enjoys, a husband who loves her, two nearly perfect daughters . . .*

He fumed all the while he dressed. Then, as he drove to his doctor's appointment later in the morning, the agonizing sorrow gripped his heart. *She doesn't love me anymore. What does a guy do when his wife doesn't love him anymore? When did it happen? How come I never noticed?*

Blaine had heard of marriages crumbling once the kids were grown and gone. He would believe it'd happen to his next door neighbors, but not to him and Krissy. They were Christians. This stuff wasn't supposed to happen to godly couples.

Perplexed, he drove into the clinic's parking structure, found a spot, and pulled his truck to a halt.

"So how's the back?" Dr. Lemke asked about thirty minutes later. The man's bald head shone like a brand-new plastic toy under the fluorescent lights in the exam room. Blaine would wager the short, stocky physician weighed about three hundred and fifty pounds, and he prayed he'd never end up fat and bald in his old age.

"Back's not so good. I'm still in a lot of pain."

The doctor glanced up. "Yes, so I see from the physical therapist's report. He states you're unable to do some pretty simple stretching and bending exercises."

"True, but don't think I haven't been practicing at home just like the therapist told me," Blaine stated in his own defense. "But the exercises aren't working."

"Hmm . . ."

Blaine watched the pen tip wiggle as Dr. Lemke scratched down what they'd discussed. Since the man was employed by the City of Milwaukee, Blaine figured he wanted to write out a return-to-work slip as soon as possible and spare further workers' compensation. In truth, Blaine wanted that too. He was growing bored at home all day.

"You're going to have to see a specialist," the doctor said at last. "Go back to the surgeon who operated. I'm afraid I can't do anything more for you."

"Sure. Whatever."

The doctor scribbled out the referral and his medical assistant made the appointment for Blaine. Sheet of paper in hand, he left the clinic and climbed into his pickup truck. He didn't care a whit about himself as he made the drive toward home. He kept thinking about what Krissy said that morning.

We're stuck with each other.

Blaine knew she meant it, too. They'd said things to each other before that they didn't mean, just like most other married couples. They'd apologized for it, then prayed together and asked for God's forgiveness, too. But given Krissy's odd behavior of late, he could tell those words had come from the very depth of her being.

Lord, what do I do? he prayed as he pulled into the driveway. Tears welled in Blaine's

331

eyes, and he couldn't even remember the last time he'd cried. *Lord, please help me. Please save my marriage. I'm nothing without Krissy.*

Did you ever tell her that?

The Voice wasn't an audible one, but it had replied to his heart just the same.

Sure I told her. Millions of times.

Millions?

And trillions.

Blaine shifted, feeling uncomfortable since he suddenly couldn't recall when he'd last shared his heart with Krissy.

How many times does a guy have to tell his wife the same old thing?

Millions and trillions.

Blaine grinned and gazed up through his sun roof and the blue, cloudless sky. "All right, Lord. I get it. You don't have to hit me over the head with a brick."

Exiting his truck, he grimaced as a shooting pain blasted down his leg. "On second thought, maybe You did."

"Mrs. Robinson, you have a phone call." Turning from the bulletin board she was decorating, Krissy forced a smile at the secretary. "I would have used the intercom system," the woman continued, "but it doesn't seem to be working. We'll have it fixed by the time school starts though."

"Thanks. I'll be right there."

The tall, slim, redhead whose age seemed unfathomable nodded and exited the classroom. Krissy had heard Mrs. Sterling was pushing sixty, yet she looked and acted no older than thirty-five. Secretly, Krissy hoped she'd be in such good shape at that age.

Setting the stapler down on her desk, Krissy followed the secretary through the hallway. They entered the office suite, Mrs. Sterling returned to her desk, and without even picking up the receiver, Krissy knew Blaine would be at the other end of the line. What had possessed her to throw such hateful words at him? She'd felt badly all the way to school and then Bruce's morning "challenge" to all the teachers had really touched her heart.

"Hello?" she answered somewhat timidly.

"Hi, Hon, what do you want for supper tonight?"

Blaine sounded like his same old self for which Krissy felt grateful. "Um, I really hadn't thought about it."

"Well, do you mind if I whip up something?"

She grimaced. Blaine was famous for his three-alarm chili at the fire station. Unfortunately, it wasn't one of Krissy's favorites. But she'd hurt him enough for one day. "Sure, make whatever you want."

"Okay."

"And, Blaine?"

"Yeah?"

Krissy glanced over her shoulder to be sure no one could overhear. Mrs. Sterling was nowhere in sight. "Sorry about this morning. . . ."

"Honey, all is forgiven, and we can talk about it tonight if you feel up to it."

"We can?" Holding the phone several inches away, Krissy stared at it like the piece of equipment had just grown a mouth of its own. "Well, all right," she said at last. "I'll see you in about an hour."

"Sounds good. And Kris . . . I love you."

She smiled, feeling guilty as she hung up the phone. Why was Blaine acting so nice after she'd been so mean? Of course, he wasn't a guy to stay angry or hold grudges, but he wasn't always so agreeable either.

"Everything all right, Kristin?" Pivoting, she glanced across the office suite in time to watch Bruce walk out of his private office. "You look like you might have had some bad news."

"No, no," she assured him. "I think the doctor just gave my husband some different pain medication. He didn't sound like himself."

"Hmm . . ." Bruce gave her a curious frown. "Pain medication for what?"

"For his back. Blaine was injured at work. He's a fireman and he fell through the roof of a two-story house. Cracked a couple of vertebrae and had surgery to repair a couple of discs that ruptured in the process."

"How horrible. When did that happen?"

"This past May."

"I see. Well, I'll pray for him. It's my belief that chronic pain often leads to drug addiction. My wife nearly became addicted to her prescription drugs. It's one of the reasons she opted for the surgery."

Krissy sucked in a breath, hoping such a thing wouldn't befall Blaine. But she quickly shook off her misgivings, realizing her husband hadn't been depressed a day in his life. As for an addiction to pain medication, he rarely took the stuff — even when he legitimately needed it.

"I didn't mean to frighten you," Bruce said, looking earnest.

Krissy snapped from her musing. "You didn't. You just gave me something to think about."

"One thing I learned from the situation with my wife is that life is short. Too short to waste on unhappiness."

Krissy couldn't help agreeing. She'd felt dispirited for over a week and it wasn't any fun.

Bruce gave her a compassionate grin. "You can talk to me anytime. I'll be here for you."

Krissy felt a blush creep up her neck and warm her cheeks. "That's very kind."

"I mean it."

"I know you do. Thanks."

Their gazes met and Krissy's traitorous heart began to hammer so loudly she felt certain Bruce could hear it. She was only too grateful when Mrs. Sterling reentered the office, carrying a stack of papers.

Krissy quickly made her exit.

Chapter 5

Krissy turned the van into the driveway and groaned at the sight of her next door neighbor, Jill Nebhardt, standing near the patio wearing khaki shorts and red T-shirt. Next she noticed the cloud of gray smoke billowing into the air and guessed that Blaine had fired up the grill. Now Jill was most likely chatting his ear off while he barbequed.

Well, at least he didn't make his three-alarm chili, Krissy mused gratefully as she killed the engine. Grabbing her purse, she climbed out of the van.

As she strode toward her husband and neighbor, Krissy experienced a twinge of guilt for not feeling very friendly. She supposed she should have compassion on the poor woman since Jill was terribly discouraged in her marriage. On the other hand, Krissy felt tired, and she and Blaine had their own issues right now.

"Hey, you're home," Blaine said as a smile split his tanned face. "I didn't even hear you pull in." His gaze flittered to Jill in explanation, and Krissy understood immediately.

"I was just telling Blaine about Ryan's new work schedule. He's gone twelve, sometimes thirteen hours a day. When he comes home, he's so crabby the kids and I can't stand to be around him. Worse, he expects dinner on the table and the house to be spotless."

"I told Jill I know the feeling since that's what you expect too, right Hon?"

Krissy rolled her eyes. "You haven't done housework in twenty years, Blaine."

"With three women around, why should I?" Pointing the metal spatula at her, he added, "And you haven't changed a flat tire in all that time. Or shoveled snow."

"You won't let me use your snow blower, otherwise I would." Krissy leaned toward Jill. "This argument could go on all night."

The younger woman chuckled. "I'm so glad to see you two aren't perfect. You seem like it sometimes. I'm really envious of your relationship." She peered into Krissy's face with teary brown eyes. "You don't know how lucky you've got it, Girlfriend."

"I remind Krissy of that at least three times a day," Blaine said.

Sudden shouts from the adjoining backyard brought Jill to attention. "Uh-oh . . . sounds like Grant and Royce are at it again. I'd better scoot. Talk to you guys later."

"See ya, Jill," Blaine replied.

"Bye." Krissy watched their neighbor jog around the house before looking back at Blaine. "Hi."

"Hi." He stepped around the smoking grill and gave her a kiss. "Have a good day?"

"Yeah, and you?"

"Okay."

"What did the doctor say?"

"He wants me to go back and see Dr. Klevins."

"The surgeon? How come?"

"Because my back isn't improving at the rate he'd like."

Krissy nibbled her lower lip in momentary contemplation. "Do you think another operation is ahead of you?"

"I doubt it. I've had a fusion, what more can the surgeon do?"

"I don't know."

Blaine looked down at whatever he was cooking.

"What are you making for supper?" Krissy asked, curious.

Bringing his gaze back to hers, he grinned. "Beef tenderloin. One of your favorites."

The news made her smile. "I've been hungry for a grilled steak. And here I had assumed you concocted your famous chili."

"You hate my chili. Why would I make it when it's just you and me for supper tonight?"

"Well, I —"

"See, I know you, Krissy. Better than you think." He raised an eyebrow as if to make his point.

"Touché." Hitching her purse up higher onto her shoulder, she couldn't help grinning. "I'm going inside to change."

"Slipping into something more comfortable, are you, Darling?" Blaine asked in a feigned British accent.

"Oh, like right." Krissy shook her head at him and walked to the side door. "I've got a mountain of things to accomplish tonight."

Entering the house, a swell of disappointment rose inside her when she realized she could sure use a romantic evening. Then, much to her shame, a vision of Bruce Sawyer and his tender blue eyes flittered across her mind.

"You're not eating."

Krissy looked up from her plate. "Everything is perfect, Blaine. The steak, the salad, the dinner rolls . . ."

"But?"

"But I feel a little down all of a sudden. I can't explain it. It's just weird."

"Maybe it's the company," Blaine quipped, setting his fork down none too gently.

Krissy stared at him ruefully. How could she make him understand what was going on inside her when she didn't understand it herself? "Blaine . . ."

"You know what," he said, an earnest light in his dusky, blue-gray eyes, "I've been in love with you since we were juniors in high school."

Krissy had to smile as mental snapshots of the past flashed through her mind. "I know . . ."

"And when you agreed to go to the prom with me that year, I felt like the luckiest guy alive. I mean, Krissy Marens . . . *the* Krissy Marens, prettiest girl in school . . . going to the prom with me . . . and I wasn't even on the football team."

Laughing, she sat back in her chair and folded her arms. "I thought you were awfully cute."

Blaine's smile faded. "Change your mind lately?"

"No . . . I mean . . ." She sighed. "I don't know . . ."

She began picking at her salad again, not willing to see the pain she probably inflicted on the man she was supposed to love unconditionally. She felt guiltier now, trying to be honest, than if she'd have just stuffed these feelings in the deepest part of her and somehow tried to forget them there.

"I can't help it that my hair is thinning," Blaine said. "This bald patch on the back of my head seems to get bigger every year."

Krissy glanced at him and smiled. "I like your bald spot. And I think your thinning hair makes you appear . . . distinguished."

"Hmm . . ." He rubbed his jaw, looking perplexed. "Maybe my five o'clock shadow bugs you, is that it?"

"No, I like your five o'clock shadow. I wish you had it all day."

"Want me to quit shaving?"

Krissy rolled her eyes. "No."

"Help me out here, Woman," Blaine cried in exasperation, holding his arms out wide. "I want to please you, but how can I when I don't know what it is that's displeasing you?"

"The paunch hanging over your belt turns me off. There. I said it."

"Thank you." Throwing his gaze upward, he shook his head. "For your information, I plan to get rid of my . . . paunch . . . just as soon as my back heals up."

"That's what I figured, so I didn't want to make a big deal out of it. But you've been wearing such sloppy clothes lately."

"My blue jeans are a little snug. Besides, they're hard to pull on with my back killing me half the time."

Krissy shrugged.

"Okay, okay, okay," he said, his palms out as if to forestall further debate. "I'll lose some weight. I'm not pleased with this extra twenty pounds either."

"You'll feel better, too. That's twenty pounds off your aching back."

Blaine humbly agreed. "Now, I need to ask you something else," he said, standing and taking his silverware and half-empty plate to the sink. "Something important."

Krissy felt horrible for ruining his dinner. "What's the question?"

"I want a totally honest answer. No beating around the bush." After depositing his dishes near the sink, he turned and faced her.

She rose and cleared her place, setting everything on the counter next to Blaine's utensils. Standing in front of him, she looked up into his eyes, unsure if she trusted herself to be as forthright as he requested.

"You still love me, Krissy?" Her brawny husband wore an expression of boyish vulnerability and the sight moved her to tears.

"Yes, I love you. Of course I love you. It's just that . . ."

"What?"

"It's just that in so many ways, Blaine, we're strangers."

"That makes no sense. We've been married for twenty years. We've known each other since high school. How can we possibly be strangers?"

"Because since the twins were born we put all our energy into raising them. We did a good job, too. But, when the girls were in first grade, I went back to school and finished my degree and from that point on, I had my career, you had yours, and our home life consisted of our daughters and maintaining a house."

Krissy expelled a long breath, hoping she was getting through to him. "I don't regret any of the sacrifices we made for Mandy and Laina, except for one. Our relationship. We lost touch, you and I, and now there's a distance between us that I don't know how to bridge."

Working the side of his lip between his teeth, Blaine seemed to be considering everything she said. Then he sighed, shrugged, and gathered Krissy into his arms. "If we love each other, which we do," he stated at last, "then we can pray about these things and work on spanning whatever gap exists."

Resting her head against the lower part of his shoulder, Krissy could hear the strong, steady beat of Blaine's heart. She could smell smoke on his T-shirt from the outside grill. It was a scent she'd become well-acquainted with over the years because of his occupation. She associated the odor with an unsettled sensation and realized that, even though they'd grown apart, she'd always concerned herself with his safety. She had fretted and prayed for him during those hours following his accident. Wasn't that love? Of course it was!

Blaine placed a light kiss on her forehead. "Everything'll be all right."

She nodded and tightened her arms around his waist. "Fall always seems like a time of change and adjustment. A different school year, new students — and this year another school altogether for me, and now Mandy and Laina are gone."

"Honey, they're not 'gone.' You make it sound like they're dead. They're just away at college. It's a temporary thing."

"Like the season."

"Right. Life's full of seasons."

Krissy nodded, wishing this one would pass quickly.

Chapter 6

It was the last day of the week and first day of September. Warm sunshine spilled through the partially cloudy sky and onto the black asphalt where Krissy's third graders were at play. Shiny new equipment in bright yellows and reds beckoned children of all ages to its monkey bars, slide, and swings. The little girl inside Krissy felt tempted to join the kids each time she heard their squeals of laughter.

"I wish they would have made gym sets like that when I was growing up," fellow teacher, Erin Latrell, said. She stood to Krissy's right, observing her second graders.

Krissy laughed. "I was thinking along those same lines." Tipping her head, she considered the young woman. Krissy guessed Erin wasn't much older than the twins, with her peaches-and-cream complexion and blue-eyed innocence framed with shoulder-length, reddish-brown hair that fell in soft curls past her shoulders.

"Mind if I ask where you attended college?"

"Not at all. I stayed right here in Wisconsin. I lived at home. Still do, but I'm getting married soon. Next summer, in fact."

"How nice." Krissy smiled, suddenly wishing she would have insisted that Mandy and Laina live at home while going to school. But as she mentally replayed the conversation she'd had with each of her daughters last night, she realized the girls were happy and enjoying campus life. Besides, they truly needed this time to blossom and grow into the young women God intended them to be.

Wistful, she returned her gaze to the children at play. *Blaine was right,* she thought, *this is just a season . . . a stormy one. And it's storming in my heart.*

The sound of hard sole shoes tapping against the pavement drew Krissy out of her reverie. Glancing over her shoulder, she saw Bruce Sawyer, dressed in a light brown suit, striding toward them. Reaching her and Erin, he grinned.

"Nice day."

Krissy smiled. "It certainly is."

Erin nodded in agreement.

"I wanted to deliver these personally," he said, handing each of them a white, sealed envelope. "They're invitations to my annual

Labor Day party this coming weekend. Time got away from me, and I didn't trust placing them in teachers' in-boxes." He paused, bestowing a warm smile on Erin, then Krissy. "I'd be honored if you would both attend."

Krissy glanced down at the envelope in her hand, not wanting to look up into Bruce's blue eyes. She was a married woman and to flirt would be very wrong, but if she wasn't mistaken, Bruce sought out her company . . . and Krissy felt more than flattered. Worse, she enjoyed it.

Oh, Lord, this is a bad situation, one I can't give in to even if I'm tempted to . . .

"May I bring my fiancé?" Erin asked.

"Of course. I'd love to meet him," Bruce replied graciously. "And, Kristin," he added, turning toward her, "I hope you'll bring your spouse."

Why had that just sounded like a question? Did Bruce care one way or the other?

Pushing her ponderings aside, she tried to attack the issue pragmatically. Would she bring Blaine? Or rather, would he deign to accompany her? In all probability, he'd elect to stay home. He abhorred attending social functions that included Krissy's co-workers. He said teachers were boring and tried to one-up each other as proof of their intellect. Of course, the same could not be said for Blaine's colleagues who played tug-of-war over mud pits and blasted each other with fire hoses on their company picnics. Over the years Krissy had gone to each and every one with Blaine, and she did so without complaint.

Mustering her courage, she glanced up at Bruce and gave him a formal grin. "I'll pass the invitation on to my husband. Thanks."

"Great," he said, but Krissy sensed the answer lacked Bruce's usual enthusiasm.

As he walked away and reentered the school, she felt her heart take a plunge from the weight of the guilt she'd been carrying around for almost two weeks. Yet, she hadn't done anything to feel ashamed about, except entertain thoughts of impossibilities. She wasn't about to leave Blaine in order to have a fling with her new principal. She was a Christian. She loved her husband. He loved her.

Krissy sighed. *So what in the world is my problem?*

Blaine wasn't sure how he felt as he drove home that Friday afternoon. Disappointed, scared, and irritated all at the same time. He'd seen the orthopedic surgeon, and after hearing the bad news, he checked in at the fire station to say hello to the guys. Next, he conversed with the captain for a long while, and at last, Blaine saw the wisdom behind taking the permanent disability the city offered, along with a compensation package the union procured for him. The surgeon had stated that Blaine would never return to work. His back wasn't ever going to be as limber and as strong as it had been before the accident. However, his physician ordered him to swim and lose weight . . . that is if he didn't want to turn into a mass of plump vegetation. Blaine knew it was sound advice, and he'd been watching his diet lately. He'd even shed a few pounds, but he had many more to lose. So, after the fire station, Blaine's next visit was to the local health club where he purchased a membership. He figured a workout would use up an hour or two, but how would he spend the rest of his days?

Lord, there has to be a job out there somewhere that I can do. A man doesn't work, he doesn't eat . . .

Blaine pulled into the driveway and parked behind Krissy's van. Climbing out of his truck, he entered the house and the aroma of sautéing garlic immediately met his senses. He followed his nose to the kitchen where he found Krissy at the stove.

"Smells great in here," he said, placing his hands on her slim hips and kissing her neck. "What are you making?"

"A stir-fry . . . with real chicken," she replied emphatically.

Blaine chuckled. "Your version of Chinese food is always tasty, Hon. It's the order-out stuff that rouses my curiosity."

"What did the doctor say?" Krissy asked in a no-nonsense tone.

He chewed the side of his lip and considered her. Was she in one of her moods again? She didn't even acknowledge the compliment he'd just paid her.

She looked at him askance. "Well?"

"I've got six months to live."

Krissy gave him a quelling look. "Don't even joke about such things, Blaine."

"Well, maybe that's what you'd like to hear," he blurted. He was getting tired of catering to her whimsical ups and downs. Didn't she care a whit about him?

Setting down the spatula, she faced him, hands on hips. "I'm not up to sparring with you, so just tell me what the doctor said, okay?"

Blaine exhaled and fought against the frustration welling inside of him. "He said I can't go back to work because I'll never be able to function in the capacity the fire department expects. So, I stopped by the station and accepted the permanent disability offer and comp package. I'm no longer a firefighter."

Krissy's jaw dropped slightly. "You're out of a job? Just like that? Can't they give you some more time to recuperate?"

"It's been three months, Kris."

"But —"

"Look, the doc said it and my captain agreed. I'm no longer physically able to perform my job. And I won't be. Ever."

Blaine saw Krissy swallow hard. "We can't live on my salary . . . and help the girls through college."

"I'll have money coming in. And I plan to find something else to do besides sit around here all day watching soap operas."

"You've been watching the soaps?"

Blaine laughed at her horrified expression. "I meant that figuratively."

She nodded, looking relieved, and began slicing the boneless chicken breasts and adding the pieces to the oil and garlic.

"Honey, don't worry. Things are going to be fine. The Lord will take care of us. He'll find me some sort of work that I can do to supplement the disability payments."

"Yes, I . . . I'm sure you're right."

Blaine folded his arms and watched his

wife prepare their meal with lackluster efforts. It just wasn't like her. Up until a few weeks ago, she'd had an unsurpassed zest for life, but now a kind of dreariness clouded her eyes. He wished he could get inside her head for five minutes. Maybe then he could understand whatever it was that bothered her . . . other than what she'd previously admitted to. He had a feeling the problem was more than just his extra poundage and the girls being away, although the combination might have been the boiling point.

"Hard day at school, Kris?"

"Not exactly."

"Well, what *exactly* is bugging you right now? Me?"

"No . . . not you. It's just that I was thinking about quitting my job until you came home with your news."

Blaine brought his chin back in surprise. "Why do you want to quit your job? You don't like the new school?"

"I don't know . . . maybe I'm just tired of teaching altogether. Maybe I've lost what it takes to be a good educator."

"That's not what you said Monday night. You said the kids seemed to adore you and that they were excited about their new third grade teacher. I really thought you were starting to snap out of this depression . . . or whatever you want to call it."

Krissy began chopping celery, onions, and mushrooms. Next she tossed the vegetables into the wok on the stove. "There's just this person at school who . . ." She swallowed and Blaine sensed she was trying to carefully select her words. "Well, I don't know if it's . . . healthy for me to work near this person."

Blaine frowned. "Not healthy?"

"Emotionally speaking."

"Hmm . . ." He thought it over. "So this person is verbally abusive or threatening?"

"Threatening," Krissy replied on a decisive note.

"You're kidding? This person is making threats? Let's call the cops!"

"No, no, Blaine, not that kind of threatening. I mean, he's not threatening me, he's just a threat to me."

"Like he wants to take over your job?"

Krissy turned thoughtful. "Something like that, I guess. He wants to take over something."

"Man, you wouldn't think that kind of competition existed in Christian day schools, but I suppose it's everywhere." He paused, thinking it over. So all this was about her career? Well, that made sense.

"Listen, Kris, if after bathing the matter in prayer, you feel you need to quit your job, go ahead. You'll find another one. Probably a better paying one, too." With that he closed the distance between them and kissed her cheek. "See? Problem solved."

Krissy watched her husband's retreating form as he left the kitchen and entered the living room. Next she heard the rustling of the paper and knew he'd taken to reading the daily local news.

Blaine thinks the problem's solved, she thought, jabbing at the stir-fry with the wooden spatula. She then placed the cover on top of the wok and allowed it to cook. *The problem is not solved. It's far from being solved. But what do I say? I'm bored with our marriage and I'm attracted to Bruce Sawyer?* Krissy shook her head. Blaine would hit the ceiling. What husband wouldn't? And here she was supposed to be a good, Christian wife.

Her spirit plummeted deeper with discouragement and shame. Not only was she a lousy wife, but she was a sorry excuse for a Christian woman as well.

Chapter 7

Krissy sulked around the house for the rest of the evening, and Blaine didn't even bother trying to cheer her up. Frankly, he hadn't the slightest clue what more to do for her, other than leave her alone and allow her to come to her own conclusions about whether she should quit her job. Meanwhile, he started his new swimming routine on Saturday morning, and after completing several laps he could tell the exercise would strengthen his back muscles. Maybe he'd take off this extra weight quicker than he anticipated. The idea encouraged him.

On Sunday morning, he and Krissy attended their usual Bible study and the service that followed. When the pastor gave an altar call, Krissy went forward, looking more miserable than Blaine had ever seen her.

Lord, I feel helpless, he silently prayed, stepping into the aisle and allowing Krissy back into the pew after she'd knelt and prayed up front. It comforted Blaine to know she, at least, communed with their Heavenly Father. God had the answers that he lacked, and the Lord would guide Krissy's steps.

Back at home, she seemed . . . happier.

"Everything okay?" Blaine asked as they stood in their bedroom. He unknotted his tie, then yanked it out from around his neck.

Krissy smiled and nodded as she changed her clothes. "Everything's fine."

"What do you want to do this afternoon?"

She stopped and glanced at him, her expression one of surprise. "You want to do something?"

"Well, yeah . . . why is that such a shock?"

Krissy laughed softly and hung up her dress. "Because you usually like a nap on Sunday afternoons."

"That's when I was a hardworking man. Now I'm footloose and fancy-free."

"Oh, brother!" She rolled her eyes.

Blaine chuckled. "And tomorrow's a holiday, so you don't need a nap either."

"We sound like two old fogies."

"We are two old fogies. So what do you want to do this afternoon, *Granny?*" Judging from her wounded expression, Blaine instantly knew he'd said the wrong thing. "Honey, I was only kidding. The granny-thing was supposed to be funny."

"I know . . . I guess it just struck me the wrong way." She gave him an earnest stare. "I'm not ready for old age."

"Well, we're not getting any younger. I mean, think about it. We could be grandparents in the next couple of years."

"Bite your tongue!"

Blaine laughed at her incredulous expression. Then she threw one of the bed pillows at him. He caught it and whipped it back, hitting her in the shoulder.

"All right, that's it. The war's on."

"Now, wait a second, here. I've got an injured back, remember?"

"Too bad. All's fair in love, war, and pillow fights . . . even when you're wounded."

Blaine grinned broadly. He hadn't seen Krissy this feisty in months. Clad in her lacy white slip, she made a fetching sight as she gathered her ammunition. He gave her enticing curves a long, appreciative glance.

Then suddenly the phone rang, intruding upon their special moment.

"Let's not answer it," Blaine said.

Krissy frowned. "But it might be the girls."

He thought it over. "We'll call them back."

She worried over her lower lip, and Blaine knew he had to answer it and put her mind at ease. Ignoring the pangs of disappointment, he lifted the portable phone from the bedside table and pushed the TALK button. "Hello, Robinsons'."

"Yes, may I speak with Kristin?" the male voice at the other end asked.

"Who's calling?"

"Bruce Sawyer. I'm the principal of Wellsprings Academy."

"Oh, right. Sure. Hang on a sec." Covering the mouthpiece, he held the phone out to his wife. "For you."

"Who is it?" she asked, sitting back on her haunches on top of the bed.

"Your new principal."

Blaine watched as Krissy paled in one second and blushed in the next. In fact, she turned scarlet right down to her collarbone. He narrowed his gaze, trying to gauge her odd reaction.

"What does he want?"

"Beats me," Blaine replied. "Should I tell him we're, um, busy?"

Krissy nodded, looking almost afraid to take the call.

Blaine put the phone to his ear. "Sorry, but Krissy's unavailable. Can I give her a message?"

"Yes, please. Ask her if she'd mind bringing a pan of brownies to the picnic tomorrow. My caterer's mother got sick, so I'm trying to put together an impromptu potluck."

Blaine pursed his lips and looked at Krissy who was staring back at him curiously. "Sure, I'll ask her."

"If there's a problem, tell her to give me a call. She's got my number."

She does? Blaine swallowed a tart reply. There was just something in this guy's tone he didn't appreciate. "Okay, I'll relay the message."

"Great. Thanks."

Blaine pushed in the OFF button with his thumb. "Who's this Bruce Sawyer anyway?"

Krissy felt as though there was a hot blade piercing her insides. Inadvertently, she placed her hand over her stomach, but then she told herself she'd done nothing to feel ashamed about. "Bruce's the principal of Wellsprings Academy," she answered honestly.

"Yeah, that's what he said. And he wants you to make a pan of brownies for tomorrow's picnic. Did I know about this picnic?"

"No, because I wasn't planning to go."

"Hmm . . . well, you'd better call the guy back and tell him. He said you've got his phone number."

Krissy frowned. "I have his number . . . ?" Then she realized what Bruce meant. "Oh!" she said with a good dose of relief. "We all have it. It's in the staff directory."

"So, why do you look so guilty, Kris?"

"I don't know. Do I look guilty? I shouldn't. I haven't done anything wrong."

Blaine sat on the edge of the bed. "Is this guy hitting on you or something?"

Krissy shook her head and glanced at the printed spread. The last thing she wanted to do was discuss Bruce Sawyer with her husband.

"He's not the one threatening you and making you feel like quitting your job, is he?"

"Bruce isn't making threats against me, no," Krissy said. How could she possibly describe the kind of threat the man posed? Bruce walked into her classroom and she suddenly felt sixteen again, all weak-kneed and nervous. When he sought out her company, she felt flattered, honored. They shared many common interests, and Krissy sensed the mutual attraction. Still, he knew she was married . . . so what was he thinking? The same thing she'd been thinking? That in another place, another time, they might have pursued a romantic relationship? But the fact remained: she was married. Very married . . . and Krissy planned to stay that way, despite her wayward emotions.

Blaine cupped her chin, bringing her gaze up to his. "Everything okay?"

"Yes," she replied, unsure if it were the truth or a lie. She felt so troubled in her heart, so stressed. Hadn't she gotten all this settled during the worship service?

"All right. If you tell me things are okay, then I believe you."

Krissy forced a little smile before Blaine leaned over and touched his lips to hers. It was like salve on a painful red welt, and she closed her eyes at its sweet familiarity.

But then all too soon, he ended the kiss. "You never answered my question," he said, wearing a silly smirk. "What do you want to do this afternoon?"

Krissy grinned as her hand clutched the corner of a pillow and before he could duck, she whacked him upside the head.

Chapter 8

Krissy leafed through the staff directory, found Bruce's phone number, then picked up the telephone and began to punch in the digits. Before she could finish, however, Blaine came up behind her and stole the phone out of her hand.

"Hey, I've been thinking . . . why don't we go to this picnic tomorrow?"

Krissy dropped her jaw. "You? Want to go to a picnic? With a bunch of teachers and their spouses?" She held her hand over her heart, feigning cardiac arrest.

He shook his head. "You'd starve to death if you went into acting."

She shrugged.

"But I'm serious. Maybe we should go. I mean, it's your new school and you're debating whether God wants you there . . . perhaps He'll show you at tomorrow's picnic."

Nice try, Krissy wanted to say. She wasn't that dumb. She knew the reason behind

Blaine's interest in attending. He was curious about Bruce. She likened it to the times she and the girls would return from an afternoon of shopping and Blaine would ask, "How much money did you spend?" to which Krissy replied, "Not much." Then Blaine would say, "Lemme see the checkbook." It wasn't that he didn't believe her or didn't trust her. He'd made that much clear over the years. And he never once berated her for overspending. Simply, he liked to see the facts for himself. In all probability, the same held true now with the principal of Wellsprings Academy. Obviously Krissy hadn't adequately hidden her feelings when Bruce phoned earlier, so now Blaine wanted to appraise the situation for himself. Unfortunately, it made Krissy feel terribly uncomfortable.

"Blaine, I don't want to attend this picnic."

"Free food. You don't have to cook . . . except for a pan of brownies."

"I'll make you your own personal pan," she promised. "And I'll make your favorite cream cheese brownies, but only if we can stay home."

"Sorry, Babe, I'm on a diet." He patted his tummy for emphasis. "Besides, you accused me of not enjoying the same things you do, so here's our chance to do something together. Something you enjoy."

Krissy inhaled deeply, then let out a slow breath.

Blaine tipped his chestnut-brown head. "Want to tell me why you're so dead set against going to this little shindig?"

She considered the request. It would be nice to clear the air. But at the same time, she didn't want to hurt Blaine by admitting her attraction to another man. Would he ever trust her again?

"Don't you think I'll understand?" he asked, his expression soft, earnest.

"No, I don't think you will."

"Well, why don't you try me and see?"

"Because I don't want to take the chance. Besides, whatever I'm going through is something very personal. It's between God and me."

Blaine folded his arms. "I feel kinda left out."

She tried to ignore the pained look on his face. "Want to go to the zoo this afternoon?" she asked, purposely changing the subject.

"Not particularly."

"I thought maybe we could even ask Jill if we could take her kids. You know, get them out of the house for awhile so she and Ryan can have some time alone."

Blaine grimaced. "I'd rather go to fifty school picnics than take a bunch of whining kids to the zoo."

"Oh, come on, Blaine, it'll be fun."

He puffed out an exasperated sigh. "How'd you manage to come up with this harebrained scheme?"

"Harebrained? Thanks a lot."

"The idea, not you, Krissy."

She folded her arms, trying to stifle her irritation. "For your information, I heard Jill and Ryan arguing at one o'clock this morning. They were in their kitchen with the window open and they woke me up. I couldn't fall back asleep, and I started thinking about how we could help them. We can't enroll them in Christian marital counseling or a Bible study because they're opposed to anything religious. But then, during the worship service, I came up with . . . with this *harebrained scheme* of taking their kids to the zoo. It's a way to reach out to our neighbors."

"The zoo, huh?"

Krissy nodded.

Blaine rubbed his stubbly jaw in consideration, then finally agreed. "Okay, I'll go to the zoo this afternoon, but only if we can go to the picnic tomorrow."

"I'll think about it. I mean, I can always phone Bruce later with our regrets."

Blaine shook his head. "No picnic. No zoo. I drive a hard bargain."

Krissy stared hard at him, and Blaine stared right back. She could see the spark of determination in his dusky eyes. Against her better judgment, she relented. "Oh, all right. We'll go to the picnic. But I don't want to hear one complaint about being bored."

He grinned wryly. "Got it."

"And you don't have to tell every stupid joke you know and embarrass me."

"Me? Tell stupid jokes? C'mon, Hon, my jokes are always hilarious."

"Yeah, right." Spinning on her heel, she marched toward the front door. "I'll go ask Jill if we can take the kids."

"Sure. And I'll be here on my knees praying she says no."

Krissy felt pleased that Jill agreed to allow her four children to go on the outing. In addition, Jill promised to spend some quality time with Ryan.

"I'm sorry we disturbed you last night," she muttered, looking embarrassed.

Krissy gave the woman a warm smile. "I wasn't so much disturbed as concerned, and I hope you don't think I'm a nosy neighbor trying to butt into your business."

"Are you kidding? You're a godsend. With the kids out of the way this afternoon, I might even accomplish a thing or two around the house and that'll make Ryan happy. He's forever complaining about the messes. But I just don't have any time to clean."

Krissy thought Ryan had better lighten up. But then she reminded herself that there are two sides to every situation, and she didn't know the other half of this one.

Sitting on a step in the back hall, she helped baby Haden on with his shoes. Then she lifted him into her arms, thinking he was about the cutest thing she'd ever seen, with his blond curls and deep brown eyes.

"Wanna go to the zoo?" she asked the eighteen month old.

"Zoo . . . Mama . . ." He pointed at Jill and Krissy wondered if he was going to cry when she took him home.

"Don't worry," Jill said as if divining her thoughts, "Haden will go anywhere with anyone — especially if his brothers and sister are along."

"Okay, then, let's go." Krissy carried the youngest on one hip while the three other kids followed her back to her house.

"I guess I wasn't praying hard enough," Blaine mumbled when she entered.

"Hi, Mr. Robinson," the oldest said cheerily. At eight years old, he was a red-haired, freckle-face kid with a smile that displayed a future need for orthodontics. "You coming to the zoo with us?"

"Yep. Mrs. Robinson is making me."

"She is?" The boy looked at her curiously.

"He's teasing you, Grant." Krissy gave Blaine a stony look.

He grinned back at her in reply.

"I like the aminals at the zoo," four-year-old Chelsea announced. Her coloring was similar to little Haden's. "I 'specially like the bears."

"I like the snakes," Royce interjected. The second-oldest, his features were a mix of his siblings'. He had reddish-brown hair and brown eyes but only a smattering of freckles.

"I like the snakes, too." Blaine grinned and pulled out his car keys. "Mrs. Robinson hates snakes, so we'll have to make her stay in that part of the zoo the longest."

"Yeah!" the two older boys agreed.

"Oh, fine," Krissy retorted, "but then I'll make you all go to the gift shop where I'll stay for hours!"

"Yeah! We like the gift shop, too!" Royce said.

Blaine laughed and headed out of the house. Krissy and the children trailed behind him. When they reached the van, the kids piled in and Krissy converted one of the back passenger benches to a child's harnessed seat into which she strapped Haden. With the task completed, she made sure the others were belted in safely before she took her place up front.

Blaine gave her a sidelong glance from where he sat behind the wheel. "You sure you want to do this?"

"Too late now."

With a sigh of resignation, he started the engine and backed out of the driveway.

They arrived at the Milwaukee County Zoo, parked, and Blaine paid the admission fee, grumbling under his breath about the cost of four children and something about highway robbery. Krissy ignored the remarks, knowing that he was only half serious anyway, and entered the gates with the children. The welcome sign proclaimed that this particular zoo was considered one of the finest in the country, and it housed approximately twenty-five hundred different animals. Krissy remembered from bringing her third-grade class here on field trips that it was virtually impossible to see everything in a span of a couple hours.

"Okay, what animals should we look at first?" she asked.

"Can we go on the train first?" Royce replied, and in the next moment the calliope-like blare from the down-sized steam locomotive heralded its arrival at the midget station.

The children were all in agreement; the train ride which circled the zoo had to come first. Blaine murmured a little louder this time as he bought the six tickets, but he seemed to enjoy the ride on this sunny September afternoon.

Krissy enjoyed it, too. Moreover, she relished holding a little one on her lap again. Her once-a-month nursery duty at church never seemed to completely satisfy the longing she'd harbored for years to have another child. Well, it obviously wasn't in God's plan. She would have to wait for grandchildren.

After the train ride, they visited the polar bears and sea lions. Then it was on to see the snakes and sundry other reptiles, all of which made Krissy's skin crawl. Next the alligators, and they finally moved on to the monkey house.

"Now you boys'll feel right at home," Blaine said as they entered the area where the chimps were swinging from tree limbs, jumping around, and picking at each other. "This reminds me of you guys playing on your gym set."

"Uh-uh," Grant said, an indignant frown furrowing his auburn brows. "We're not monkeys."

"It's a joke," Krissy assured the boy. "Mr. Robinson is always making bad jokes."

"Uh-uh," Blaine mimicked juvenilely.

"You're more trouble than these kids," she whispered, giving him an elbow in the ribs.

"Oh, yeah?" He caught her arm in fun and drew her tightly to his side. "Well, just for that little comment, you get to buy us all popcorn and soft drinks."

She shrugged, figuring it was the least she could do. Overall, Blaine was being a good sport.

A half hour later, they sat on a park bench, munching on popcorn and watching the children who were preoccupied with the elephants.

"You know, that little guy is awfully cute," Blaine remarked.

"Haden? Yes, he sure is."

"I used to often wish I had a son . . . not that I ever felt displeased about our twin daughters. But I prayed hard and long for a boy. Guess God answered that prayer with a 'no.' "

Krissy whipped her gaze around and stared at him. She would have never guessed Blaine harbored such a desire all these years. He had never said a thing. "We could have adopted. We still could, I suppose."

"Naw, I don't have the energy or the patience for kids anymore."

"That's just because you're out of practice."

"Yeah, maybe."

A rueful smile tugged at the corners of her lips while she studied Blaine's profile. Did he have any other regrets? The very question seemed like evidence enough that she really didn't know this man the way she ought to.

Two sides to every situation, she thought, recalling her speck of wisdom concerning her neighbors. And in that moment, Krissy realized how one-sided, how self-focused she'd been. Blaine was hardly some amoeba, like the kind scaling the aquariums here at the zoo. He was a man with emotions, ideas, feelings, and . . . disappointments.

"I'm sorry I never gave you a son," Krissy said. "I would have loved one, too."

He glanced at her, and with his sunglasses hiding his eyes, she couldn't quite make out his expression. But if she had to guess, she'd define it as surprise. "It's not your fault." He turned his line of vision back to the kids. "Just wasn't meant to be. I accepted that a long, long time ago."

Acceptance.

Oddly, the word seemed to cling to Krissy's heart for the remainder of the afternoon.

Chapter 9

Blaine groaned and then stretched out on the sofa and placed his head in Krissy's lap. "I think I outdid myself at the zoo today. My back is killing me."

"Oh, I'm sorry," Krissy replied, feeling guilty for insisting they go. "Sometimes I forget you're recuperating."

"Sometimes I do, too, and therein lies the problem."

Smiling at the retort, she ran her fingertips through Blaine's chestnut-colored hair. It felt thick and coarse, and although he kept it cropped short for the most part, he really had quite a lot of it around the sides and on top of his head.

"Say, Blaine, can I ask you something?"

"Sure you can." He peered up at her expectantly.

"I've been thinking ever since you said you wished we'd had a son . . . well, do you have any . . . regrets?" she asked on a note of hesitancy.

"Regrets about what? Our relationship or life in general?"

"Life in general."

"Sure I do. Who doesn't?"

Krissy grew more curious. "What do you regret?"

"Not becoming a Christian sooner in life for one thing. The girls were, what, in second grade or something when we accepted the Lord?"

She nodded, recalling how the twins had gone to vacation Bible school one summer and how at the closing program she and Blaine had heard the gospel preached for the first time. Neither had any trouble accepting the Word of God as truth. Each had been raised to revere the Bible and God; however, they had both trusted in something other than Jesus Christ for their salvation.

"On occasion I think that if we'd known then what we know now . . ." He chuckled. "What's that old cliché? Hindsight is twenty-twenty vision?"

Krissy had to agree. "What about our relationship, Blaine? Any regrets there?"

"None whatsoever. And you?"

"No . . ." She hedged slightly.

"That didn't sound very convincing, Kris."

Contrition filled her being. "Sorry. It's that I'm a different person today with different interests, likes, and dislikes. I'm not the same woman you married."

"Tell me one person who stays the same over twenty years' time." Blaine frowned.

"But that's what I mean . . . if we had to do it all again, would we?"

"That makes no sense," Blaine said on a note of exasperation. "The fact is, we can't do it all again, so why even bother speculating?"

"You're right."

"You know as well as I do that we can't change what's happened in the past. We can only go forward."

"True."

Krissy continued to caress his scalp, running a finger down the side of his face and around his ear. It obviously felt good because Blaine closed his eyes, looking like he might fall asleep. She wondered if he were right that perhaps she had begun to dwell on things beyond her control . . . and imagine things she had no right thinking about, such as Bruce Sawyer. Try as she might to rid her thoughts of the tall, broad-shouldered man with a sparkling blue gaze, it seemed impossible. Was she obsessed, or was this something that happened to people at one time or another during their marriage?

"Can I ask one more thing?"

"Shoot."

"In all the years we've been married, were you . . . well, did you ever find yourself attracted to another woman?"

Blaine cocked one eye open. "Nope."

"Oh, come on, you're a red-blooded man and you're not blind."

"Sure, but I don't allow myself any appreciative glances. It's like Pastor once said from the pulpit. The first look is accidental, the second look is sin." Blaine grinned. "On my life, Kris, I never needed to take a second look. I've got it too good at home."

His words should have comforted her, but instead they caused Krissy to feel even more guilt-ridden.

Blaine pushed himself into a half-sitting position and searched her face. "Are you feeling insecure about us? I mean, you don't think I'm doing something I shouldn't . . . do you? Was it because Jill came over that day I was grilling? Honestly, I wouldn't dream of —"

She placed her fingers over his lips. "The thought never even entered my mind. I trust you. Completely. The truth is, I trust you more than I trust myself."

Confusion swept across him. "What's that s'posed to mean?"

"I . . . well . . . I . . . I guess I don't know how to explain it."

"Try." He narrowed his gaze speculatively. "Does it have something to do with your not wanting to go to this picnic tomorrow?"

"Yes."

A glacier of fear suddenly began to slide from his forehead, down his face, neck, chest, and spread to his limbs. What was Krissy getting at? Was she trying to tell him that she'd been unfaithful?

Tamping down his anxiety, he knew he had to stay calm. If Krissy sensed his upset, she'd shy away and wouldn't confide in him.

"Tell me, Krissy," he whispered.

Tears filled her eyes. "I want to tell you, Blaine, because after today I realize that I . . . I need your help."

"Okay." He felt willing to help her any way he could.

She swallowed hard. "But I'm afraid you'll hate me if I tell you. I hate myself."

Blaine thought this might be as bad as he feared. Swinging his legs off the sofa, he stood and walked to the large picture window on the far wall of their living room.

He stared out across the lawn, noticing that the leaves on the trees were starting to change colors.

Change. It was frightening, and Blaine felt like he had an icy death grip around his neck. Prayer seemed impossible. But after several long moments, he took a deep breath and turned back around. "Honey, I could never hate you," he said sounding more composed than he actually felt. "You're the love of my life."

Rising, Krissy strolled slowly toward him, wiping a tear off her cheek. "You know I've been in this funk since the girls went away to college."

Blaine nodded.

"Well, then I began teaching at the academy where I met . . . the principal, Bruce Sawyer. Almost immediately we discovered that we had common interests. What's more, Bruce listened to me and validated my feelings, and he wasn't so macho that he couldn't share his . . . and he did."

Blaine bit his bottom lip, struggling to keep his temper in check. He suddenly felt like hopping in his truck, driving to the guy's house, and knocking his block off. "So how far did it go?" he heard himself ask.

"How far did what go?"

"The affair."

A look of horror crossed Krissy's features, and Blaine felt mildly relieved.

"You didn't have a fling with this guy? That's not what you're trying to tell me?"

"No, Bruce has never touched me."

"You gave me heart failure for nothing?"

"It's not 'nothing.' " Krissy threw her hands in the air. "See, that's what you do. You make light of everything important to me. I'm torn in two over this. Doesn't that matter?"

"Of course it does. I'm not taking any of this in stride. I'm merely trying to understand."

After an audible sigh, Krissy sniffed back the remainder of her tears. "I'm attracted to Bruce. I know it isn't right and our friendship is inappropriate at best, but there's this part of me that enjoys his company . . . and I know he enjoys mine. That's why I don't want to attend the picnic tomorrow. I don't want to see him and be reminded of all these crazy things I feel — and I certainly don't want them to develop. You're my husband, Blaine, and I'm committed to our marriage no matter what. It's just that . . ."

"It's just that your heart isn't in it anymore," he finished for her.

Looking ashamed, she bobbed her head in silent affirmation, and Blaine felt tears prick his own eyes. The admission wounded him; however, it wasn't nearly the travesty he'd first imagined. For that he felt grateful. But even if it were, he would have fought for his marriage, and with God on his side, he would have won, too.

Tell her that.

The inner prompting was so strong, Blaine didn't dare ignore it.

"Come here, Sweetheart," he said, although he didn't give Krissy a choice in the matter as he pulled her into his arms.

"You must be so angry with me."

"No, not angry . . ."

"I'm sorry, Blaine. I didn't want to t–tell you be-cause I didn't w–want to h–hurt you."

"It's all right," he said, kissing the top of her head while she sobbed into his sweatshirt. "I'm glad you told me. I love you and I want you to be happy." He pushed her back slightly and gazed down into her tear-streaked face. "But I want your heart, Krissy. It belongs to me and I want it back." With his thumb, he gently brushed away the sadness marring her lovely countenance.

"I want you to have my heart, too, Blaine."

"Okay, well, your willingness is half the battle, I guess . . ."

He pulled Krissy close to him, feeling like an apprehensive soldier. The war was on . . .

But could he win?

Chapter 10

The sound of children laughing outside her bedroom window awoke Krissy from a sound sleep. It took a moment, but then she realized the kids next door were playing in their yard.

With a yawn, Krissy rolled over and glanced at the alarm clock on the bedside table. Surprised, she lifted her head from the pillow and stared hard at the glowing numerals. Could it really be 10:30 in the morning? She looked at the vacant place beside her and the obvious registered; Blaine had gotten up already.

Climbing out from under the bedcovers, she strolled to her closet and pulled on her robe for warmth. The house felt chilly, but since it was only September, Blaine wouldn't want to turn the heat on yet. However, it wouldn't be long. Winter was rapidly approaching.

She stopped in the bathroom, freshened up, and brushed out her hair. Then she made her way to the kitchen where she found Blaine, standing in front of the sink, holding a cup of coffee in his hands, and gazing out the window.

"G'morning."

He turned around and gave her a tiny smile. "It's about time you woke up, Lazybones."

Krissy scrunched her countenance in a sassy reply and walked toward him. "Any more coffee?"

"Uh-huh." He handed her a mug from the cupboard.

"Blaine," she began, as she poured the fragrant dark brew from the carafe, "you haven't said a whole lot since our discussion yesterday evening. Does that mean you're upset?" Taking a sip of coffee, she turned to view his expression. It was thoughtful, serious.

"What guy wouldn't be upset?"

Krissy grimaced. "I know . . ."

"But I'm glad you told me. And I've given the matter a lot of thought. I didn't sleep much, and with every lap I swam this morning, I asked the Lord what I should do about the situation."

"And?"

"Well, first let me tell you what I *wanted* to do. I wanted to phone Sawyer and tell him that not only are we unable to attend his picnic today, but that you aren't returning to work tomorrow . . . or ever." He sighed. "It took every ounce of strength I had not to give in to the urge. But the Lord showed me that I really need to trust you and let you decide how to handle this situation."

Krissy's heart warmed to his words. "I've got good news for you. I'm not going back to the academy. I've already decided that much. I'll call Bruce today and let him know, and I can clean out my desk tomorrow morning before school starts." She paused, encouraged to see a look of relief on Blaine's face. "But I want you to know that I could probably face anything now, knowing that you're praying me through it." She took a step closer. "With you and God on my side, I can do anything."

Again just a hint of a smile. "I'm glad you're feeling better, Hon."

"But you're angry, aren't you? I can sense it."

"Yeah, I'm angry . . . at him! The jerk." A muscle worked in Blaine's jaw. "He knew you were married all along. He should have kept his distance."

"I'm not exactly innocent. I should have kept my distance, too."

"True, but I've got a hunch that guy

wouldn't have minded busting up our marriage."

Krissy didn't agree. She rather thought Bruce fell into the situation just as she had. It wasn't a premeditated thing. The attraction, the chemistry between them, had been apparent from the beginning.

"Listen, I'm a man, so I know how men think. The thrill of a conquest and all that. But as a Christian, Sawyer shouldn't have ever befriended you. I mean, if I sensed a woman was attracted to me, I wouldn't go out of my way to discover all the great things she and I had in common."

Mulling it over, Krissy had to admit he had a point. She took another sip of coffee and recalled the many times Bruce had sought out her company. She'd rationalized it away, feeling badly for him because of what he'd gone through with his wife. She thought he merely wanted someone to talk to — a comrade; however, she'd mistakenly opened her heart to him when her heart belonged to Blaine.

Krissy shut her eyes and anguished over this whole mess. "I'm so sorry." Sudden tears threatened to choke her. "Can you ever forgive me? Can you ever trust me again?"

"I can, yes, on both accounts."

She peered forlornly into her black coffee. "But it'll take time, won't it?" When Blaine didn't answer, she looked up at him.

"It's going to take more than time, Kris," he said, his dusky eyes darkening in earnest. "It's going to take patience, communication on both our parts, commitment to our relationship, and . . . last but hardly least, it's going to take a lot of love."

Krissy felt oddly impressed by his answer. It sounded rehearsed, but that only meant he'd really been giving the matter his utmost attention. Finally, he was taking her thoughts and feelings — he was taking her! — seriously!

"I'm willing," she said, setting down her mug on the counter. She slipped her arms around Blaine's midsection and smiled despite her misty eyes. "I do love you. And I think you're pretty terrific to put up with me."

He set his forearms on her shoulders, coffee cup still in hand. "And I think you're pretty . . . period."

She tipped her head, feeling both flattered and surprised. "You really think I'm still pretty?"

"No, actually I think our girls are pretty. You're . . . beautiful."

Her smile grew. "It's been a long time

since you told me that."

"I tell you all the time."

"No, you don't."

"Well, I *think* it all the time."

Krissy shook her head. "Too bad I can't read your mind."

Blaine looked properly chagrined. "Okay, so I should say what I'm thinking more often. I'll try."

"That's all I can ask for."

He nodded. The pact was sealed. Then, as Blaine regarded her, a tender expression wafted across his features and deepened the hue of his eyes. Slowly, he lowered his mouth to hers. On contact, she closed her eyes, deciding this was the most pleasurable kiss he'd given her in a long while. Gentle, undemanding, yet heartfelt and sincere.

After several long moments, Blaine lifted his chin and kissed the tip of her nose, then her forehead.

"You smell like chlorine," Krissy blurted.

"From the pool."

"Kind of a different smell for you." At his questioning frown, she added, "I'm used to you smelling like smoke."

"Those days are gone."

"And I'm glad. No more fretting over you fighting fires."

A wry grin curved the corners of Blaine's

lips. "So now that we're both unemployed, what do you want to do with all the time we're going to have together?"

"The rest of our lives," she murmured. Funny how the thought didn't seem so oppressing anymore. She grinned up at him. "Blaine, I'm sure we'll think of some way to amuse ourselves."

That evening, Krissy watched Blaine stack kindling in the fireplace and light it. Then she glanced across the dimly lit room at their neighbors who sat together on the love seat, sipping hot cocoa, and she marveled at the turn of events this afternoon. While Blaine had manned his post at the grill, slopping thick barbeque sauce on fat spare ribs, Ryan had sauntered over and began complaining about wives, kids, and marriage in general. After a lengthy discussion, Blaine had invited Ryan and Jill and their brood over for supper.

That was the first thing to blow Krissy's mind. Blaine had always acted more irritated by the Nebhardts than concerned for them and their marriage.

The second thing that sent her reeling was when Blaine suggested the younger couple get a sitter and come over after their children were settled. Surely, he would have much preferred to plant himself in front of the television tonight rather than entertain Jill and Ryan.

But when Blaine sat down at the piano and began to play for their guests, Krissy's head really began to spin. She hadn't heard him play in years.

"I wrote this piece just after I left for college," he'd announced. "I hated leaving Krissy behind. So I composed this sonata. I called it 'September Sonata.'" He grinned over his shoulder at his audience. "It was the very piece that made her say, 'I do.'"

His fingertips danced across the ivory keys of the baby grand in the corner of their living room and Krissy's face flamed with self-consciousness. The stirring melody evoked a host of memories that she didn't feel like reliving in front of her neighbors. That sonata — an instrumental musical composition consisting of three or four movements — how like their relationship it seemed. From falling in love to their perfect wedding day, to becoming parents and watching their daughters mature into lovely young women, their song of life had now begun to play a tune of rediscovery.

Suddenly their future together looked more than promising. It seemed downright exciting.

Krissy felt proud of Blaine, and the Nebhardts seemed impressed with his talent and applauded when he finished playing. Suddenly embarrassed, he announced he'd make a fire.

Brushing the wood dust from his hands now, Blaine walked over and claimed his place beside Krissy on the couch. It may have been her imagination, but she thought his blue jeans fit a little better and instead of wearing one of his usual, worn-out sweatshirts, he wore a dark gray pullover which he had neatly tucked into his pants. Making himself comfy, he stretched his arm out around her shoulders.

"You guys are so cute together," Jill remarked. "Like newlyweds or something."

"Well, we are . . . kinda," Blaine said, giving Krissy a meaningful wink.

"So you survived raising kids, huh?" Ryan asked.

"Just barely," he replied. "And if I've learned anything, I've learned I need to cherish my wife." Looking at her, he added, "If I ever lost her, I'd have nothing. I'd be nothing. I only wish I would have realized it years ago. I wish I would have made time for her . . . for us . . . in spite of our hectic schedules."

There beside him, Krissy felt like her

wanderlust heart had come home. Blaine wasn't a man to make public professions, especially when they pertained to his personal life. He had sincerely meant every word he'd just spoken.

She glanced up at him in a measure of awe, and for the first time in years, she felt unmistakably loved — and, yes, even cherished.

Epilogue

Icy fear gripped Blaine Robinson's heart as he raced down the hospital corridor. He'd been conducting a routine insurance inspection for the company at which he'd been employed for the past year when he'd gotten Krissy's page. He had left right away, but was he too late?

A nurse in lime-green scrubs and a matching cap stepped into his path. "Can I help you, Sir?"

"My wife," he panted, "her name is Krissy Robinson."

"Right this way."

Blaine followed the woman through a set of doors and down another hallway.

"If you want to go in with her, you'll have to put a gown over your clothes."

"Fine." Blaine didn't care what he had to do; all he wanted was to be with Krissy.

The woman handed him a blue printed gown and he immediately pulled it on and tied it at the back of his neck.

"Okay, you ready?" The nurse smiled.

"Ready as I'll ever be, I suppose."

"Aw, come on now," she said with a teasing smile, "you've got the easy job."

"Yeah, so I've been told."

She laughed and escorted him into the birthing room where Krissy reclined in a specialized delivery bed.

Blaine rushed to her side. "I got here as soon as I could." He noticed the beads of perspiration on her brow as he bent to kiss her forehead.

Krissy held out her hand, and he took it. "The contractions came on so fast."

"No kidding. You were fine this morning."

"I know . . ."

Her body suddenly compelled her to bear down hard, and she was helpless to do otherwise. A moment later, she collapsed against the back of the bed, letting go of the hand grips.

"Okay, this is the big one," Dr. Herman announced, her soft voice carrying a note of excitement to Blaine's ears. Despite Krissy's routine ultrasound exams, they had decided against learning the sex of their unborn child. "Another push. That's it."

But this was the part he hated, those agonizing last few minutes. Standing by Krissy's side, he knew his "job" was to encourage her, except it was hard to get past the feeling of utter helplessness.

Krissy squeezed his hand and cried out in final travail before falling back against the bed again. Blaine brushed the hair from her face and then the newborn's squall filled the room. Exhausted, Krissy went limp.

"I'm too old for this."

Blaine grinned, then looked at the doctor with anticipation coursing through his veins. "Is it a he or another she?"

The woman's round face split into a smile. "It's definitely a he!"

"Are you sure?" After he'd spoken those words, Blaine felt like an idiot. The doctor's incredulous glare only confirmed it.

"Of course I'm sure!"

"Don't mind him, Dr. Herman," Krissy said. "I think my husband is just over-whelmed."

"To say the least," Blaine admitted. He had to take several quick swallows in order to keep his emotions in check. He and Krissy had prayed for a son ever since they discovered she was expecting. Now that God had answered that fervent request, Blaine could scarcely believe it. He never thought this day would come and over the past seven months, he had found himself praying like the man in the Gospel of Mark:

"Lord, I believe; help thou mine unbelief."

One of the nurses placed the baby on Krissy's abdomen. She clamped the cord in two places, then offered the scissors to Blaine. He took it and cut the umbilical cord, feeling glad that the hospital staff allowed men to take such an active role in the birth of their children. He'd read everything he could find on the Internet pertaining to pregnancy and childbirth, he'd monitored Krissy's diet, and he had even attended the birthing classes with her. But now he felt cheated because he'd arrived so late. He had looked forward to assisting with the delivery.

However, his disappointment paled beside the joy he felt at having a son. Putting an arm around Krissy, he watched as she cradled him. Blaine reached out and touched the infant's tiny hand, marveling at God's phenomenal creation of life.

"Let's call him Luke," Blaine said.

"Sounds good to me."

Leaning forward, he gave Krissy a kiss. "I love you," he whispered in her ear.

"I love you, too." She placed one hand against Blaine's face. He kissed her palm. "This is one of the happiest moments of my life."

"Ditto."

Krissy smiled. "We have our little boy at last."

Blaine's eyes grew misty.

"And you know what else?"

"Hmm . . . ?"

"You're my very best friend, and I couldn't stand the thought of bringing our baby into the world without you by my side. I tried my best to hold back the labor, but I couldn't fight the inevitable for long."

"You did just great, and God saw fit to get me here in the nick of time." He gave her shoulder an affectionate squeeze. "And for the record, Kris, you're my best friend, too. Want to know something else?"

"What?"

"It's going to stay that way, despite diapers, bottles, and frenzied schedules. Neither your day care center nor my part-time job . . . nor our precious children will come between us as long as I'm alive and have something to say about it."

Krissy smiled and glanced down at their latest little blessing who had fallen asleep. Looking back at Blaine, she said, "That's a promise I'm going to hold you to."

"Good."

Several moments passed before Krissy spoke again. "This marks a whole new season of life for us. We've got a baby again."

"You're just realizing that now?" he teased, although he knew what she meant. God was still composing their life's sonata. . . .

And this was simply the next interlude.

About the Author

Andrea Boeshaar has been married for twenty-five years. She and her husband, Daniel, have three adult sons. Andrea attended college, first at the University of Wisconsin-Milwaukee, where she majored in English, and then at Alverno College, where she majored in Professional Communications and Business Management.

Andrea has been writing stories and poems since she was a little girl; however, it wasn't until 1984 that she started submitting her work for publication. In 1991 she became a Christian and realized her calling to write exclusively for the Christian market. Since then Andrea has written articles, devotionals, and over a dozen novels for **Heartsong Presents** as well as numerous novellas for Barbour Publishing. In addition to her own writing, she works as an agent for Hartline Literary Agency.

When she's not at the computer, Andrea enjoys being active in her local church and taking long walks with Daniel and their "baby" — a golden Labrador-Retriever mix named Kasey.